THE
SLAYING
OF THE SHREW

Also by Simon Hawke

A Mystery of Errors

THE
SLAYING
OF THE SHREW

Simon Hawke

A TOM DOHERTY ASSOCIATES BOOK

NEW YORK

THE SLAYING OF THE SHREW

Copyright © 2001 by Simon Hawke and William Fawcett & Associates

This book is printed on acid-free paper.

A Forge Book
Published by Tom Doherty Associates, LLC
175 Fifth Avenue
New York, NY 10010

www.tor.com

Forge® is a registered trademark of Tom Doherty Associates, LLC.

Library of Congress Cataloging-in-Publication Data

Hawke, Simon.
    The slaying of the shrew / Simon Hawke.—1st ed.
        p.   cm.
    ISBN 0-312-87894-X
    1. Shakespeare, William, 1564–1616—Fiction.   2. Great Britain—History—
Elizabeth, 1558–1603—Fiction.   3. Dramatists—Fiction.   4. Weddings—
Fiction.   5. Actors—Fiction.   I. Title.

PS3558.A8167 S58 2001
813'.54—dc21

                                                                2001040479

First Edition: December 2001

Printed in the United States of America

0   9   8   7   6   5   4   3   2   1

For

Brian Thomsen

With friendship, gratitude, and respect

THE SLAYING OF THE SHREW

1

✳

THE PLAGUE SEASON WAS A good time to be out of London, especially since it often meant the closing of the playhouses. And although Smythe much preferred the excitement of the city and working at James Burbage's Theatre to the quiet, uneventful country life he'd left behind, carts passing by outside one's window loaded with stinking corpses rotting in the summer heat had a way of mitigating London's worldly charms. Nevertheless, when he found out that the Queen's Men were going on the road, he was much less concerned about the plague than the possibility that he might not be asked to come along.

He was not, after all, a shareholder in the company or even one of the key supporting players. The boy apprentices who played the female parts were of much more value to the Queen's Men than he was as a mere ostler who only played occasional small roles and helped out with odd jobs around the playhouse. He had no stake in the profits of the company, other than wishing they'd do well, and to date, the only roles that he had played were small and insignificant, mere walk-ons of the sort given to ordinary hired men such as himself. Even those, as undemanding as they were, he knew he'd botched, for the most part. If not for his friend, Will Shakespeare, whom the company had learned to value for his versatility, he was convinced they would have let him go by now.

"Nonsense," Shakespeare said, when Smythe confided his worries to his roommate. "There's always a place in the theatre for a handsome lad with a good leg, a stout chest, and a fine, strong pair of shoulders." He spoke without putting down his pen or looking up from his small writing desk, which was pushed up against a bare wall opposite their bed in their lodgings at The Toad and Badger, in St. Helen's parish.

Smythe frowned. The poet's wit often had a biting edge and he could wield it as adroitly as a cutpurse used his bodkin. He was not sure if the remark was meant to chide him. "And just what do you mean by that, pray tell?"

The irritation in his tone caused Shakespeare to look up from his work and sigh, then glance back at him over his shoulder. His large, unusually expressive dark eyes, the poet's dominant feature in a somewhat sallow face that was otherwise not especially remarkable, held a look of exasperated resignation. "I mean, Tuck, that there are other attributes to be valued in a player aside from his ability to act. And 'tis indeed a fortunate thing for you, my friend, for of a certainty, you are no great threat to Ned Alleyn and our colleagues at the Rose."

The company was still smarting from the defection of Edward Alleyn, formerly their featured player, to the Lord Admiral's Men, who played at the Rose Theatre. Together with the recent death of the long-ailing Dick Tarleton, whose comedic talents had been a large factor in their company's success, Alleyn's departure had been a severe blow to the Queen's Men. They still had their enviable name, for there could be no more august patron than Her Royal Majesty, but their fortunes had, of late, been on the decline. Smythe knew that the frustration of seeing a rival company's star in the ascendant while theirs was on the wane was in part responsible for his friend's sarcastic remark. But he also knew the larger fault was his own, not only for interrupting Will while he was trying to work, but for putting him in the awkward position of standing up for an inferior actor simply because that actor happened to be his roommate and his friend.

"Well, I deserved that, I suppose," Smythe said, glumly.

Shakespeare sighed again and put down his pen. He pulled off his ink-stained, calfskin writing glove, which had no mate for he had made it for himself for this specific purpose, dropped it on the table and then turned around to face him. "Right then," he said, placing his hands upon his knees and regarding him with a steady, direct gaze. "Let's have it. Out with it."

"Out with what?" asked Smythe.

"Whatever matter stalks the labyrinthine mazes of your mind like some perturbed spirit," Shakespeare replied, dryly. "Give vent to it, for 'tis clear that I shall have no peace til you have unburdened yourself."

"Nay, Will, I have distracted you enough already with my own concerns. You must return to yours and work upon your sonnets, for 'tis that work which pays our rent."

"You contribute your fair share," Shakespeare responded. "And in truth, 'tis not as if this sort of work requires great labor, though it does seem laborious, betimes. A poet who sings the praises of some aristocratic popinjay for a few pounds is little better than a trollop who kneels for a few shillings. Yet if fortune must condemn me as a dishonest sonneteer, at least I am an honest strumpet in giving forth to the best of my ability. But now we stray. Of late, my friend, you have been ruled by a most bilious humor. Ever since you learned that the Queen's Men were going on the road, you have been sulking like an errant schoolboy sent indoors to learn his hornbook. This sullen truculence of yours is most unseemly. What ails you, Tuck?"

"I have already given you the cause of my distemper."

"And I have sought to reassure you. Never fear, Tuck, you are coming with us, that I'll warrant. With Ned Alleyn and Dick Tarleton both departed, one for a more prosperous venue and the other, presumably, for a more virtuous one, the Queen's Men need all the help that they can muster."

"But, Will, I can scarce replace either Dick Tarleton or Ned

Alleyn," Smythe replied. "I can neither clown or dance a jig, nor, in truth, can I act with any great ability."

"Well, in truth, you cannot act with any ability at all," said Shakespeare. "As for clowns and jig dancers, they have had their day. The groundlings may still find some amusement in the brainless caperings of that oaf Kemp and his ilk, but it shall not be long ere that sort of thing begins to pall upon them. One can only see so many clownish jigs and pratfalls before the novelty wears off. On the other hand, people never seem to tire of comely lads and lasses, and you, young Symington Smythe, are a fine, handsome figure of a man whom lads and lasses both find comely. What is more, you not only have a way with horses as befits a proper ostler to the gentry and nobility, but are a skilled farrier and smith to boot, and have the strength of a bull, qualities always of great value to any company of players on the road."

"So then, you hold that my only attributes are my strong body and good looks?" asked Smythe.

"Well, for my own part, I find many qualities in you to value as a friend, but so far as the company may be concerned, it does help to have some attractive people on the stage. And aside from one or two apprentices who have the comeliness of youth, the Queen's Men, sad to say, are not a very comely lot."

Though he knew that Will meant well, Smythe did not find the poet's words encouraging. Ever since he had seen his first play put on in the courtyard of a village inn by a traveling company of players, the very Queen's Men who now played at the theatre where he was employed, he had nursed a childhood dream of becoming a player himself, but unfortunately, his father had not supported him in that ambition.

A man with considerable ambitions of his own, Symington Smythe the elder had been scandalized at the notion that the son who bore his name wanted to become something as disreputable and low class as a player. He had secured his own status as a gentleman with great expense and much currying of favor and had his eyes set upon a knighthood. Having his only son wishing to become a player was simply unacceptable. Instead, in the belief that some hard work would knock some sense into his head and at least teach him a decent and respectable trade, he had him apprenticed to a smith, his own less fortunate younger brother, Thomas, who had not stood to inherit the estate.

Living with his uncle, a strong, but steady-tempered, patient and amicable man, Smythe had learned the craft of smithing, growing ever stronger as he grew ever more adept. He always had a love for horses and a natural way with them, which had also made him a good farrier. But above all else, he learned something from his uncle that few people could teach and fewer still could master.

The art of making blades was Thomas Smythe's true passion. He could work metal with extraordinary skill and had taught his nephew almost everything he knew. His Uncle Tom believed he had a gift for it and a good future in the guild, but though he had picked up his uncle's love for the demanding craft of metalworking, Smythe's dream of acting on a stage had never left him. When at last he learned that his father had bankrupted himself in his vain and injudicious pursuit of a title, he decided there was nothing left to prevent his setting out for London to pursue his dream.

A series of serendipitous events had brought him closer to the realization of that dream than he would have thought possible after so short a time in London. While still en route, at an inn near the outskirts of the city, he had met a fellow traveler named Will Shakespeare, himself on the way to London with hopes of finding work with a company of players. They fell in with each other and decided to share quarters and expenses, since neither of them had much money. Soon afterward, a chance encounter with none other than the flamboyant and controversial poet, Christopher Marlowe, had gained them an introduction to Richard Burbage, whose father owned the theatre where the Queen's Men played. However, though they had found employment at the Burbage Theatre, Smythe's first attempts at acting as a hired man had revealed a shortcoming of which he had not previously been aware. He had, it seemed, virtually no talent as an actor.

"Do you see no hope at all for me as a player, then?" asked Smythe, morosely.

"*No* hope?" Shakespeare shrugged. "Well, I would not wish to see a man left hopeless, least of all my closest friend. Nor would I wish to lay the burden of false hope upon him, either. Let us say, instead, that I see *little* hope. But do not despair, Tuck, for by the same token, I see little hope for myself, as well. Methinks I might fare better as a poet than a player, but 'twould seem Chris Marlowe has little more to fear from me than Ned Alleyn has from you. Yet, be that as it may, 'tis grateful we should be, for we have work while many others in these hard times go a'begging."

"True," said Smythe, folding his arms behind his head as he lay upon the bed, staring at the ceiling. Times were hard in England. People were flocking to London from all over the country, desperate to find work. It was difficult enough just finding lodging in a city where small rooms such as their own were often occupied by entire groups of unrelated people, sleeping on the floor and making do as best they could. As if in afterthought, he added, "I should be thankful, I suppose."

Shakespeare stared at him for a moment and then shook his head. "That is not the end of it, methinks. There is something else that troubles you, quite aside from your apprehensions about your standing with the company. The very air around you is oppressive with your melancholy. What disturbs you, truly?"

Smythe grimaced. "Nothing, really. Except . . . well . . . I was thinking of Ned Alleyn."

Shakespeare frowned. "*Alleyn?* Why, Alleyn's gone now. What has he to do with aught?"

"Well . . .'twas more in the way he went."

Shakespeare frowned. "He went because he could not improve his fortunes further here and had an opportunity to do so elsewhere. He was a shareholder in the company, but then he could rise no further. He knew full well that Dick Burbage stands to inherit the Theatre from his father, while Philip Henslowe has no son to take over the Rose, only a daughter who . . . *Ahhh! Now* I see it! You still have your mind upon that dewy girl, Elizabeth! You think that if Ned Alleyn can succeed in marrying a theatre owner's daughter, why then, perhaps you might do the same with the daughter of a wealthy merchant who owns a part of ours."

"Well—"

"Well, nothing. I advise you to put that thought straight out of your mind, my friend. You have about as much chance of taking Elizabeth Darcie to wife as I have of gaining immortality."

"But what of Alleyn, Will? Was not his situation much the same as mine in most respects?"

" 'Twas nothing like," said Shakespeare, with a snort. "For one thing, Ned Alleyn, for all of his insufferable pomposity, happens to be the greatest and most celebrated actor of our time. While you, you great buff . . ." Shakespeare stopped, cleared his throat, and then continued. "Well, you are my friend, Tuck, but we have already dispensed with our discussion of your dubious abilities upon the stage. Philip Henslowe knows full well that Alleyn will draw audiences to the Rose, much to our disadvantage, and it only stands to *his* advantage to seal Ned to the Rose through marriage to his daughter. For his part, Ned Alleyn stands to gain, as well. Henslowe's daughter, from what I hear, is a buxom, young and pretty lass with a most amiable disposition, but the main attraction is, of course, the Rose, which Alleyn would then stand to inherit through the marriage."

"Aye," said Smythe, "which was precisely why I thought that a player and the wealthy owner of a playhouse and other diverse ventures could, perhaps, despite differences in class—"

"Henslowe is a wealthy man, I'll grant you," Shakespeare interrupted, "or at least he seems wealthy to the likes of us, but remember he is not a gentleman and has no real ambitions to rise above his class. He is the owner of a brothel, for God's sake. Henry Darcie, on the other hand, is *truly* wealthy, one of the most successful merchants in the city, and he longs to improve his lot in life with all his heart and soul. Already, he stands well above you, and through his daughter, hopes to rise still higher. Having her become involved with a mere player would work contrary to those hopes, regardless of how skilled or popular that player might become. And in your case . . . well, the less said of that, the better. In any event, Henslowe's interests are not the same as Darcie's. Were you to bring in audiences ten times as large as Ned Alleyn might attract, 'twould still make no difference in the end. Through hard work and diligence, and perhaps a minor miracle or two, there may yet be some small hope for you as a player, Tuck, but as a suitor for Liz Darcie, you have none. None whatever. You may as well give it up, my lad. The girl may have graced you with a smile or two, but she is unattainable, believe me."

Smythe was moved to argue, but he checked himself. On the face of it, there was nothing Will had said that he could logically dispute. And yet, despite that, he was certain that Elizabeth had feelings for him. That day when they first met at the theatre, there had been a spark between them, he felt certain of it. And then later, when she had found herself caught up in a web of intrigue, a devilish plot designed to turn even her own family against her, she had come to him in desperation, seeking help, and once more, Smythe had been convinced that something quite significant had passed between them.

When he spoke to Will about it, the poet had done his best to dissuade him, arguing that Elizabeth Darcie had felt threatened and so had instinctively resorted to the age-old tricks inherent in her gender, using her seductiveness and vulnerability to gain a strong protector. And, Shakespeare had argued, it had worked.

"She drew you into it, despite your better judgement," he had said, "and before the thing was ended, the entire company was placed at risk and I was very nearly murdered!"

Smythe did not need to be reminded of how assassins had attacked them in the middle of a production at the theatre. He would not soon forget that! But at the same time, Elizabeth was not to blame. She had been an innocent, a mere pawn in a complex foreign plot with implications that had reached to the very highest levels of the government. The role that they had played in helping to defeat that plot had gained them a powerful friend at court in the person of Sir William Worley, the master of the celebrated Sea Hawks and the right hand man of Sir Francis Walsingham, one of the queen's chief ministers and the head of Her Royal Majesty's most secret service. Smythe knew that Shakespeare did not truly hold Elizabeth to blame for that devilish affair or the attempt upon his life, but he also knew that Will was not without some rancor when it came to the fair sex.

He did not know why, precisely. Shakepeare was rather close-mouthed on the subject, save when he was in his cups, and even then, he revealed very little. Smythe only knew that Will had left a family behind in Stratford when he came to London, a wife and children whom he never visited, but to whom he sent a good portion of everything he earned, for which reason, despite a very frugal disposition, he never had any money and was always struggling to earn more. Hence, his "strumpet sonneteering," as he called it, writing verse in praise of various courtiers who collected such fawning scribblings, paid for them, and often had them bound into small volumes which they then passed amongst themselves and exhibited in their homes like treasured trophies taken in some hunt. Smythe found it all quite comical and even childish, yet foolish as it seemed, in such trying times, it could provide some much needed income and, to a fortunate few, even a decent livelihood if their reputations grew and printers sought their work to offer for sale in the book stalls at St. Paul's.

The true prize for an ambitious poet lay in securing the patronage of an aristocrat, as some of the university men had done. Many noblemen had their own pet poets, as Smythe thought of them, and in return for their support, these well-educated men of letters wrote paens of praise for their well-heeled patrons, likening them in fulsome, cadenced terms to gods or heroes from Greek mythology or ancient history. Smythe had read several such slim volumes that Shakespeare had brought home. He had been amazed that men would pay good money for such drivel and had said so.

"Drivel it may be," Shakespeare had replied, "but if 'twill help to pay our rent and put food into our empty, growling bellies, then to drivel shall I fix my compass and grandly sail forth."

And so he did, often working late into the night by candlelight, writing at his desk, a small, crudely made trestle table now covered with candle wax and ink stains. He was often writing when Smythe fell asleep, and sometimes was still to be found writing come the morning. To date, he had not yet managed to find a wealthy patron, but he had sold some sonnets to a few well-born young gentlemen, thanks to an admiring word or two dropped casually by Sir William at court, and his name was beginning to become known as a rising young poet. He was yet a far cry from being a rival to the likes of Robert Greene or Thomas Lodge, but then he was still new in London and did not have the advantage of a university degree to buttress his ambitions. However, he did not let that deter him, not when it came to writing sonnets, nor when it came to writing plays.

Thus far, he had yet to write a complete play of his own, though he had made extensive notes on various ideas. Shakespeare's first opportunity to show the company what he could do came when Alleyn left them in the midst of a production that had not been working to begin with. It was unclear who was the original author of the play, for companies frequently performed plays that were rewritten from earlier versions, which were often rewritten from earlier versions still, which in turn often came from other sources. The original author was often impossible to pinpoint, though as Smythe recalled, this particular production had all the stamp of Robert Greene upon it.

Though he could not say that it was Greene for certain, the play had a pomposity and a pretentiousness, a smug condecension in its mocking attitude towards the rising middle class that had all the earmarks of the university men — Greene, in particular — who seemed to despise the very audience for whom they wrote. Or perhaps, as Shakespeare had put it, for whom the companies performed the plays, for Will believed that the university men actually wrote less for the playhouse audiences than for one another. Therein, he insisted, lay their true failing.

For the Queen's Men, the problem was, perhaps, less clearly defined, but nevertheless immediate. The play was a disaster and their featured player had summarily quit them for a rival company. Something needed to be done, and quickly. Seeing his opportunity, Will had stepped forth, volunteering to try his hand at doctoring the play. Dick Burbage had decided they had nothing to lose by letting him try. If the young ostler fancied himself a poet, Burbage had told the others, then why not see what he could do? So what if he was not a university-trained man of letters? Who was to say that he might not come up with an amusing verse or two that could add some much needed spirit to improve the play? It certainly could not, Burbage had admitted wryly, be made a great deal worse.

Shakespeare had not only improved the production by deleting a few lines here and adding a few there, rewriting the most troublesome scenes, but he had continued to rewrite in stages, after each performance, until an almost entirely new and much improved play had emerged. The company was so well pleased with the result that they gave him the opportunity of looking over the other plays in their repertoire, to see if they might be improved, as well.

For Shakespeare, this had brought about a change in fortune that had elevated him from the lowly post of ostler at the Burbage Theatre to book-holder and sometime actor. Both positions carried more prestige within the company and brought with them slightly better pay, but as book-holder especially, Will now had a great deal more responsibility. While not quite as important as the role of stage-manager who assembled the company, assigned all the parts, and saw to it that all the actors received their parts in manuscript sheets of paper pasted together to form rolls upon which were written each actor's cues and speeches, the book-holder worked closely with the stage-manager, assembling all the properties and keeping them in good order for every performance, as well as acting as a prompter and arranging for all the music, fanfares, alarums, stage thunder and other incidental noises, and keeping track of all the cues and entrances and exits during the performance.

Smythe, meanwhile, remained an ostler, though more and more, he found himself performing menial work around the theatre, sweeping and maintaining the stage, and making sure there were fresh rushes strewn across the yard for each performance. It was not quite the glamorous life he had envisioned for himself when he had embarked for London. Instead of basking in the warmth of audience applause, as he had so many times imagined in his daydreams, he often sweltered in the all too real stench of what they left behind after each performance.

From time to time, there was a small part for him to play, but the company had learned not to depend upon his ability to memorize his lines, nor upon his execrable sense of timing. Smythe was at a complete loss to explain these shortcomings. His memory never seemed to fail him save for when he stepped out upon the stage, at which point it inexplicably went blank and he could not recall even the simplest, briefest line. As a result, he was never sent out on stage alone. To make certain he did not miss his cue, Will was usually there to shove him out in the direction he needed to go, and whoever was already on stage always stood prepared to prompt him if the need arose, as it usually did. For Smythe, it was exasperating, but he seemed completely helpless to overcome the situation.

"Stage fright," Dick Burbage called it. " 'Tis a thing to which most players fall victim at one time or another. To some, it means merely an unsettled stomach and a slight trembling of the hands or knees, a sort of giddy, momentary weakness overcome the moment they step out onto the stage and plunge into the role. For others, it is a nearly unbearable, oppressive pressure in the chest, the heart beating like a wild thing trying to claw its way free of the flesh, violent shaking and cold sweats, a paralyzing fear that becomes completely all consuming. And yet, for all that, it often goes away once they step out onto the stage and become caught up in the play. Most players get over it in time. Still, with a few. . . . it never truly goes away."

"What do such people do?" Smythe asked him.

"Well, if they wish to remain actors, then they must *act* as if it does not bother them," Burbage had replied.

"And if they cannot?"

Burbage shrugged. "Then it must inevitably become evident to them that they might well become good ostlers, or perhaps masons, or smiths or carpenters or coopers, or else merchants, ironmongers, jewelers, butchers, saddle-makers, rivermen or scribes, but sadly, they never can be players. Lack of talent may be compensated for to some degree with industry and diligence, but nothing in the world may compensate for lack of courage. Mind you now, having courage does not mean having a lack of fear. It means having the ability to persevere in spite of it. The principle is the same, you see, whether one stands upon the stage or upon the field of battle. The soldier who faces enemy troops and quails before them is, in some respects, no different from the player who faces an audience and is struck with fear. The singular difference between them is that in the soldier's case, the fear might well cost him his life. And thus far, Tuck, I have never heard of an audience so hostile that they have actually killed a player. Still, there is always a first time, I suppose. . . ."

"Look, Tuck," Shakespeare said, interrupting his thoughts, "I have written enough for one night. I need a respite. Let us go downstairs and have some ale. You need to stop this lying about and moping. Most of the others will be down there still, discussing their preparations for the journey. At least, the ones who have not yet drunk themselves insensible. You need to get your mind on other things. There will be other girls in other towns, doubtless a few pretty enough to make you forget all about Elizabeth Darcie. And they will doubtless be much more accessible."

"Perhaps, but they shall not be Elizabeth," Smythe said. " 'Twould never be the same."

"Blow out the candles, then," Shakespeare replied, wryly. "All cats are gray in the dark, my friend. Come on, let us go and have ourselves a drink or two or three."

They made their way downstairs to the alehouse of the Toad and Badger, where they found most of the members of the Queen's Men still enjoying one another's company after their last performance and their ordinary supper of meat pies, ale and cheese. Beer, the poor man's drink, was filling the small hours as they smoked their pipes and eagerly discussed their forthcoming departure.

"Ah, Will, Tuck, come join us!" called John Fleming, waving them over to the table where they sat. "Dick has just been telling us about our new engagement at the commencement of our tour!"

"What new engagement?" Shakespeare asked, as he signalled the tavern maid for a drink.

"We are to be performing at a wedding," said George Bryan, a recently hired member of the company who had come to them from another troop of players that had been disbanded. There were fewer acting companies now that licensure was being more strictly enforced, especially in London, and only those companies with aristocratic patrons were licensed to perform.

Smythe sat down next to Bryan and at once found a tankard of beer placed before him. He reached for it, thinking that he never used to drink anything but milk, water or his special infusion of herbs until he came to London, where no one seemed to drink anything but wine or beer or ale. Here, water was only used for cooking or else washing up. No one ever thought to drink it. Wine and ale, however, flowed as freely as the Thames and drunkenness was so common in the city as to be completely unremarkable. It was not unusual to see men lying passed out on the streets, utterly insensible with drink and vulnerable to any pickpocket who came along to lift their purses. Most citizens generally gave these supine souls a wide berth, however, especially at this time of the year, for it was by no means certain from outward appearances, unless one made a risky close inspection, whether it was a drunkard fallen into stupor or else a victim of the dreaded plague.

Each year, when summer came, the plague took a heavy toll among the citizenry. There were so many new graves in St. Paul's Churchyard now that the minister complained about the stench of all the decomposing bodies. Smythe grimaced at the thought and took a drink, enjoying the feeling of the rich and heavy brew sliding down his throat. He had developed a taste for it, but reminded himself to be sure to visit Granny Meg so that he could obtain a fresh supply of dried herbs for his infusion, a recipe taught him by another cunning woman from back home. He had been strong and healthy when he came to London and he intended to do everything he could to stay that way, even if it made everyone think he was peculiar for imbibing a hot beverage brewed from weeds. However, the ursine Courtney Stackpole would not countenance such a curious concoction in his tavern, and so Smythe drank beer as he listened to Fleming and the others, anxious for more news about their tour.

"There is to be a wedding celebration held at the estate of one Godfrey Middleton, a wealthy merchant and projector," said Richard Burbage, "who is a good friend of Henry Darcie, well known to us all as my father's partner and thereby part owner of our illustrious theater. 'Tis through the good offices of Henry Darcie that this special engagement has been arranged for us."

"So then we are to be performing at some fat merchant's wedding?" Shakespeare said, with a noticeable lack of enthusiasm. " 'Tis to be a private performance for the guests, held in some dim, stuffy, and ill-suited hall?"

"Nay, 'twill be the wedding of his eldest daughter, Catherine," said Dick Burbage. "And the performance will be held out of doors!"

"A grand pavillion and a stage shall be built especially for the occasion on the grounds of the estate," said Robert Speed, another member of the company, who had the singular ability of speaking lucidly and clearly no matter how drunk he became. His bleary-eyed gaze was the only indication of his inebriated state as he raised his tankard in a toast to the efforts that would be made to ensure a fine performance and a memorable wedding. "Separate pavillions shall also be erected as banqueting houses and galleries to house the audience," he added in stentorian tones, "all of whom will come barging down the river in a grand progress like Drake's own bloomin' fleet after the defeat of the Armada! 'Ere's to 'em all, God bless 'em!" He emptied his tankard and belched profoundly.

"There are to be three hundred guests or more, most of whom shall be participating in the progress," explained Burbage. "There shall be work aplenty for the rivermen, what with boats and barges all assembled in a flotilla to bear the wedding guests. And the theme for this grand celebration shall be that of Queen Cleopatra greeting Julius Caesar."

"Oh, what rot!" said Shakespeare, rolling his eyes.

"Indeed," said Kemp. "One would think that it was some elaborate court masque held in honor of the queen, herself!"

"Very nearly so," said Burbage. "Godfrey Middleton seems intent on putting on a lavish spectacle in honor of his daughter, who is marrying into the nobility, thereby doubtless improving his own prospects for an eventual knighthood."

"Ah, just what we need, more knights," Will Kemp said, puffing on his long clay pipe. "At the rate that knighthoods are being handed out these days, they shall soon be stacking them up like cordwood in the church."

"Oh, and speaking of knights, there is to be a joust, as well," said Burbage.

"A wedding joust?" said Shakespeare. "Well, why not? 'Tis an apt metaphor for the combative state of holy matrimony. Has a decision yet been made about which play shall be performed? Perhaps the groom, as Caesar, could be stabbed to death on stage while the bride, as Cleopatra, made a complete asp of herself in front of all the wedding guests."

"I vote for that one," Speed said gravely, raising his tankard once again and quaffing it in a single swallow.

"We *have* been asked to submit a number of suggestions for plays that would be *appropriate* to the occasion." Burbage said.

Fleming added, "Master Godfrey, in his anxiety that everything should be just so, has apparantly appointed himself our personal Master of the Revels for this particular occasion."

"We could perform *The Unconstant Woman*," Shakespeare said, with a straight face.

Will Kemp snorted. "That should prove a popular choice with Master Middleton." The others chuckled.

"You think perhaps *The Holy State* would be appropriate?" asked Bryan, seriously.

"With Nashe's long, windy soliloquies and moralistic pedantry?" said Shakespeare. "Do you wish to entertain the wedding guests or stupify them all into a slumber?"

"Well, then, what would you suggest, Will, as our aspiring resident poet?" Fleming asked, wryly. "Which play from among our vast repertoire do you suppose would be the best for such an occasion?"

Fleming might have meant the remark somewhat in jest, thought Smythe, but at the same time, he marked the fact that no one laughed. It was the first time that anyone had suggested, seriously or not, that Will might one day hold such a position in their company and that no one laughed at the idea was evidence of just how much Shakespeare had risen in their general esteem. He felt pleased for his friend, but at the same time, he felt a little envious.

"Well, to be serious for a moment—but only for a moment—I am not certain it is needful that our choice of play reflect on the occasion," Shakespeare replied. "That sort of choice would not be without its risks, you know. After all, what gentleman would wish to see a group of motley players make comment, through their sport, upon his daughter's marriage? Were we to play something comedic concerning the general state of matrimony, then Middleton might feel that we were poking fun at his own family. On the other hand, if we chose something like Nashe's play to perform, for all its fine, moralistic sentiments and tone, then he might perceive his daughter and her husband were being preached to by their inferiors. Namely, ourselves."

"Aye, he makes an excellent point," said Burbage, nodding. "While this shall not be a court performance, there shall nevertheless be a great many powerful and wealthy people in attendance. We want to make this occasion a memorable one, to all of them as well as Master Middleton, and not for all the wrong reasons."

"Well, why *not* a comedy?" asked Kemp. "We could play something spirited and amusing that has naught to do with marriage, and yet would still entertain the better sort of people with its subject matter. *The Honorable Prentice* would be an excellent choice, methinks."

In other words, something that would play more to his talents as the company's clown and jig-dancer, Smythe thought. It was a predictable response from Kemp, who liked anything that would showcase his abilities, but at the same time, it was not without merit. An idea suddenly struck him.

"What about that new play you have been working on, Will?" he said, turning to Shakespeare. "You know the one, you have read me portions of it."

"What new play?" asked Burbage, immediately interested. "You have been working on another adaptation?"

Shakespeare glanced at Smythe with irritation. "Well, no . . . not quite. 'Tis something new, entirely of my own composition. . . ." His voice trailed off and he looked a bit uncomfortable.

"Indeed?" said Fleming, raising his eyebrows. "What is the matter of it?"

Shakespeare cleared his throat and took a sip of wine. He did not seem anxious to discuss it. Nevertheless, he answered Fleming's question. "It concerns a matter of identity," he said, "something I have been playing about with in a sort of desultory fashion."

"Go on," said Burbage. "Tell us more. How does it begin?"

Shakespeare paused a moment, collecting his thoughts. "Well . . . it begins with an itinerant young tinker, an impoverished wastrel by the name of Christopher Sly, who is thrown out of an alehouse by his hostess for drunkenness and loutish behavior and for refusing to pay his bill . . ."

"A sly wastrel named Christopher?" said Fleming, smiling. "A bit of a dig at young Marlowe, perhaps?"

Speed belched ponderously. "Sod Marlowe."

"Bestill yourself, Robby," Burbage said. "Thus far, it seems a good beginning. Go on, Will. What happens next?"

Shakespeare took another drink and cleared his throat once more. "Well, Sly staggers about and rails at her in a roaring, drunken speech in which he foolishly claims noble descent from the Norman conquerors and so forth, taking umbrage at her treatment of him. . . ."

"One could have some fun with that," interjected Kemp, clearly imagining himself in the role.

". . . and then he falls into a drunken slumber in the road." Shakespeare continued, "whereon a lord and his hunting party arrive upon the scene. Finding him thus disposed—or indisposed, as the case may be—this lord, for want of some amusement, decides to play a trick upon the drunken tinker and instructs his retinue accordingly. They shall remove the tinker to this lord's estate, where they shall strip him of his clothing and place him in the lord's own bedchamber. All within the household are carefully instructed, when the tinker wakes, to treat him as if *he* were the lord himself who, having fallen into some madness for a time, had forgot himself and was now miraculously and mercifully restored to his wits . . . and to his loyal servants. And so, when the tinker comes to his senses, he is at first confused by all that happens, but soon comes to believe he truly is a lord, because all around him assure him it is so, even the lord himself, who plays the part of a servant."

"Oh, I like it!" Burbage said. "It has great possibilities for witty banter and tomfoolery. I think we should submit this play to Master Middleton as our first choice! What say you, lads?"

"Aye, 'tis a lighthearted and amusing sort of thing," said Bryan. "I can see how it would be received. I like it, too."

Shakespeare looked dismayed. "But . . . but, my friends . . . the play is not yet finished!"

"Well, we need not submit the entire book to Middleton for his approval," Burbage said. "I do not think that he would have the time or even the inclination to read it, in any event, what with all the preparations he must see to for the wedding celebration. A brief summary of the story should suffice."

"Aye, a man of Master Middleton's position would not be bothered with trifling details," Fleming agreed. "There is quite enough there from what Will has already described to satisfy him, I should think, and if there should be anything in the final book he may find disagreeable, why, we could always change it in rehearsal, as we often do."

"Indeed, it sounds like a fine idea to me," said Kemp, nodding with approval. "Put in a few songs, then add a jig or two, and it should prove just the thing to entertain the distinguished wedding party."

Seeing the stricken expression on his roommate's face, Smythe suddenly realized that for all his good intentions, he had made a serious mistake, though he did not quite understand just what it was. Yet it seemed quite clear that what he had thought would be a welcome opportunity for his friend to have one of his own plays acted by the Queen's Men, and in front of an influential audience, at that, was instead regarded by him as a horrible disaster. And when he turned towards Smythe amidst the general discussion of how they might present his play, Smythe saw in his face a look that struck him to the quick. It was an expression of great alarm . . . and of betrayal.

2

THE CATHEDRAL OF ST. PAUL, KNOWN simply as "Paul's" to the native Londoner, did not present the sort of quietly spiritual surroundings that Smythe had learned to associate with church during his boyhood in the country. Like the city over which it loomed magnificently, Paul's was a curious amalgamation not only of architectural styles, but of the spiritual and the temporal as well, the exhalted simultaneously sharing space with the debased.

Surrounded by a stone wall, the churchyard of St. Paul's was a bustling place of business, full of crowded market and book stalls past which Smythe wound his way as he entered through one of the six gates leading into the enclosure. Within the courtyard, to the northeast, stood Paul's Cross, which always made him think of a miniature tower with its Norman-styled wooden cross atop a conical lead roof over an open pulpit built atop stone steps. Here, outdoor services were held at noon on Sundays, and important proclamations were read out to the citizenry. In the northwest corner of the yard stood the Bishop's Palace, near the college of canons and several small chapels. Here, too, could be found Paul's School, and the bell tower and the chapter house, incongruously elegant and solid compared to the hodgepodge of crudely fashioned merchant stalls thrown up all around the noisy churchyard.

The interior of St. Paul's, much to Smythe's surprise the first time he had seen it, was no less a bustling place of business than the cacophonous outer churchyard. The middle aisle of the Norman nave was known popularly as "Paul's Walk," and merchants as well as other, less desirable sorts routinely plied their trades there, even while services were being conducted, so that the choir frequently had to compete with the shouts of sellers hawking their various wares, like the Biblical moneylenders in the temple, whose spiritual if not lineal descendants also could be found doing a brisk business in Paul's Walk, counting out their coins upon the fonts.

Each supporting column in the cathedral was known for a type of business that could be transacted there. Various handwritten or printed bills were posted on the columns, people looking for work or else advertising one service or another. Smythe passed one column around which several lawyers were meeting with their clients or else negotiating with roisterers and layabouts who sold their honor for a shilling or two to bear false witness against someone in a case. Nearby, an ale seller had set up several small casks beside another column and was offering hardened leather drinking horns to passersby to taste his wares. Beside him, at another column, loaves of fresh baked bread were being sold, and the next column over was a place for buying books and broadsheets. Nearby, small portraits of the city's aristocracy were being sold, including, of course, all the fashionable courtiers and Her Royal Majesty, Elizabeth the Virgin Queen.

Smythe passed several small tables made of wooden planks placed atop empty wine casks where tailors sold their wares, and further on, men and boys looking for work vied for the attention of prospective employers, who in turn were being distracted by the prostitutes parading up and down the aisle of the cathedral, meeting every strolling gallant's eye with a bold gaze, a bawdy comment, a hipshot and a wink.

Over the echoing din, Smythe heard the sharp, staccato sounds of hoofbeats on the cathedral floor and quickly moved aside as a cloaked rider in a rakish hat went trotting past him down the center of the aisle, sword swinging at his side. Out for a casual morning canter through the house of God to look over the whores, thought Smythe. While he was certainly no papist, nor especially religious one way or another, Smythe could not help but think that the Dissolution over which the queen's father, King Henry VIII, had presided had become truly dissolute, indeed. He did not think that he would ever grow fully accustomed to the way that things were done in London.

"*Tuck*! Over here!"

He turned towards the familiar voice, smiling when he saw Elizabeth waving to him. She was dressed in a long, voluminous, hooded cloak of green velvet that stood out from her body where her whalebone farthingale held her skirts out from her waist, making her seem to glide across the floor as she approached, and she held before her face on a slim rod a fashionable mask of green brocade and feathers, as many ladies did when they went out in public, especially if unescorted. But mask or no mask, Smythe would know her anywhere. Each time he saw her, he was reminded of the first time they had met, and how she had struck him nearly speechless with her beauty.

It had been at the Theatre, shortly after he had started working there with Will, and she had arrived in Sir Anthony Gresham's coach. Smythe had not known whose coach it was, only that it bore the same crest upon its doors as the coach that nearly ran them down on a country road while he and Will were on their way to London. In the heat of his anger, Smythe had forgotten himself completely as he ran up to the coach and threw open its door, fully intent on dragging out its occupant and thrashing him, gentleman or not, only to be brought up short at the sight of Elizabeth sitting there alone. She had taken his breath away, and Smythe found that familiarity had not diminished in the least the effect she had upon him.

She was nineteen, the same age as he, with pale blond hair, fair skin, and eyes so blue they almost seemed to glow. She was easily the most beautiful woman Smythe had ever seen, and he could scarcely believe that she was still unmarried, despite all her father's efforts to secure a husband for her. She was stunningly attractive, with a prominent, wealthy merchant for a father, and it seemed as if there would have been no shortage of eager suitors wanting to take her for a wife. However, anxious as he may have been to get his daughter married off, Henry Darcie would not accept just any suitor. In order to be suitable, a suitor for Elizabeth's hand in marriage had to be a gentleman, and preferably a titled one who could serve Darcie's desire for advancement. That alone narrowed down the field considerably, but Elizabeth herself narrowed it down still further.

For one thing, she was tall for a woman, though not as tall as Smythe, who stood over six feet, and most gentlemen who were conscious of appearances—and what gentleman was not?—would not wish to have a wife who towered over them. For another, she was rather willful and independent—some would say spoiled, though Smythe did not find her so—qualities generally far less desirable in a gentleman's wife than compliance and amiability. And then there was the matter of her age, which could give a prospective suitor pause.

With most young women being betrothed at eleven or twelve and married at fourteen or fifteen, unmarried women of seventeen or eighteen were often considered to be approaching spinsterhood, especially if they came from a good family. And for prospective suitors, aside from the obvious desirability of a more youthful maiden, there was also the lingering question of why Elizabeth was still unmarried at nineteen. A man of position had to wonder what could be wrong with her that she was still unmarried, despite her dowry and her beauty. Immediately suspect would be her disposition. No gentleman of means and social prominence wanted to be married to a shrew.

For her part, Elizabeth did not hesitate to exploit such masculine concerns, for the truth was, as Smythe knew, she had no great desire to be married, unless it were for love. Even then, she had her reservations, especially after the near disaster of her betrothal to Sir

Anthony Gresham, which at least for the present had cured Henry Darcie of his desire to see his daughter quickly married off. But if he had become more cautious concerning potential suitors for his daughter, Henry Darcie had become no less so concerning Smythe's involvement with her.

While he was grateful for the service Smythe had performed in saving his daughter from a terrible fate and himself from playing an unwitting part in a devilish foreign plot against the realm, which could easily have destroyed all hope of his advancement, Darcie was nevertheless not so grateful as to lose all sight of propriety, so Smythe and Elizabeth had to arrange to see each other on the sly.

"Elizabeth!" Smythe said, taking her hand in his and raising it gently to his lips.

"I have missed you," she said in that forthright manner that he found so absolutely charming, lowering her mask so he could see her lovely face.

"And I you," he replied. "I was so glad to get your message. I trust that nothing is amiss? Your family is well?"

"All is well at home," she said. " 'Twas kind of you to ask about them, as they do not inquire about you." She smiled, mischievously. "You have heard about the wedding of Godfrey Middleton's eldest daughter, Catherine?"

He nodded. "I have. The Queen's Men have an engagement to entertain the wedding party with the performance of a play."

She gazed at him anxiously. "I know. So then . . . you are going to be there?"

"Yes, I shall." He frowned. "Why? Are you not coming?"

"Of course I will be there," Elizabeth replied. She took his arm and they started walking slowly down the aisle, past the busy market stalls. "I am to be the maid of honor to the bride. Catherine Middleton is my very good friend. But the last time that you and I spoke, Tuck, you seemed uncertain about your standing with the company and I did not know if things had changed for you since then."

"Well, they have not dismissed me from their service yet, if that is what you mean," Smythe said. "For all of my appalling lack of talent, it appears I am still useful to them, albeit mostly in roles that do not require my presence on the stage."

She rolled her eyes. "You know, I do not think that you are nearly so inept as you portray yourself."

"There is an entire company of players who would give you a good argument upon that score," said Smythe, with a self-deprecating grin. "And as my Uncle Thomas used to say, ' 'Tis a wise man who knows his limitations.' I am well aware of mine, Elizabeth, for better or for worse."

"Then why do you persist in your desire to be a player? You told me once that you had learned the craft of smithing from your uncle, and that he had also taught you how to forge fine blades. Both pursuits are honorable trades. Why, a good armorer could, with the right patronage, achieve a reputation and advance himself into the gentry. That would not be out of your reach, you know. My father is already indebted to you, as is Sir William. Both men, I am quite certain, would be more than willing to assist you if you wanted to set up in trade. And if you were to become a gentleman, why then, Father could have no possible objection to our seeing one another."

"Elizabeth," said Smythe, squeezing her arm gently, "your father has objected to more than one gentleman already. And aside from that, becoming a gentleman does not always solve one's problems. My father is a gentleman, with his own escutcheon, for all the good that it has done him."

She stood and stared at him, startled. "What! But you have never told me this!"

He merely shrugged. "I saw no reason to make mention of it."

"No reason! No reason, indeed! You mean to tell me that you come from a good family? That your father is a gentleman, a country squire, and you came to London to become an *ostler*?" She stared at him with disbelief.

"I came to London to become a *player*."

"Well, you were an ostler when we met and, in any event, a player is not much better than an ostler in my father's eyes. But do not try to change the subject! Why did you not *tell* me?"

"Because I do not see what difference it could possibly have made," said Smythe.

"To me, none," Elizabeth replied, "but 'twould have made a world of difference to my father!"

"Methinks not," said Smythe. " 'Twould only have made matters worse, if your father knew the truth of it."

"Whatever do you mean? What truth?"

"My father is a very vain and foolish man," said Smythe, without any trace of bitterness or rancor. "I know 'tis disrespectful to speak so of one's parent, but if it makes me a bad son to speak the truth, so be it, then. The truth is that my father wanted so to be a gentleman, to have an escutcheon of his own that he could blazon upon the windows and the mantle and the entryway, embroider upon the blue coats of his servants and gild upon his coach, that he spent a goodly portion of his inheritance in currying favor and paying bribes and buying influence. In time, and at no little cost, he was able to achieve his goal and was eventually granted his escutcheon by the heralds, which he then proceeded to affix to everything you could imagine, from his pewter cups to his gauntlets and his handkerchiefs of Flemish lawn and sarcenet. Meanwhile, my Uncle Thomas, to whom I had been sent for rearing, had no such lofty ambitions or pretensions. Even if he had, he could ill afford them, for 'twas my father as the eldest who had been favored in the will."

"And you mean to say he never helped your uncle?" asked Elizabeth.

"That matter was never formally discussed with me, but I am as certain that my uncle never asked as I am that my father never offered," Smythe replied. "Who is to say but that had my father raised me, instead of Uncle Thomas, then perhaps I might have turned out more like him, so I am grateful that my uncle was much more of a father to me than the man whose name I bear."

"But it nevertheless is the name of a gentleman," Elizabeth said.

"Aye, a gentleman who was not satisfied with having achieved the rank that he had bought so dearly and instead newly set his sights upon a knighthood. To which end, he spent himself very nearly into debtors' prison. He is now little better than a pauper, and the truth is I rather doubt your father would find very much about him of which he could approve."

"For all that they seem to have so much in common," Elizabeth said, wryly, referring to her father's own considerable social ambitions. "Oh, but Tuck, why did you never tell me this?"

"As I have said, I saw no reason for it. My father is my father, for better or for worse, as I am myself. I have no part of his accomplishments or failures. I prefer to be judged on my own merits, or the lack of them, whichever the case may be. And 'twas never my desire to be like my father, or my Uncle Thomas, for that matter, for all of the respect and love I bear him. Toiling at a forge is hard and honest work, good work, and I believe I am an able craftsman, but the truth is that it has never been my passion. Ever since I saw my first play acted out upon a tavern stage, I have wanted to become a player. 'Tis all I ever wanted. Nothing more."

"And your father did not approve, of course," Elizabeth said, nodding with understanding.

"Aye, he did not. He stormed and thundered, threatened to disown me, but I would not give up my dream, and in the end, when he had squandered what was left of his inheritance — and mine — I realized at last that there was nothing left to hold me, and so I left home and came to London to pursue my dream. Perhaps I am as vain and foolish in that as my father was in his pursuit of social position and a knighthood, so who am I to judge him?"

Elizabeth smiled and placed her hand upon his as he held her arm. "I would not call you a bad son," she said, softly. "I think you are a far better one than he deserves."

"Well, that is neither here nor there," said Smythe, a bit uncomfortably, though it felt wonderful to hear that from her. "The point is, whatever I am to make of myself, I must do it by myself."

"I understand how you must feel," she said, after a moment's pause, "but I do not think I can agree."

"Indeed? And why is that?"

"Because I can see no particular virtue in refusing help when it is offered, or in refusing to take advantage of social connections. We live, after all, in a society where such connections are pursued with vigor and people are often rewarded not for merit, but for the relationships that they have cultivated. Why, even the queen bestows rewards upon her favorites, who vie with one another for position. I have seen my father thrive in such a fashion, which is how he has built his business and his fortune."

"And I have seen *my* father bring himself to ruin doing just the same," said Smythe.

"Because he did not do it wisely," said Elizabeth. "You said yourself that he had tried to buy his way into a knighthood. I was not trying to suggest that you should attempt to purchase favor, as he did, merely that you should not scorn the favor you have already *earned*. Consider your friend, Will."

"What has Will to do with any of this?"

"He serves well to illustrate my point. The part he played in helping me resulted from his desire to help *you*, because you are his friend. In turn, by assisting you in helping me, he has also helped Sir William, though that merely came about by happenstance. And despite the fact that Will Shakespeare did not set out specifically to help Sir William, Sir William was nevertheless appreciative, and he, in turn, has helped Will Shakespeare by mentioning his name at court and praising him as a poet, which has already begun to bring him some commissions and earn him something of a reputation. Sir William would be no less willing to help you, for your help to him was even greater than your friend Will Shakespeare's. There is no dishonor in any of this, Tuck, no injury to pride. No one has tried to purchase favor, and no bribes have been offered or accepted. 'Tis merely a matter of people helping one another. Just as you helped me when I came to you because I had nowhere else to turn."

"Well, to be completely honest," Smythe said, "I cannot claim that I was moved to help you entirely out of the goodness of my heart. 'Twould be base of me if I were to deny that, at least in part, I did have somewhat baser motives."

She smiled. "And what makes you think that I did not, as well?" She chuckled at the surprised expression on his face. "You look as if I have just sprouted horns. Why do men always presume that only *they* can think and feel such things?"

"I am not sure that we do presume so," he replied, recovering. "It is just that we are unaccustomed to hear women speak of them. Especially with such frankness."

"And why should a woman not speak as frankly as a man?"

"Well, because 'tis not very womanly, I suppose," he replied, with a smile.

"Now you sound just like my father," she said, with a grimace. "The queen speaks frankly, from everything I hear, and yet no one thinks *her* any less womanly for it."

"Well, that is different; she is the queen," Smythe said.

Elizabeth looked up at the cathedral ceiling as if seeking deliverance and shook her head in exasperation. "Again, that is just what my father would have said. 'Tis a most unsatisfactory and unreasonable reply. It does not even address the question. You say 'tis unwomanly for a woman to speak frankly. I tell you that the queen speaks frankly and yet she is a woman, and you respond by saying that it is different because she is the queen. Where is the sense in that? *How* is it different?"

"I should think the sense in my reply should be self evident," Smythe said. "The queen is not like ordinary women."

"Indeed. Does being the queen make her any less a woman?"

"Certainly not. Quite the contrary, I should say."

"So then if being the queen makes her more of a woman, then does speaking frankly make her any less the queen?"

They made the turn on the Walk and started heading back arm-in-arm the way they came. Smythe could not help but notice how men turned to stare openly at Elizabeth as they went by. "Of course not," Smythe replied, feeling distracted and somewhat irritated. "As queen, 'tis her royal perogative to speak in whatever manner she should choose."

"Why then would she choose to speak in a manner that makes a woman seem less womanly, rather than more?"

Smythe frowned. "Because she is the *queen*, and cannot be judged by the same standards as ordinary people like ourselves. Indeed, 'tis not for us to judge her in any way at all, for she rules by the divine grace of God."

"And yet, strange as it may seem, God made her a woman," Elizabeth replied.

"Do you presume to question *God*?" he asked, raising his eyebrows.

"Why is it that whenever a woman presumes to question men, they act as if she has presumed to question God?" Elizabeth replied. " 'Tis most vexing and exasperating. I truly thought you would be different, Tuck, but I see now that my friend Catherine was right."

"*Catherine?*" Smythe said, frowning. He could not understand why their conversation had taken this peculiar turn, or how it had turned into an argument, but it seemed as if Catherine Middleton was somehow behind it all. Until the previous day, when he had learned that the Queen's Men would be playing at her wedding, he had never even heard of her. Now, suddenly, she was Elizabeth's "very good friend." He could not recall Elizabeth ever even mentioning her name.

"She said that men are all alike in that aspect," Elizabeth continued.

"And what aspect is that?" he asked, confused.

"That if a man spoke frankly and asserted himself, then he would be regarded as bold, intelligent, and forthright. Yet if a woman were to do the very same, she would be branded a truculent scold and a shrew. And to think I disagreed with her and insisted you were different! Oh, you should have heard her laugh!"

"She laughed at *me*?"

"No, at *me*! Why must you think 'tis always about *you*? 'Twas my innocence that so amused her. She told me that at my age, one would think I would know better!"

"And what is Catherine's age, if one may be so boorish as to ask?"

"She is seventeen years old."

"Two years younger?" Smythe said, mildly surprised. "Why, from the way she spoke to you, I would have thought she was much older."

"She makes me feel as if she is," Elizabeth replied. "For all that she is younger, she is much more clever and spirited than I."

"She sounds rather arrogant to me," said Smythe. "And rather graceless and ill-mannered, too."

"You *see*?" Elizabeth said, breaking away from him. "You have just given the very proof of her perception!"

"I see nothing of the sort," he replied, angrily, feeling the color rising to his face. "What I see is that this girl has been filling your head with all sorts of arrant nonsense. I have never met Catherine Middleton, nor has she even laid eyes upon me, and yet despite this, she apparently deems herself fit to sit in judgement over my character, and not only mine, which is presumptuous enough, but all men in general. Would that I had such wisdom at the age of seventeen! Odd's blood! With such sagacity, by now I could have been not only a gentleman in my own right, but a privy counselor and doubtless a peer of the realm! Indeed, perhaps we should recommend your friend Catherine to Sir William, so that he, in turn, can recommend her to the queen, for 'tis clear that she should be advising her along with Walsingham and Cecil as one of her chief ministers."

"Oh, now who is spouting arrant nonsense?" Elizabeth retorted. "You are speaking like a simple, addle-pated fool!"

"Well, you might recall that 'twas this 'simple, addle-pated fool' to whom you turned for help when you were in your desperate hour," Smythe replied, stung by her words. "And when all else seemed convinced that you were taking leave of your senses and would soon be bound for Bedlam, 'twas this 'simple, addle-pated fool' alone who listened to you and believed in you and helped you. Well, fool I may be, milady, but I shall tell you who is the greater fool, and that would be the man whose supreme folly shall be to say 'I do' to Catherine Middleton, for in his 'do-ing' shall come his undoing, mark my words."

"He shall be marrying a shrew, is that your meaning, then?" asked Elizabeth, archly.

"'Twas you who said it and not I!"

She shook her head. "You sorely disappoint me, Tuck. I expected rather more from you. But then 'tis I who am to blame for having expectations. Women who have expectations of men are often doomed to disappointment."

"And did your clever friend Catherine say that, too?" asked Smythe.

"As a matter of fact, she did," Elizabeth replied. "I disagreed with her in that, as well, and told her that *you* lived up to *all* my expectations. 'You will see,' was all she said. And so I have. Would that I had not. Good day to you, sir."

She abruptly turned and walked away with a firm, purposeful stride.

Smythe was so taken aback, he simply stood there motionless, staring after her, caught in the grip of indecision and conflicting emotions. A part of him wanted to go after her, but he was not sure if it was to apologize or else continue the argument until he could make her see his side of it. Yet another part stubbornly resisted, telling him to let her go and let the devil take her. He felt very angry, but at the same time, he was filled with regret and self-reproach. And he did not understand what had just happened.

They had never argued like this before. Elizabeth had never be-

haved like that before. It was a side of her that he had never before
seen. Granted, she was willful and possessed of strong opinions, but
he had never known her to be so utterly unreasonable, so stubbornly
obstinate, so . . . shrewish.

The corners of his mouth turned down in distaste as he thought
of Catherine Middleton, a young woman whom he did not even
know, but whom he already disliked intensely. She appeared to be
trying to poison Elizabeth's mind against him. And apparently, she
was succeeding.

"Oh, you were so right, Catherine!" Elizabeth said. "He behaved
just as you predicted!"

"Well, that is because men are so utterly predictable," Catherine
Middleton said dryly, as the tailor and his apprentices busied themselves with the fitting of her wedding gown. "*Ow!* Have a care, you
clumsy oaf! You stuck me again!"

"Forgive me, mistress," said the young apprentice, around a
mouthful of pins, as he draped cloth over her farthingale. "I shall
try to be more careful."

"That is what you said the last two times," replied Catherine,
noting that he did not sound especially contrite. "I am not here to
be your pin cushion, you fumble-fingered rogue." She turned to the
tailor. "If you cannot find any male apprentices who are less ham-
handed, then perhaps you should seek to employ women, so they
can perform the job properly!" The cloth slipped from the farthingale as she turned, causing the apprentice to step back, throw up his
hands and roll his eyes at his master in exasperation.

"The seamstresses who work for me do the job very properly,
indeed, milady," said the tailor, in a haughty tone, as he stood back
with his arms folded, surveying the scene with a critical eye. "However, the fitting must perforce be done properly for them to do their
job the way they should. And that requires a certain degree of cooperation from the *wearer* of the dress, you see."

"The wearer of the dress shall not survive to wear it if she is bled to death by your incompetent apprentices," Catherine replied, dryly. "*Ow*! Now you did that on *purpose*, you miserable cur!" She shoved the offending apprentice away and he lost his balance, falling hard on his rump, venom in his angry gaze.

"I must insist that you desist from abusing my apprentices, milady," the tailor said.

"Then kindly instruct them to keep their oafish hands to themselves!" Catherine replied, jerking away from another young apprentice as he fumbled at her extremely low-cut bodice. "You think I do not know what they are about, the knaves?"

"Here, here, what's all this row?" demanded Godfrey Middleton sternly as he entered the room. "Catherine, I could hear you railing clearly all the way from the bottom of the stairs!"

"Well then, Father, I am pleased that you shall hear more clearly still now that you are here," Catherine replied.

Elizabeth had to bite down on her knuckle to keep from chuckling. She knew her own father thought that she was spoiled and willful, but she would never have had the courage to speak to him as Catherine did to her father. Not that Catherine was truly rude or disrespectful. She managed somehow to be defiant without openly appearing to defy. It was, however, a fine line that she walked, and Catherine sometimes seemed balanced quite precariously.

"I have heard clearly enough already," Middleton said, with a sniff. "There is no excuse for this cantankerous behavior, Catherine. These men are merely trying to do their job."

"Trying is truly what they are," said Catherine. "They are trying my patience sorely with their pricking pins and groping fingers. I find this entire process vexing and outrageous beyond measure."

"Milord, upon my oath, I can assure you that my apprentices and I have exercised the utmost care and taken absolutely no untoward liberties," the tailor said, in a gravely offended tone. "Indeed, if any injury has been sustained here, it has been to young Gregory, yonder, who was just assaulted in a most unseemly manner by your daughter."

"Aye, 'twas most unseemly," echoed Gregory, looking like a little dog that had been kicked.

"I'll give you unseemly, you lying little guttersnipe!" said Catherine, raising her hand at him. Gregory cowered, as if in fear for his very life.

"That will be quite enough, Kate!" her father said.

"I *hate* it when you call me Kate," she replied, through gritted teeth. "My name is Catherine!"

"I should think I ought to know your name, girl, I bloody well gave it to you."

"Father!"

"Be silent! God's Wounds, I shall be eternally grateful when at last you have become your husband's baggage and not mine. These seventeen long years I have put up with your sharp tongue and it has exhausted all my patience."

"Really, Father, it cannot have been that long, surely. For the first three or four of those seventeen years, I could scarcely even speak."

"You learned soon enough and well enough to suit me," Middleton replied, dryly.

"I have always sought to please you, Father," Catherine said. " 'Tis a source of great discomfort to me that I have always failed to do so. Would that I had been a son and not a daughter, then doubtless I would have found it much less of a hardship to find favor in your eyes."

"Would indeed that you had been a son and not a daughter," said her father. "Then I would not have had to pay nearly a king's ransom to get you married off."

Gregory, the young apprentice, chuckled at that, but Catherine ignored him. The only evidence she gave that she had heard him was a tightening of her upper lip. Elizabeth thought it was insufferable that her father should speak to her that way in front of strangers. She felt awkward being in the same room with them herself.

"And yet you are paying merely in coin and a vested interest in your business," Catherine said, "while I am paying with my body and my soul and all my worldly goods. If the shoe were on the other foot, and 'twas I who paid the dowry to have *you* married off, then which of us, I wonder, would you think was paying the greater price?"

"The greatest price, I fear, shall be paid by poor Sir Percival, who shall be marrying naught but trouble and strife," said Middleton. "My conscience is clear, however, for none can say that I made any misrepresentations at all in that regard. Indeed, I made a point of it to acquaint Sir Percival in full with the nature of your disputatious disposition, so that no claim could afterward be made that I was not forthright in all respects concerning this betrothal and this union, and so that no rancor ever could be borne."

"And that is very well, for I would not wish you to bear Sir Percy's rancor, Father," Catherine said. "Better by far that a husband should bear rancor towards his bride than towards his father-in-law. 'Tis well that you have so fully acquainted him with the nature of my disposition, as you say, for now at least one of us shall know something of the one with whom we are to say our vows."

Her father harrumphed and frowned, looking as if he were about to make a sharp rejoinder, but instead chose to direct his comments towards the tailor. "Are you finished yet with all this bother? God's Wounds, one would think that you were costuming the queen herself!"

"A moment more, milord," the tailor said, fussing about and hovering around Catherine like some great predatory bird. He made a few final adjustments, stepped back to admire his handiwork, nodded to himself with satisfaction and then clapped his hands, signalling his apprentices to finish and pack everything away.

"At last!" said Catherine, with a heavy sigh. "I was beginning to feel like some bedraggled scarecrow in the field."

"Would that your dress were no more expensive than a scarecrow's," said her father. "With what this fellow charges for his work, I could attire at least half the court."

"Milord, I *have* attired at least half the court," the tailor responded stiffly, "and upon occasion, even Her Majesty herself, as you must surely know, for you had inquired about my work before you ever came to me. If a gentleman wishes to have nothing but the very best, then he must be prepared to pay for nothing but the very best. I can assure you that once the work is done, and your daughter in her wedding dress would make the goddess Aphrodite blush for the meanness of her own apparel, I am confident that you will consider the money to have been well spent, indeed."

"Spent is just how I shall feel when all of this is over," Middleton replied. "No sooner shall I have recovered from the ordeal of marrying off my eldest daughter than I shall have to contend with marrying off my youngest, who already has suitors flocked about her like hounds baying at the moon. A day does not go by, it seems, when some young rascal does not come pleading for her hand."

"Well, be of good cheer then, Father," Catherine said, "for at least you have never been beleaguered so on my account."

"Had you a sweeter and more amiable disposition, like your sister, you might have been married sooner, Kate," her father replied.

"Never fear, dear Father," Catherine said pleasantly, with only the barest trace of sarcasm in her voice, "I shall be married soon enough, and sweet and amiable Blanche will surely follow hard upon, for all the panting swains who trip over themselves to find her favor. Then, when you are at long last rid of both your daughters, doubtless you shall find the peace and carefree solace you have always longed for."

"Indeed, the day cannot come soon enough for me," he said, stepping aside to let the tailor and his apprentices out the door. He wrinkled his nose as they passed and raised a small pomander on a gold link chain to his nose. The little golden ball was perforated, so that the scent within could escape and help mask offending odors. "Good evening, Elizabeth."

"Good evening, sir," she said, lowering her head, though not so much out of respect as to conceal her smile and barely-suppressed giggle at Catherine's face, which was perfectly mimicking her father's expression of distaste behind his back.

"I could just scream," said Catherine, after he had left and shut the door behind him. She rolled her eyes. "The way he goes on over this wedding, one would think he was out at the elbows."

" 'Tis a most elaborate and costly affair, though, you must admit," Elizabeth said. "Her Majesty's own tailor makes your wedding gown, a grand, costumed progress on the Thames is being planned, to say nothing of the players and the fair being held to commemorate the occasion . . . indeed, your father spares no expense."

"But do you think any of it is truly for *me?*" asked Catherine, as her tire woman helped her out of her large hooped, canvas and whalebone farthingale, which she had worn over a simple homespun long tunic for the fitting. "He does it all only for himself, so that all of London shall talk of nothing but the wedding of Godfrey Middleton's daughter. Such a spectacle! So grand! So fabulous! And to think what it must have cost him! That, my dear Lizzie, is the true object of this entire exercise."

"But everyone knows full well how rich your father is," Elizabeth replied, with a slight frown. "How does he profit by reminding them?"

" 'Tis not everyone he wishes to remind," said Catherine, as she removed her long tunic and was assisted into a simple kirtled skirt of marigold velvet accented with gold and silver embroidery. "Mind you, he wishes everyone to speak of this Olympian wedding festival for months on end, but only so that an important few may hear."

"But why?" Elizabeth asked.

"Well, you know, of course, that each year at about this time, the queen sets out upon her annual progress through the countryside," Catherine replied. "She takes a different route each time, one

year moving with her entire court from Whitehall to Suffolk, then
to Norfolk and from there, on to Cambridgeshire, perhaps. Another
year, she will travel from Westminster to Sussex to Kent, or else
to Northhamptonshire, and then on to Warwickshire and Stafford-
shire . . . but each and every year, with never an exception, she begins her progress the same way. Her first stop is always at Green
Oaks, where Sir William Worley entertains her lavishly. And each
and every year, Elizabeth, at about this very time, my father nearly
wears his teeth down to the gums for gnashing them because the
queen has chosen to sleep beneath Sir William's roof instead of ours.
He would do anything to have her stay at Harrow Hall, instead,
even if 'twas only once, for once is all that it would take to vault
him into the vaunted ranks of the queen's favorites. And once he
can number himself amongst that exclusive company, he will have
attained influence at court, prestige, and power, which is what he
desires above all else. Meanwhile, what his daughter may desire concerns him least of all."

"I know only too well how you must feel," Elizabeth said, sym-
pathetically. "Your father and mine have much in common, which
is doubtless why they are good friends. They understand one another."

"As do we, dear Lizzie," said Catherine. " 'Tis a pity they do not
understand us as well. But then, they do not truly wish to understand. Men never do."

And thinking of her argument with Smythe, Elizabeth sighed
and said, "No, it seems that they do not."

3

ODFREY MIDDLETON'S STATELY, TURRETED STONE manor was elegant testimony to his success in business, thought Smythe as their little caravan turned up the winding road leading to the estate. It was dramatic evidence of how the world was changing, when a "new man" like Middleton could, with luck and industry, pull himself up by his own bootstraps and enter the new—and much despised by some—English middle class, though there was nothing at all middling about Middleton's estate.

Located a few miles to the west of Westminster, Middleton Manor overlooked the Thames, fronting on the river's north bank. The large river gate gave access to several terraced flights of wide stone steps that led up to the house, and it was this way that most of the wedding party would arrive during the grand nautical progress that was planned. Part of the duties of the Queen's Men, aside from putting on a play, would be to act as costumed greeters for the wedding guests, so they had been provided with a map drawn up especially for the occasion, showing the general layout of the estate, with instructions as to where their stage should be erected, as well as where the pavillions and the booths for the fair would be set up.

The house was set back a considerable distance from the road, on the crest of a gently sloping hill. The narrow, winding drive that led up to the imposing stone house from the main thoroughfare curved around a copse of good, stout English oaks and shrub thickets that hid a large pond from view from the road. They saw it as they came around the bend, where the road ran below and past the house for a short distance and then doubled back to the top of the hill, leading past lushly planted gardens and an elaborate maze with its tall hedges carefully clipped to perfection. As the road curved around the side of the house, leading towards the front entrance on the river side, it gave way to a cobblestoned plaza large enough for a coach to turn around.

Past the stables and some outbuildings, on the gentle slope to the east of the house, they could see the gayly striped and beribboned pavillions for the wedding and, just beyond them, in the field, the stalls for the fair were being erected. Already, merchants were arriving and setting up their tables. Most came by boat, disembarking and unloading their goods at the ornately carved stone river gate, but others, eager for an opportunity to sell their wares to some of the wealthiest citizens of London, were braving the road in carts and wagons, taking their chances not only with highwaymen, but with the weather as well, which could easily render the road from the city impassable in the event of rain. The river was by far the preferable and most reliable way for most people to travel in the environs of London, but unfortunately, it would not serve a company of players setting out upon a wide-ranging tour of the surrounding countryside.

"Quite the hurly burly," Shakespeare said, as he observed all the activity. "That ground will be all churned up into mud by the time this festival is over. I do not envy the groundskeepers all the work that they shall have to do to put it right again."

"They shall doubtless merely plough it up for planting," Burbage said. "There shall not be too much damage, as this is only a small, private fair, a social event for the wedding guests alone," Dick Burbage said. "The merchants are allowed to participate by invitation only."

Smythe shook his head. "Even so, I should not wish to clean

up after all of this. How many stalls and tents are they erecting? It seems I can count at least thirty or so from here. That does not seem like a small fair to me at all."

Burbage laughed. "You will not say that after you have lived awhile in London, country boy. Bartholomew's Fair boasts many more stalls and tents than you shall see here by a good measure, and the Stourbridge Fair, near Cambridge, is larger still. You would never see it all properly in just one day. However, I would wager that the goods you shall find for sale here will come a great deal more dearly than the run of what you might find at Bart's or Stourbridge. These boys will all be charging as much as the traffic will allow, and you may be sure the purses here shall all be rather heavy ones."

They were riding together at an easy walk, three or four abreast, with a wagon and two carts following behind, giving them the aspect of a small gypsy caravan. On the road, a company of players traveled as lightly as possible, but they still needed to bring all of their costumes and their props, as well as the materials to put up their stage and effect any necessary repairs to their equipment while they were out on tour. Sometimes it was necessary to send a rider or two on ahead to make preparations for their arrival in a town or at some country inn, and so they travelled with several spare mounts in addition to the cart and wagon horses. The wagon was painted with their name in ornate, gilt-edged letters, so that all would know the Queen's Men were approaching, and they proudly flew their swallowtailed banner, as well.

As they approached the house, it took on even more grandeur up close than it had possessed from a distance, seen from the road. The carved stonework between the vast array of mullioned windows was now clearly visible and the sheer size of the place impressed itself upon them even more.

"Odd's blood, 'tis less a house than a small castle," Shakespeare said. "It seems to lack only the moat and battlements and crenellations. 'Twould not surprise me to find a ghost or two stalking the halls at midnight. How would you say this place compares to Sir William's estate, Tuck?"

"Oh, quite favorably, indeed," replied Smythe, very much impressed. "Only this has the aspect of a much newer construction. And I do believe 'tis somewhat larger than Green Oaks, unless I miss my guess."

"Your eyes serve you well," Burbage said. "From what my father tells me, Middleton Manor was completed only four years ago, by the same architect who had built Green Oaks for Sir William Worley, save that Sir William's house had been extensively refurbished, while Middleton Manor was newly built in its entirety. My father said the architect had been specifically instructed to surpass what had been done at Green Oaks, with no heed whatever to the cost. And from what I see before me, judging only by the exterior of the house, it would seem that little heed was paid, indeed, if any."

"Middleton must have spent a goodly fortune on this place," said Smythe. "I would swear there are more chimneys rising from this roof alone than could be found in my entire village. I will wager that each room has its own fireplace. And just look at all that glass! There are even bay windows in each turret! The morning light within must be quite blinding."

As they proceeded around the side of the house, the river came into view below them, where the bank fell away sharply from the terraced slope. The sight that greeted them as they made the turn and saw the river made them all pull up short and stare.

Below them, a small flotilla of boats was approaching from the east in what looked like a carefully arranged formation. Most of the boats were being rowed by rivermen, but some of the larger ones were under sail and there were two barges being towed in the midst of the motley looking fleet. Both barges had been modified so that they had the aspect of craft that would convey Egyptian royalty, or at least someone's idea of what such a vessel might have looked like. A large afterdeck had been erected on each barge, each with a dais and elaborate canopies of purple cloth fringed with gold, and benches had been placed along each deckrail for "slave rowers," though it seemed that the oars were only for show. They appeared much too short to be very functional, scarcely brushing the surface of the water. And after a moment's observation, it became evident that they were not functional at all, but nailed in place, for none of them moved at all. In one of the lead boats, a man was standing and shouting commands through a large horn as the boats bobbed in the choppy current, trying to maintain position relative to one another.

"What in God's name are they doing?" Smythe asked, perplexed.

"We, of all people, should be able to tell that," Shakespeare replied. "They are rehearsing."

"Oh, of course," said Burbage. "They are preparing for the wedding progress. The theme, remember? Queen Cleopatra comes to visit the Emperor Julius Caesar."

John Fleming shook his head as he rode up beside them to watch the nautical maneuvering. "Methinks Cleopatra could use a better steersman," he observed, dryly. "Her barge seems to be in the process of ramming her own escorts."

Several of the boats had indeed suffered collision with the barge as Fleming spoke. The barge had drifted into them, and a number of the others steered quickly out of line to avoid the mess. One of the smaller boats was foundering and the man with the horn seemed to be having fits. He was holding the horn with one hand, shouting into it at the top of his lungs, and waving directions frantically with his free hand.

"I, for one, find that rehearsal with a company of unruly players on a stage poses challenges enough, without having to concern myself with the disposition of a small fleet," said Burbage, with a chuckle.

"What concerns me more," said Shakespeare, with a trace of anxiety in his voice, "is how our play shall compare with this elaborate nautical spectacle, to say naught of the distractions of the fair. I fear that we may have no easy task before us, my friends."

As he spoke, the queen's barge kept on drifting, sliding sideways in the current and bumping into two other small boats that were not quick enough to get out of the way, no matter how desperately their boatmen rowed. The man in charge of directing the flotilla began leaping up and down in a frenzy, shouting himself hoarse into his horn.

"He is going to upset that boat if he does not watch out," said Speed.

The little boat was rocking violently and the boatman started shouting at his frantic passenger, who spun around angrily to shout back at the boatman and, in the process, lost his balance and plunged headlong into the river.

"Man overboard!" Will Kemp cried in his ringing stage voice, from his seat beside Speed in the wagon.

They all burst out laughing heartily, but Smythe's laughter died abruptly in his throat when he saw the stricken expression on his roommate's face. Shakespeare alone was not laughing. He was watching it all with a look of chagrin and, for a moment, Smythe could not account for it. He gazed at the poet with puzzled concern, and then a moment later, comprehension dawned.

Had he not known Will Shakespeare as he did, Smythe would not have understood, but all at once he realized that his friend was viewing the disaster down below—and especially their laughter at it—as a harbinger of things to come. Shakespeare had no confidence in the play that he had written. He had not wanted it performed. Indeed, he had kept insisting that it was not finished, but his concerns had been dismissed as nothing more than the natural hesitancy of a poet before the first performance of his work. If there were any problems, the Queen's Men were confident that they could be fixed during rehearsal. After all, they had seen Shakespeare rewrite plays already in their repertoire at a lightning pace, often making extensive changes overnight, or even inbetween performances, and those changes were always for the better. It occurred to Smythe that

Burbage and the others all took this ability for granted. The only one who apparently did not was Shakespeare.

It had become evident now that the barge was drifting due to the parting of one of its tow ropes. As they watched it skewing sideways, Smythe understood that Shakespeare was envisioning a similar disaster on the stage and seeing himself in the role of the unfortunate fellow with the horn. The man was being assisted back into the boat as they watched. Somehow, he had managed to retain a grip on his horn, but now, in a fury, he tossed it violently overboard.

"I would not concern myself overmuch with competition from that sort of spectacle, if I were you," Burbage said to Shakespeare, leaning over in his saddle slightly and reaching across to clap him on the shoulder. "If they manage to pull it off without sinking themselves like Drake sank the Armada, why then at best, it shall be merely a parade of boats and two silly looking barges, one bearing a bride dressed like an Egyptian queen and the other conveying the wedding party. By the time they reach the river gate down there and disembark, all watching will have wearied of the sight. And if they repeat this sorry show, why, they shall merely amuse the audience and prime them for our own merrymaking. Odd's blood, if the Queen's Men cannot easily surpass a little water pageant, then we should all start looking for something else to do."

They were met by the steward of the estate, a gaunt, balding and smugly self-important man who introduced himself as Humphrey. Like many of the wealthy middle class, in imitation of the aristocracy, Godfrey Middleton divided his time between residence at his country estate and a home that he maintained in the city. Even though it was less than a day's ride to London, with his business concerns keeping him in the city much of the time, it was necessary for Middleton to have a capable steward in charge of his country house. It was a large responsibility, and Humphrey's manner indicated he was quite aware of that and thought everyone else should be, as well. He was neither rude in his greeting of them nor was he dismissive, but he nevertheless gave the impression that he was a very busy man with many more important things to do, which was doubtless true, thought Smythe, at least under the current circumstances, considering all the preparations that he had to oversee for the wedding and the fair.

Without wasting any time, Humphrey rattled off their instructions. They were to proceed directly to the stables, where their horses and equipment would be put up by the grooms, and then immediately set about their preparations for the staging of their play, which was to take place on the morrow, in the late afternoon, following the wedding. It meant that they would not have much time, if any, to rehearse. If they were quick in setting up, then there might be an opportunity to get in one quick rehearsal in the evening. In the morning, they would all be busy greeting the wedding party as they arrived.

"Costumes shall be provided for you," Humphrey stated curtly, with a slightly preoccupied look, as if ticking off a mental list. "You shall be receiving them this evening while you are setting up your stage and can then divide them amongst yourselves, accordingly."

"What sort of costumes?" Burbage asked, with a slight frown. "I was not aware that we would be donning any costumes other than our own. Surely, there cannot be any time for fittings?"

"Fittings shall not be necessary," Humphrey replied. "The costumes are merely simple white robes that drape over the body. You shall be Roman senators, welcoming our distinguished guests as they arrive and helping them disembark, then escorting them up to the house, where my staff shall take over their charge."

"Ah, of course," said Kemp. "As everyone knows, the august members of the Roman Senate always took the part of porters at the docks whenever important guests arrived to visit Caesar."

Humphrey arched a disdainful eyebrow at Kemp's sarcasm and then more than matched it with his own. "If you prefer, we could make you a Nubian slave, strip you to your waist, darken your skin with coal dust, and have you walk behind the guests, carrying an ostrich feather fan."

"Methinks I would just as soon serve in the Senate," Kemp replied, with a sour grimace, as the others chuckled.

"The schedule of events does not leave us much time to rehearse," said Burbage.

The steward's expressive eyebrow elevated once again. "Well? You are the Queen's Men, are you not, the self-proclaimed masters of tragedy and comedy? I was informed you were the best players in the land."

"Aye, we are proud, indeed, to have that reputation," Burbage replied, puffing himself up. "Nevertheless—"

"Well then," Humphrey interrupted, "Master Middleton has paid for the best, and so he expects the best, and nothing less. 'Tis in your own interest, therefore, to live up to your stellar reputation. Look to it."

"That had almost the aspect of a threat," Shakespeare said to Smythe as they left Humphrey and proceeded toward the stables. "Do you suppose they might set the dogs on us if our performance is found wanting?"

"I doubt that Master Middleton would waste his sports upon the likes of us," said Smythe, with a straight face. "I think it more likely he would dispatch a phalanx of footmen armed with cudgels to urge us on our way."

"Well you may jest," said Shakespeare, "but these moneyed sorts would do just that sort of thing and not think twice of it. I do not trust that Humphrey fellow. He has a lean and hungry look. I much prefer a well-fed man. Corpulence has a tendency to make one indolent and indolent men are much less likely to be moved to violent action."

"Like our late King Henry, you mean?" said Burbage. "Now there was a sweet, pacific soul for you. Anne Boleyn found him rather corporal in his corpulence, as I recall."

"Aye, imagine what his humor might have been if he were thin," said Smythe, grinning.

" 'Twould have been much worse, I have no doubt of it," Shakespeare replied. "Had he been a leaner and more spirited man, like Richard Lionheart, then instead of merely breaking with the Church of Rome, he might have launched his own crusade against it."

"Now you know, there might be a good idea for a play in that," said Smythe.

"God's wounds!" said Burbage. "We do not have enough trouble with the Master of the Revels? Do us all a kindness, Will. Should you by any chance decide to pen a play about an English king, then try to choose one whose immediate descendants do not at present sit upon the throne, else we might all end up with our heads on London Bridge."

"Sound counsel, Dick," Shakespeare said. "I shall endeavor to keep it in mind."

"And you, Smythe," Burbage added, "leave the playwriting to Shakespeare and stick to what you do best."

"Aye, whatever that may be," said Kemp, getting down from his seat up in the wagon as they reached the stables and dismounted. "Lifting heavy objects, was it not?"

"Indeed, I do believe that you have struck upon it, Kemp," said Smythe, turning towards him. "And since there is nothing heavier than your own weighty opinion of yourself, I think I shall indulge in a bit of practice at my skill." With that, he seized Kemp and hoisted him high into the air, holding him at arm's length overhead.

Startled, Kemp yelped, then started blustering. "Put me *down*, you great misbegotten oaf!"

"As you wish," replied Smythe, and tossed him straight into the manure bin.

Kemp landed in the odiferous mixture of soggy straw and horse droppings to the accompaniment of uproarious laughter from his fellow players. He arose like a specter from the swamp, bits of soiled straw and dung clinging to his hair and clothing. Outrage and embarrassment mingled with anger and disgust, overwhelming him to the point of speechlessness.

"I have had my fill, Kemp, of your snide barbs and venomous aspersions," Smythe said. "That you are more talented than I is something I shall not dispute. The least talented member of this company is a better player by far than I, much as it saddens me to say so. I am quite aware of my shortcomings. Be that as it may, I carry my weight and I work as hard as you do, if not harder, and I challenge any member of this company to say that I do not. I am not, by nature, hot-tempered, but neither will I suffer myself to be abused. The next time you provoke me, I shall put you through a window, and the landing may not be as soft. Find another target for your caustic wit, for I have had enough of it."

There was complete silence as everyone waited for Kemp to respond. It was a side of Smythe they had not seen before, and it took them all aback a bit.

"Well . . ." began Kemp, awkwardly, " 'twas never my intention to do you any injury. I never meant to give any offense, you know. 'Tis just my way . . . to chide people a bit, good-natured like. I never knew that it discomfitted you. You should have said something." He tried to meet Smythe's gaze, but his eyes kept sliding away. He looked, Smythe thought, rather like a guilty dog that had been caught stealing a meat pie.

"I have said something, just now," Smythe replied. "And I trust that there shall be no need for me to say it once again."

Later, when they were brought to their quarters in the servants' wing on the ground floor of the mansion, Shakespeare and Smythe found themselves sharing once again a small room, little larger than a closet. There were always some spare rooms in the servants' quarters of the larger homes for visitors who travelled with liveried footmen or tirewomen or the like. The accomodations were hardly luxurious, but they were still a sight more comfortable than what most working-class people in the city could afford, many of whom had to crowd together into tiny rented rooms and share sleeping space upon the floors.

"I was wondering when you would finally have your fill of Kemp and clout him one," said Shakespeare.

"Now I never clouted him," protested Smythe.

"No, what you did was much worse. Or much better, depending on one's point of view. You humiliated him. Plucked him up as if he were a daisy and threw him straight into a pile of shit. 'Twas quite lovely, really. Wish I had thought of it myself, save that I would have lacked the strength to hoist him up like that."

Smythe grimaced. "I probably should not have done it. But I was sick of him constantly picking away at me."

"Well, rest assured, he shall not do it anymore, but you have made an enemy for life."

"You think?"

"Oh, aye. You can best a man and he will like as not forgive you for it, but humiliate him and 'tis a sure thing that he will hate you til he dies. And I suppose that one can say the same for women, when it comes to that. Man or woman, either way, hate shall not discriminate."

Smythe nodded. "I cannot disagree. But I do believe that Kemp had hated me right from the very start, or at the very least, disliked me a great deal. I could not have made things that much worse. I had held my temper with him in the past, but that only seemed to encourage him. At least now, I might save myself having to listen to his noise. Nevertheless . . . perhaps I should not have done it."

"No, 'twas the right thing you did," said Shakespeare, thoughtfully, as he stretched out on the straw mattress and put his arms up behind his head. "You are a strapping lad, Tuck, powerfully strong, but that strength shall only be respected when there is a threat that it might be employed. If a man like Kemp perceives that he can bait you with impunity, why then you might be twice his size and it shall not discourage him. He was always pricking you with his nasty wit, we could all see that. If you had not thrown him in the shitpile, or else clouted him a good one, 'twould have only gotten worse."

"I think so, too," said Smythe. "Though, in truth," he added, somewhat sheepishly, "I cannot claim to have thought the matter through that way before I acted."

"Betimes a man may think too much," said Shakespeare. "Clarity is often better found in action than in thought. Hmm, that's a good line. Let me set it down 'ere I forget."

He got up from the bed and rummaged in his bag. As Shakespeare searched for his papers and his pens and ink, Smythe took his place and stretched out on the straw bed. "In truth, Kemp was only a small part of my distemper. I keep thinking that Elizabeth is here somewhere and but for our foolish argument, I might have found an opportunity to spend a bit of time with her before we went on tour."

"So what prevents you?" Shakespeare asked. "Go and search her out. Or else send word to her by one of the household servants."

"You forget," said Smythe, "we argued."

"About what?"

Smythe frowned. "For the life of me, I cannot now recall." He snorted. "Foolish."

"Most quarrels between men and women are over foolish things," said Shakespeare. "Especially if they are lovers."

"But we are not lovers," Smythe protested. "We have never . . . Well, we have never."

"Then that is even more foolish," Shakespeare said, impatiently. "I have told you afore this to get that girl out of your head, because she is too far above you, but if you intend to be stubborn about it, then you might as well tup her and have done with it. If you can manage to avoid having your ears and other parts of your anatomy sliced off by Henry Darcie, it might get her out of your system."

"Mmm, I see. Was that how it worked for you in Stratford?"

"Swine. Do I toss your poor past judgement in your face?"

"Aye, all the time."

"Lout. Aha! Here we are!" He brought forth his papers and a

small box containing his inkwell and his pens. "Now . . . what was that line I wanted to set down?"

Smythe shrugged. "I dunno."

"God's wounds! You have forgotten?"

"You said you wanted to set it down; I recall that much. You did not say you wanted *me* to remember it for you."

"*Argh!* I can see that you are not going to be of any use to me at all until you set your mind straight about that girl. Folly. 'Tis all folly, if you ask me. Go, find her. Find her and make it up to her. Abase yourself before her and tell her what a mighty goose you have been and how you should have known better, but were utterly blinded by your vanity and foolishness. A woman loves to hear a man admit to being a fool; it confirms her own opinion and lends credence to her judgement. Go and find her and plead for her forgiveness."

"But . . . I had done nothing truly wrong," said Smythe.

"Did you *speak?*"

"Well, aye, but—"

"Then you undoubtedly did wrong. Either way, it matters not. You shall not mend fences by stubbornly standing on your pride. Go on, get out. Leave me in peace. I must try to somehow make a play out of this dross that I have penned and must now see performed, thanks to your kind offices."

"I never meant to cause you trouble, Will. I was only thinking that it might be an opportunity for you," said Smythe.

Shakespeare sighed. "I know, Tuck, I know. And that is why I cannot be angry with you for it. I know that you meant well. As I, too, mean well when I tell you to go and tell Elizabeth that you are sorry for your quarrel. I still think that no good can come of this infatuation, but then I am like as not the last who should advise anybody on such matters."

Smythe took a deep breath. "I do not know, Will . . . I am not even certain where to go and look for her."

"Well, considering that they are setting up a fair outside," said

Shakespeare, "might not a young woman wish to be among the first to do a bit of shopping?"

It was drawing on towards evening, but the fairgrounds were still abustle as late-arriving merchants hurried to set up their stalls. Others, whose goods had already been displayed, were making last minute adjustments to their tables or else dickering with guests who had already arrived and were taking advantage of the warm and pleasant evening to peruse the tented and beribboned booths. Unlike other fairs that were open to the public, there was no official opening time. The invited merchants were free to begin selling as soon as they set up their stalls, so long as they refrained from remaining open during the wedding ceremony scheduled for the following day. It was a small enough concession, Smythe thought, considering the wealthy customers to whom the merchants would be given access and they were all doing their best to make the most of the opportunity by arriving early and setting up their stalls as soon as possible. And other than the singular oddity of this fair being held on the grounds of a private estate and restricted only to invited guests, it reminded Smythe of the one held at his village, or at least it did until he got a closer look at some of the goods being offered and heard the asking prices.

All fairs, large or small, had certain things in common, such as the sale of foodstuffs. Already, Smythe could smell the savory aromas of fresh fruit pies baked earlier in the day and carefully packed up for the journey to the fair. He could smell roast chicken and game birds cooking over braziers, as well as venison pastie. And much like the fair at home, there were merchants here selling bolts of cloth and ribbons, as well as finished goods, but only the very finest kinds.

There were bolts of three-piled velvet and Italian silk, as well as Flemish damasks and French lace, much finer than anything Smythe had ever seen at the country fairs back home. Expensive pewter bowls and plates and drinking goblets were for sale at one booth, fancy embroidered doublets at the next, and jewelry at the one past that. There were heavy gold rings and enamelled chains and bracelets and brooches all set with precious stones, the work of the city's finest artisans. There was even an armorer's stall where Smythe stopped to stare at the highly polished and extravagantly engraved armor of the queen's own champion on display. Nearby, a booth with weapons laid out on the cloth covered tables and hung up on pegs affixed to slanted display boards drew his attention. He gazed with interest at the great double-handed swords and Scottish basket-hilted claymores, war axes, spiked morning stars and triangulated maces, all of which, in these times of peace, were far more likely to be purchased for display upon some wall rather than for potential use in battle. He paid closer attention to the more practical swords and daggers suitable for daily wear, such as the gleaming Toledo blades and Italian stilettos, their hilts wrapped with fine gold and silver wire; slim and graceful ladies' bodkins with hilts of bone or ivory and precious jewels set into their pommels and crossguards; purposeful looking swords and knives from the best artisans of Sheffield, as well as elaborately-wrought cup and basket-hilted French poignards and rapiers and main gauches. Save for a venison pastie, perhaps, or a roast goose drumstick, Smythe saw absolutely nothing that he could afford on his meager player's pay.

As he wandered among the stalls, he suddenly caught a glimpse of a familiar-looking hooded cloak of green velvet. It was the same one Elizabeth had worn when they had last seen one another at St. Paul's. The day that they had quarrelled, Smythe thought, ruefully. She had often worn that cloak; it was her favorite. He was about to call out her name, but then thought better of it and caught himself in time.

This was not the yard of St. Paul's, he reminded himself. This was a private celebration at the estate of Godfrey Middleton, one of the richest men in London, and all about him, aside from the merchants and their apprentices, were some of the most wealthy and influential people in all of England. It was not a place where Elizabeth would wish to call attention to her friendship with a lowly ostler and a sometime player, assuming, of course, that their relationship had not been irreparably damaged by their foolish quarrel.

The thought gave Smythe a sharp pang of anxiety. Friendship was probably the most that he could ever hope for with Elizabeth, although he longed with all his heart and soul for something more than that. But Shakespeare was right, she was too far above him. And if their relationship continued, she doubtless stood to lose far more than he did. The smart thing, the best thing, perhaps, would be for him to simply put her out of his mind, but what was simply said was not so simply done. Perhaps Shakespeare was right, he thought, and nothing good would come of it, but good or bad, either way, nothing would come of it at all if he did not go to her and beg for her forgiveness.

He hurried after her. A moment later, he lost sight of her among the stalls and tents, but then he caught a glimpse of green and spotted her again. She was moving quickly, purposefully it seemed, and he trotted after her. In his haste, he collided with someone and the man fell sprawling to the ground, landing flat on his back in a puddle of mud and horse manure that made a mess of his fine clothes.

"Your pardon," Smythe said over his shoulder as he hurried to catch up with Elizabeth.

"Damn your eyes, you ruffian!" the man called after him, angrily. "Look what you've done! Come back here! Come back here at once, I said! Somebody stop that man!"

Smythe quickly put as much distance as possible between them, ducking between the stalls and tents. The last thing he needed now was to be taken for a thief, especially amongst this company! He could still hear the man blustering behind him, but he seemed to have made good his escape. Except that now, once again, he had lost sight of Elizabeth. He seemed to have come almost full circle around the fairground. He now found himself standing on the perimeter of the tents and stalls, among some carts and wagons. To his left, some thirty or forty yards away, were the wedding pavillions and the house. To his right, the field continued to slope away towards the pond and the road leading up to the house from the main thoroughfare. Behind him was the fairground, and further on, the river. And to his front ran the road, and beyond it, just below the house, were the gardens and the maze. And as the shadows of dusk lengthened, Smythe caught a glimpse of Elizabeth's green cloak billowing in the evening breeze, just before she disappeared from sight on the stone steps leading down to the gardens and the maze.

Once again, he felt tempted to call out to her, and once again, he hesitated. Where was she going? And what was she doing, going down to the gardens all alone at this hour? He frowned and started after her.

The sun was going down, and the merchants would soon be closing down their stalls until the morning, camping out with their goods or in their wagons. Already, he could see a few lanterns and torches being lit in the fairground behind him. It would not be long before it would grow dark. Smythe started to run.

He reached the top of the terraced steps from which he could look out over the garden below. As with his elegant manor home, Middleton had clearly spared no expense with his gardens. Even in the fading light, Smythe could see that a great deal of time and attention had been lavished on them. There were several garden plots spread out below in a circular pattern, each exquisitely laid out and painstakingly maintained. There were stone benches and ivy-covered bowers placed along gently curving flagstoned pathways. And just beyond the gardens, disappearing into the entrance to the tall and perfectly clipped hedges of the maze, was the billowing swirl of a cloak.

4

HERE COULD ONLY BE ONE reason why Elizabeth would be coming out to the gardens alone at this time of the evening, Smythe thought, and it was not to smell the flowers. She had come to meet someone. Why else make the pretence of going out to see the merchants' stalls, only to circle round them and make her way clandestinely down to the gardens? As Smythe ran down the steps after her and along the garden pathways leading to the maze, anger and jealousy flared within him.

Was this why she had picked a fight with him at Paul's? It had made quite a convenient excuse for her not to see him at the wedding of her friend. Now that he thought of it, he recalled that the first thing she had asked him then was if he would be coming with the Queen's Men to the wedding celebration. And when she found out that he would, indeed, inconveniently be there, she had started an argument with him that gave her an excuse to walk out on him angrily. And after such a heated quarrel, what reason would he have to think that she would bother to find time for him while they were at the Middleton estate?

He stopped for a moment to catch his breath as he reached the entrance to the maze, and in that moment, his initial burst of anger, spent partially in his run down the steps and across the gardens, began to give way to hesitance and indecision. Just what, exactly, was he doing? After all, what right had he to feel jealous or possessive of Elizabeth? She was not his wife nor was she his betrothed. She was not even his lover. The truth of the matter was that they had no formal understandings between them of any sort, nor had they made any promises to one another. As Shakespeare had pointed out to him on more than one occasion, there could be no hope of any match between them. They had never even spoken of it. In truth, they had not spoken of anything that could define any relationship between them, other than simple friendship. So what, after all, was Elizabeth to him or he to Elizabeth?

Nevertheless, since he had helped her out of her predicament with an arranged marriage that she did not desire and that would, as it turned out in the end, have had her wed to an imposter and an enemy of England and thereby imperilled her very life, they had afterward contrived to see each other whenever the opportunity arose. Perhaps, thought Smythe, it was only gratitude or a sense of obligation that made her seek or at the very least tolerate his company, but even if they had spent their time merely strolling together or perusing the book stalls of St. Paul's while making idle conversation, were those not assignations? Did he tell his friends—well, anyone else save Will—where he was going? Did she tell her friends or her parents? Or were not plausible stories invented on both sides so that they could be with one another? For that matter, Smythe thought, would they have argued as heatedly as they had if there had been no feelings of any sort between them, other than mere friendship?

No, there was something more there. From the first moment they had met, Smythe felt something pass between them, a sort of spark, a momentary incandescence that they had both acknowledged without ever speaking of it openly. They had flirted in a harmless sort of way, but beneath their witty badinage was a subtext of something more significant.

Infatuation, Shakespeare had called it. "Aye, 'tis infatuation, nothing more," he'd said. " 'Tis much too innocent in its own way to call it lust, although I daresay it may come to that, should the two of you decide to stop acting like a coy pair of besotted children. However foolish it may be, there is an innocent sort of sweetness to it, but the world, I fear, does not long tolerate innocence and sweetness."

Perhaps Elizabeth could no longer tolerate it, either, Smythe thought. Maybe she had found something that she could believe was not doomed to failure and frustration. And if she had found something . . . someone with whom she could have a future, then who was he, an impoverished ostler and sometime player, to deny her? He had nothing, nothing whatsoever to offer her.

He stood for several moments, hesitating at the entrance to the maze, looking back over his shoulder and watching the lights coming on inside the house as darkness gathered and the candles were brought out. Tomorrow, there would be a wedding and two people would be beginning a new life together. And what might be happening right here, right now, he thought, was not a beginning, but an ending. He had to know for certain. He stepped into the maze.

It became immediately darker as he stood between two tall rows of hedges, clipped into the form of straight, rectangular walls that rose above his head by several feet. Before him was a solid wall of leafy green shrubbery so thick that he could not see through it. There was no question of pushing his way through to the other side. He could go either to his left or to his right, down a grassy passageway between the hedges wide enough to accommodate two people walking side-by-side. He had no idea which way Elizabeth had gone. When he ran after her, he had closed the distance between them, but in the moment or two that he had hesitated at the entrance, she had moved ahead, intent on her errand and doubtless unaware that she was being followed. But which way had she gone?

Smythe knelt to examine the grass. What little light remained was fading quickly and while he had grown up in the country and spent his share of time out in the woods, he was no tracker.

It was growing darker, so that he could scarcely see more than several feet ahead of him now. It was impossible to discern any sign of which way Elizabeth may have gone. In a little while, it would be pitch black and he would be reduced to feeling his way along the pathways. It struck him that he might have some difficulty finding his way back out again. What, he wondered, could Elizabeth be thinking? But at the same time, it occurred to him that this was the home of her good friend, and she had almost certainly visited here before. She probably knew her way through the maze. Why else would she have chosen such a place for a discreet rendezvous? He listened intently for any sounds, but now the crickets had begun their song and it was difficult to hear anything else.

He made a few more turns and still there was no sign of her. Here and there, stone benches had been placed throughout the maze and he chose one and sat down, frowning, trying to get his bearings. It had seemed simple and straightforward enough at first. Simply remember the turns that he had made and then, on the way out, reverse them. But by now, he had made so many turns that he was no longer certain of their order. He had no idea how far into the maze he'd gone. Once within it, the maze of hedgerows seemed somehow much larger and more labyrinthine than it had from the outside. He had been certain that he would have caught up to Elizabeth by now, but instead, all he had succeeded in doing was getting lost. He was about to get up and start moving once again when he heard the sound of voices approaching.

At first, he could not make out what was being said, only that it seemed to be two men in quiet conversation. A moment or two later, as they came closer, the dialogue became more clear.

". . . and with Catherine gone, my way at last shall be made clear with Blanche, so that with fortune's blessing, I shall ere long succeed in securing the old man's consent."

"Aye, the one impediment shall have been removed, perhaps, but the other yet remains. However shall you circumvent the matter of your more than modest means?"

The first speaker, Smythe surmised, was fairly young, perhaps of an age with him, if not a little older. He spoke with the firm, brash confidence of youth and if it could be said that one could have a cocksure swagger in his voice, then this man had that very quality. The second man sounded somewhat older, with a voice that had something of an aspect of consideration and reflection, though in tone, he seemed to defer to his companion.

"Rest assured that I have thought of that, as well. You did not think I would venture into this without taking all into account? I do not play at being fortune's child, old sod, I work at it."

"Aye, that you do, beyond a doubt, and I have seen your efforts bear fruit on more than one occasion. Yet at the same time, I have seen that fruit consumed without your taking any care to plant some of its seed so that still more could sprout."

"Well, that, my friend, is because I am not a common plough-man. I would much sooner seek to find an orchard ready planted, so that I could make my choice of only the ripest fruit, rather than squander all my time and effort ploughing furrows and planting seed, not all of which may sprout, and of that which sprouts and flourishes, not all of which may bear rich fruit. 'Tis entirely too much labor for not enough reward."

They sounded close enough by now that Smythe was surprised that he could not yet see them, even in the darkness. Yet a moment later, he realized why he could not. They were almost exactly abreast with him, strolling at a leisurely pace, but on the opposite side of the hedgerow, and though he was aware of their presence because he could hear them speaking, they seemed completely unaware of his.

Indeed, Smythe thought, there was no reason for them to assume that at this late hour, in the darkness, there might be anyone within the maze except themselves, and yet, apparently unbeknownst to them, there were at least three others—himself, Elizabeth, and the still unknown individual with whom she came to rendezvous. Unless, of course, that very unknown individual happened to be one of these two men.

Curious to find out, Smythe fell in step with them, pacing them on his side of the hedge. The moist grass underfoot and the chirping of the crickets masked any sounds his footsteps might have made, although he still walked softly so as not to give himself away.

"I have a plan," the first man continued, "that by its very boldness should succeed and leave no room for suspicion."

"But in time, the truth will out," the second man replied. "What then?"

"Why, by that time, it shall no longer matter," the younger man said, with a chuckle. "For by the time the truth can be discovered, I shall be long gone with Blanche, and with her dowry. The old man can raise a hue and cry, for all the good that it shall do him, for by then I shall be well beyond his reach or the reach of any authority that he might try to bring to bear against me."

"And what of the girl?"

"What of her?"

"Well, what should she think when she learns the truth?"

"What matters that to me? Faith, by the time she learns the truth of things, she shall be my wife. As such, she is my goods, my chattels, and my house, my household stuff, my field, my barn, my horse, my ox, my ass, my anything. What should she think of the truth? Why, sink me, only what I tell her she should think and there's an end to it!"

Now there's a charming fellow, Smythe thought, with a grimace of distaste. And something of a scoundrel, from the sound of things. But whoever he was, at least he had answered one of Smythe's unspoken questions. It seemed clear that he had not come here to meet Elizabeth after all, for it was somebody named Blanche on whom he had apparantly set his sights. And from what Smythe had overheard, this Blanche was in some way a relative of Catherine's, perhaps a sister or a cousin, but undoubtedly the reference was to the very same Catherine Middleton whose wedding they had all come to attend. And the next exchange he overheard confirmed it.

"Well, you seem confident enough of bringing her to heel," the second man replied, "but afore that can be done, you must first bring her to the altar, and I daresay you will have a deal of competition there. Blanche Middleton is as well known for all the suitors trailing after her as she is for her beauty. How will you be able to assure that above all those who clamor for her hand 'twill be yourself who shall find her father's favor and win out?"

"As I have told you, I do not leave such things to chance," the first man answered him. "I have a plan. Now whom do you suppose a rich merchant with aspirations to improve himself would favor most as a suitor for his youngest daughter's hand, some young, ambitious roaring boy looking for a leg up on his station as well as on the wench, or some corpulent, newly wealthy tradesman with a grossness of class exceeded only by the grossness of his girth or, perhaps, the dashingly handsome and courtly mannered son of an aristocrat?"

"What, *you*?"

"I and none other."

"But, Odd's blood, your father, rest his soul, was no aristocrat! He was a ruffler and a cozener who was drawn and quartered and had his head displayed on London Bridge!"

"I know not of whom you speak. My father stands before me."

"Merciful God preserve us! *Where?*"

The reply was mocking laughter. "Cast not about in search of ghostly spirits, my friend. 'Twas *you* I meant."

"*Me!*"

"Aye, my father stands before me in your person."

"Good God! Have you taken leave of your senses?"

"On the contrary, what I propose is emminently sensible. If one is going to brew up a bit of cozenage, then there is little to be served in making it small beer. A fine and heady ale is called for. What I intend to do is—"

The statement never was completed, because Smythe had grown so fascinated in listening to the intriguing conversation that he had neglected to observe what, in the darkness, he might easily have missed in any case . . . some clippings from the hedge, dead branches taken off earlier that afternoon and raked together into a small pile on the path preparatory to being gathered in a wheelbarrow and removed. Whether by chance or by design, they had been left there, and as Smythe kept pace with the two men on his side of the hedge, he stepped straight into the clippings, and the dry branches under-foot made a sharp, crackling sound that was easily audible over the chirping of the crickets.

For a moment, there was utter silence. Even the crickets had seemed startled by the sound. And then, as Smythe glanced down and stepped back quickly, there came an angry oath from the other side of the hedge and, almost at the same time, a blade came plung-ing through. That single step back was what had saved him. Smythe felt the sharp steel of the rapier graze his stomach, close enough to slice through his leather doublet and draw a little blood.

As quickly as it came stabbing through, the blade was drawn back again through the hedge and Smythe danced back out of the way as another lunge came at him through the shrubbery. The thick-ness of the hedge impeded the assault, but it was no less deadly if the blade happened to strike a vital spot. Unarmed save for the dagger that he always carried with him, Smythe was under no illu-sions as to its efficacy against a sword, much less a pair of swords, for it seemed now that there were *two* blades stabbing at him through the hedge, not one. Smythe decided that the only prudent thing to do was run for it. The only problem was, he was not really sure where he was going.

He would have found it difficult enough to retrace his steps without two assassins in pursuit of him. Running in the darkness only made things worse. However, if racing headlong through the dark corridors of the grassy maze confused him, then it also served to confuse those who pursued him, for it struck him that as visitors to the estate, they were probably no more familiar with the maze than he was. What at first must have seemed to them an ideal place to discuss their plans in secret now became a maddening im-pediment to their need to eliminate an eavesdropper. Smythe heard them furiously cursing behind him as they apparently missed a turn and ran blindly straight into a hedge. A moment later, he did almost exactly the same thing as he missed a turn and stopped only at the last instant, narrowly avoiding running straight into a wall of thick shrubbery.

He could no longer hear his pursuers, but logically surmised that it was not so much because he had outdistanced them as for their sudden stealth in movement. It must have occurred to them that the less noise they made in their pursuit, the better they could hear whatever sounds he made in his flight and thereby locate him in the maze. They had made it abundantly clear that they were in deadly earnest. If they caught him, he knew that they would do their very best to kill him . . . and anyone else who happened to get into their way.

The realization that Elizabeth was in grave danger if she were still within the maze filled Smythe with a concern bordering on panic. Alarmed, he almost called out a warning to her, but caught himself just in the nick of time. Calling out her name would not only serve to reveal his position to the two men who pursued him, it would also alert them to her presence in the maze.

Smythe took a deep breath in an attempt to steady his nerves, his thoughts racing in an effort to decide upon the best course of action. For all he knew, during the time that he was blundering about inside the maze, Elizabeth might already have accomplished her purpose and gone back to the house. If so, then she was safe and the two men trying to kill him would never suspect that she had also been in the maze with them tonight. On the other hand, if Elizabeth was still there and they encountered her, then they might easily assume that it was she who had overheard their plans and whom they had been chasing. And there was only one thing Smythe could think of to prevent that.

He took a deep breath and shouted out, as loudly as he could, "Help! Help! Robbers! Assassins!"

In calling out, he knew that he had given away his position, and if his pursuers were close by, then they might find him within moments and fall upon him. But the important thing was that they had heard a male voice calling out, and so would not suspect a female, even if they happened to catch sight of Elizabeth in or near the maze. At the same time, if Elizabeth was within earshot of his voice, his crying out would serve as a warning to her, one that he desperately hoped she would hear and heed.

"Help!" he called out again. "Brigands! Thieves! Murderers!"

In the distance, he heard answering shouts from the direction of the fairgrounds. If he had been heard back there, then surely Elizabeth must have heard him if she was still inside the maze. He could only hope that by now she had already gone back up to the house, but he had no way of knowing. He could not take that chance. He called out once more, as loudly as he could, and then stood very silent and absolutely still, balancing lightly on the balls of his feet, listening intently. Almost at once, he heard a rustling behind him and spun around, jumping to one side as he did so, and just as he expected, a rapier blade came plunging through the hedge, stabbing at the place where he had stood an instant earlier. This time, however, he was prepared with a riposte.

He had drawn his dagger, the only weapon he had with him, and as soon as he saw the glint of steel in the moonlight, he plunged his arm through the hedge up to his shoulder, using the rapier's blade as his guide. They struck almost simultaneously. He felt the resistance of the narrow, thickly growing branches as he pushed his knife blade through the brush, but was rewarded by a yelp of pain and a furious oath from the other side. He pulled back his knife and saw, with grim satisfaction, a dark smear of blood upon the blade.

"Take that, you craven bastard," he said.

He backed off a pace, making sure that he was well out of reach in case they struck again, then started moving to his left, listening intently and glancing all around. By now, his vision had grown somewhat accustomed to the darkness and the moonlight helped, though it was still difficult to see inside the tall walls of the maze.

He had lost all sense of direction. He tried to gauge where his opponents might be on the other side of the hedge, but wherever they were, assuming they were still together, the two men were now taking care to move as quietly as he did. For all he knew, they had split up in an effort to converge upon him. It would have been the logical thing for them to do.

He heard more shouting coming from the direction of the fairgrounds, only now it sounded closer and it allowed him to reorientate himself. It seemed that someone back there had determined the approximate direction from which his shouts had come and they had started searching. It would not be long before they thought to look within the maze. There was nothing that would so quickly galvanize a group of merchants into action as a cry of "Thieves!"

Smythe could feel his heart pounding inside his chest, as if it were some wild thing trying to beat its way out through his ribcage. His breathing was coming in short gasps and he tried to steady it and keep it quiet, lest the sound of it should give his position away. It sounded unnaturally loud to him. At the same time, he tried to listen for any sounds his antagonists might make as they stalked him. He moved lightly on the balls of his feet, prepared to spring instantly to either one side or the other to avoid a deadly thrust coming through the hedge, while at the same time watching for the openings in the hedgerows that gave access to another corridor.

He had to find his way out of the maze as quickly as he could. Help would be arriving shortly, but at the moment, that was not foremost in his mind. He knew his only chance to learn who his pursuers were lay in his finding his way out of the maze before they did, so that he could watch for them as they came out. And of course, he realized, the same thing must have occurred to them, as well.

It struck him that if those two men found their way out of the maze before he did, then there was nothing to prevent them from joining with the searchers from the fairgrounds when they arrived and pretend to have responded to his shouts along with them. He would then be found, and they would be among those who would find him, at which point they could easily turn the tables on him, claiming that it was one of them who had called out for help and that he was the assailant. At night, and from a distance, one shout sounded much like any other. He would be able to prove nothing. He knew that he had managed to blood one of them, but that in itself would constitute no proof that they had attacked him. They could just as easily claim that he had struck first.

On the other hand, he thought, they did not really have to do anything. If they got out of the maze before he did, there was nothing to prevent them from blending in with the searchers when they arrived and then simply wait for him to be found. The one he had blooded might not have his wound in some easily visible location, or else he might leave to have it tended to while his companion stayed behind to mark him and find out who he was, so that they could pick their time and dispose of him at a more opportune moment. Either way, he thought, it made no difference. If they got out of the maze first, the odds became entirely in their favor.

He called out several more times, despite the risk, then used the answering shouts to help him find his way. It was all too easy, especially under the circumstances, to make several turns through the maze and then lose track of direction. That was the idea, after all. These arboreal mazes were all the rage among the idle rich, and so of course Godfrey Middleton absolutely had to have one that was larger and more intricate than anyone else's, for which Smythe roundly cursed him as he kept turning through the corridors, trying to keep his mind on which side of the hedge walls lay towards the exterior and which were towards the center. He tried not to think about Elizabeth, difficult as that was. He could only pray that she was safely gone by now.

Then, suddenly, he was out. It took him by surprise when he stepped through a break in the hedgerows and abruptly realized he had come out. For an alarming moment, he felt exposed and vulnerable. He crouched, instinctively, holding his dagger out before him, glancing quickly to his left and to his right, but there was no sign of anyone. Then he heard shouting and saw figures in silhouette against the light coming from the house as they moved towards the steps leading down to the gardens.

Quickly, he moved away from the entrance to the maze, keeping it in sight to see who might come out behind him. He went a short way down the garden path, keeping to the shadows, still in a position to see anyone who came out of the maze, but he could see no movement there. He hesitated to go any further, because as it was, he would not see anyone come out of the maze until they came away from the entrance and moved out onto the garden path. It would be difficult, if not impossible, to get a good look at anyone in the darkness.

There were several people running down the steps now, entering the garden.

" '*Allo!* '*Allo!* '*Allo!* Who called for help? '*Allo!* Are you there? '*Allo?*"

There was still no sign of anyone coming out of the maze. Smythe swore under his breath. Could he possibly have missed them? Or had they managed to get out ahead of him?

" '*Allo! Where are you?*"

Smythe was about to call out in reply when something else occurred to him. If those men had managed to get out of the maze before him, then for all he knew, *they* could be the ones who were calling out to him right now. He would reply, and they would come running up to him, and he would think that they were coming to the rescue, when in fact . . .

" '*Allo!* '*Allo!*"

Smythe bit his lower lip. He had no time left to deliberate. He could hear running footsteps approaching. Quickly, he stepped back off the flagstoned path and concealed himself among the shrubbery just as several dark figures came running around the bend. He had a tense moment, wondering if they had seen him, but they ran right past his hiding place, heading towards the maze. He could hear them calling out to one another, asking if anyone had seen anything, and they kept calling out to him, as well. However, he would give no answering shouts this time, for he did not know for certain who they were.

He headed towards the steps, ducking back out of the way at least twice more to avoid being seen, then made his way back to the servants' wing of the house without further incident, for which he was profoundly grateful. He had experienced quite enough excitement for one night.

"God's breath!" Shakespeare exclaimed, when Smythe had finished telling him what happened. " 'Tis a wondrous miracle you were not slain! What manner of deviltry have you stumbled into this time?"

Smythe shook his head. "I know not the whole of it, but I know something of their plan, enough at least to warn our host what they intend. And by God, I shall do that, you may be sure of it! I am of a mind to go at once to Master Middleton and tell him all I heard. Will you come with me?"

"Well, soft now," Shakespeare replied, stroking his chin thoughtfully, "let us pause a bit to consider these events before we rush to raise any alarums. There is nothing to be served by undue haste, and methinks nothing that shall not keep til morning. To be sure, with his daughter being married on the morrow, Master Middleton should not receive us very cordially if we were to call upon him at this late hour."

They sat together in a tiny room on the first floor, in the servants' quarters. It was illuminated only by one candle stuck into a small, saucer-shaped brass sconce. The other members of the company were all abed by now, distributed throughout several rooms within the servants' wing. Some of them had been put up four or five to a room, because as players they did not rank above servants and, in truth, generally ranked well below them. Nor did any of them complain, for the accomodations that they had received were in fact better than those they often got, and in this case, certainly better than the merchants, who slept either in their tents or in their wagons, where they could keep close to their goods. Shakespeare and Smythe had a bedroom to themselves, though that was only because, as Shakespeare had earlier observed, calling it a room at all would be allowing it pretensions of grandeur. It was actually little more than a small closet, with two beds close together upon the floor. There was room for little else save for a small nightstand, a washbasin and a candle. That candle was now burning very low, for it was well past midnight.

When Smythe returned, Shakespeare was still up, hunched over some papers. Squinting in the insufficient light from the candle on the little nightstand, he sat cross-legged on the bed, having improvised a writing desk with a wooden trencher he had borrowed from the kitchen. He was, even at this last moment, still working on the play they were to perform the following day. Since this was to be a private performance, taking place outside the city of London, there had been no need to submit a fair copy of the play to the Master of the Revels, as would have been necessary for a performance at their theatre, but at the same time, the more changes he would make at this late stage, the more burden would be placed upon the players, who would quickly have to memorize new lines and adapt themselves accordingly to any changes he might make in the stage directions. Shakespeare knew all this, of course, but still, he was not happy with the play. He was more than happy, however, to have an excuse to put it aside for awhile and discuss Smythe's fascinating situation.

"I do see what you mean," Smythe said. "The last thing the father of the bride would need on the night before the wedding was a hue and cry raised about an overheard conversation in a garden. Still, it has a most intimate bearing on his family, and were it my own daughter who was being so intrigued against, I would most certainly wish to know!"

"Indeed," Shakespeare agreed. "However, let us first examine what you *do* know."

Smythe frowned once more. "But . . . what do you mean? Did I not just tell you?"

"You told me that you had overheard a conversation," Shakespeare replied, "but between whom?"

"Why, the two men in the maze!"

"What were their names? What did they look like?"

"Why, how in the world should I know? I do not think that either of them used the other's name. And as for what they looked like, I never even caught a glimpse of them!"

"Precisely," Shakespeare said, with a wry grimace. "You have overheard a conversation which may lead you, justifiably, to make an accusation, but against whom?" He shrugged. "There are many visitors here. This is the largest wedding the society of London has seen since . . . well, certainly since we have been in London. And what have you to go by to identify these men save for the sounds of their voices? For that matter, unless a voice should have some marked characteristic that renders it uncommon, one voice often sounds much like another. Can you be certain, beyond *any* shadow of a doubt, that you could pick these two voices out from all the rest? Or from one that may sound similar?"

" 'Sdeath! You have me there. I should think that I would know them if I heard them once again, but to say they are the ones beyond any shadow of a doubt . . . but wait . . . there is one thing! I know that they plan to pose as a nobleman and his son! That should enable us to identify them!"

"Indeed?" said Shakespeare. "And how many noblemen do you suppose will be in attendance at this wedding, hmm? Considering, of course, that this celebration is to be the single most significant social event of the season. And how many of them, do you suppose, shall bring their sons along, as well, especially considering that the extremely, one might even say obscenely wealthy Master Middleton still has an emminently marriageable and, by all accounts, extremely beautiful younger daughter?"

"Ah," said Smythe, weakly.

"Ah, indeed."

"So then . . . what are we to do?"

"Well, 'twould seem to me that you have a number of things to consider before we can answer that question," Shakespeare replied. "For one thing, you seem to have neglected, at least for the moment, the matter of what brought you out to the garden maze last night in the first place."

"Elizabeth!"

"Precisely. Now, can you be certain that she is not somehow involved in this?"

"*Elizabeth*? I could never believe that of her!" Smythe replied. "Not after what she went through herself! Zounds, does *anyone* get betrothed in London without all manner of plots and counterplots?"

"One might say that marriage is a plot in and of itself, but that is neither here nor there," said Shakespeare, wryly. "If you are going to be reporting what you heard tonight to Master Middleton, or to anyone else, for that matter, then quite aside from being questioned closely about what you had heard, you will doubtless be questioned about why you were out there in the first place, especially at such an hour. Now, would you be comfortable saying that you were there because you had seen Elizabeth entering the maze alone and therefore followed her? For if you were to say that, then chances are it would cast suspicion upon her, and she would be summoned to explain why she went out there all alone, with darkness falling."

"I would like to hear that explanation, myself," said Smythe.

"Ah, but are you *entitled* to it?" Shakespeare countered. "And even if you were, which is certainly open to argument, then how do you suppose Elizabeth would feel about that?"

"She would probably be furious with me," Smythe said, glumly. "She does have quite the temper."

"Mmm, don't they all?" said Shakespeare.

"What are we to do then?"

"*We?*" The poet raised his eyebrows. "I thought 'twas *your* problem that we were discussing. How does it happen, Tuck, that I always manage somehow to be pulled into your intrigues?"

"Because you are my friend," said Smythe.

"Aye, worse luck."

"And because you cannot resist it. You are as curious as a cat, Will."

"True, and worse luck, still," said Shakespeare, with a grimace. "So then, where does that leave us?"

Shakespeare sighed. "Well . . . it leaves us with not one, but *two* puzzles, it would seem. The first, and the most immediate, since it nearly resulted in your getting skewered tonight, is the matter of these two mysterious and rather unpleasant gentlemen and their plot involving Blanche Middleton. The second is the question of what Elizabeth was doing out in the maze tonight, and whether or not her business there had aught to do with these two gentlemen. I know that you do not believe it, but we cannot dismiss the possibility. We must keep our heads about us and not allow our feelings to influence our better judgement. You say that you neither saw nor heard her after you had entered the maze yourself?"

Smythe shook his head. "No. It seemed to me that she must have known her way around in there, for I lost track of her and became confused myself."

"You became what you had already become, else you would not have gone out there in the first place," Shakespeare said, dryly.

"Are you going to help me or criticize me?"

"I criticize you only to help you, my lad," the poet replied. He took a deep breath. "That girl is going to be the ruin of you yet. But . . . you are my very best friend, Tuck, for better or for worse, and so, as I am a loyal friend, your ruin shall be our ruin, and we shall both go down magnificently."

Tuck rolled his eyes. "You are being melodramatic."

"Of course, I am being melodramatic, you ninny. I am a poet."

"And a player."

"Aye, and thus stand doubly damned. Well then, what shall we do about this curious predicament?" He stroked his beard and thought for a moment. Then he nodded to himself. " 'Twould seem to me that saying anything to Master Middleton at this point would serve no useful purpose. We do not know enough to tell him anything of substance. That someone might plot to take advantage of him and his daughter, to marry her for money, well, that is something that any man in his position would readily surmise and take steps to prepare for. And who are we, after all, to be pointing accusatory fingers at any of his guests? We are but two lowly players, whose own motives might easily be suspect. We need much more than just the few remarks you overheard tonight before we can go to Master Middleton."

"But we are only here for one more day," said Smythe. "Or two, at most, if we depart the day after our performance."

"Which argues well for doing nothing," Shakespeare replied. "This is truly none of our affair."

"When someone tries to run me through with a rapier, I consider that very much my affair!"

"Oh, very well, then. If you insist. We shall have to see if we can discover anything about who Blanche Middleton's suitors might be, and who, among them, is an aristocrat—or pretends to be one— and who, among those, may be here together with his father—or a man who pretends to be his father. Then you must listen to them speak and see if you can recognize their voices. And 'twill be interesting to see if they can recognize yours, as well, for if so, then that may suit our purpose admirably."

"And just how would it do that?" asked Smythe, frowning.

Shakespeare shrugged. "Well, they have already tried to kill you once. They would doubtless try it once again to ensure that you did not give them away. And doing so, they might well give themselves away. And that would suit our purpose, you see?"

" 'Twould not suit *my* purpose very well if I were killed!"

"Quite. Therefore, we shall endeavor to keep you alive as long as possible. Long enough, at least, to get to the bottom of this nefarious intrigue and find out if Master Middleton is grateful enough to offer some reward."

"I see. So I should therefore place *my* life at risk so that *you* might collect a reward from Master Middleton?"

"Well, I would share it with you, of course. Assuming you survived, that is."

"How good of you."

"Think nothing of it. What are friends for?"

"For getting other friends killed, it would seem."

"Look, did I *ask* you to go out to the maze tonight on the trail of some pouty girl? Or did you, in fact, come to *me* to help you out with this?"

Smythe made a sour face. "I came to you," he admitted.

"Indeed. 'Tis not too late to change your mind, however. We could still choose to act as if none of this had ever happened and blithely go about minding our own business as if we were naught but mere players hired to perform a foolish little play for the amusement of the wedding guests, then take our bows, and pack our things, and continue on our merry way to new adventures and amusements. And I, for one, would have no trouble whatsoever if we were to do precisely that. So then . . . what shall it be?"

Smythe sighed. "You know, Will, you can be a very irritating person."

"I know. My wife used to say exactly the same thing, which is why she lives in Stratford and I live in London, where I can no longer irritate her."

Smythe shook his head. "The devil take it all. I started this, I may as well see it through. Although I have a feeling we may both regret this."

"Anything worth doing is often worth regretting," Shakespeare said. "And we can start tomorrow."

5

THE MORNING BROUGHT A BUSTLE of activity throughout the household as the staff arose well before dawn to begin making the final preparations for the wedding. The kitchen was in full roar well before sunrise, with the cooks bellowing at their helpers like sergeants on the battlefield barking out orders to their troops. The cleaning maids scurried throughout the house with feather dusters, polishing cloths, straw brooms and fresh rushes. The grooms and stable boys fed, curry combed and brushed the horses they were stabling for the guests and shoveled out the stalls for additional arrivals, although it was expected that most of the remaining guests would be arriving by boat, rowed out from the city by the rivermen.

Outside on the fairgrounds, the activity among the merchants seemed more leisurely compared to the frenetic atmosphere inside the house, but they, too, started very early. Most of them arose well before dawn, just like the household staff, and got their cook fires going, then started opening their tents and stalls and laying out their goods for market. By sunrise, the displays were all prepared and the goldsmiths could be heard tapping their hammers in their stalls; the weavers were click-clacking their looms; the tailors had their dummies set out and dressed with the finest doublets in their stock and the potters had their wheels spinning. Even the well-heeled guests who were accustomed to rising late had risen early—if not quite so early as the help—to breakfast in the hall, so that they could go out to the fairgrounds and get first crack at the merchandise, or else simply wander around and enjoy the spectacle.

Godfrey Middleton had certainly done himself proud, Smythe thought. An elaborate, gala wedding celebration for his eldest daughter, complete with a nautical procession worthy of a display for the queen's own court, and along with that, a private fair open only to his guests, a joust, and the premier of a new play staged especially for the occasion all made for an event that would have everyone in London talking about it for months. All those who had not been in attendance would feel that they had missed something very special and momentous, especially those noble hangers-on who had gone along with the queen's court on Her Majesty's progress through the countryside.

The queen herself would be certain to hear of it, and with her well known fondness for masques and jousts, theatricals and balls and entertainments of all sorts, it was almost a foregone conclusion that next time she would include Middleton Manor on her itinerary, instead of Sir William Worley's Green Oaks. And then once he had played host to the queen for a few weeks, which would be an even more expensive proposition, Godfrey Middleton would be well on his way to the knighthood that he coveted. It was all going to cost him a great deal of money, Smythe thought, but doubtless he considered it money very well spent. Especially since he had it to spend.

The Queen's Men had their duties already set out for them in their instructions from the steward. They had a light repast with the serving staff in the kitchen, which with all the frenetic and boisterous activity going on around them was rather like eating breakfast in the middle of a battlefield, then changed into their costumes and made their way down to the river gate, where they would await the remainder of the guests and, finally, the wedding party. First, however, they all lined up in their white senatorial robes for inspection by the steward, Humphrey, who walked up and down the line like a general and looked them over with a sort of disdainful resignation, adjusted the fold or drape of a robe here and there, then sniffed and pronounced that they "would do."

"There goes a man who has missed his true vocation," John Fleming commented wryly after Humphrey had dismissed them and they began to make their way down to the river. "With that bilious disposition, the man is a born critic if ever I saw one."

Smythe chuckled, but Will Kemp's perpetual grumbling and grousing forestalled his response.

"These costumes are ridiculous," Kemp said. "Roman senators, indeed! We look more like a bunch of cadavers wrapped up in shrouds."

"In your case, that would be particularly true," Robert Speed replied.

"At least my talent is alive and well, which is certainly more than I can say for yours," Kemp riposted, contemptuously.

Speed raised his hand and snapped his fingers, as if ordering up a tankard of ale. "Gentlemen, a shroud for Master Kemp's talent, if you please?"

"We should have asked for some flasks of wine or perhaps a small keg of ale," John Hemings said, as if prompted by the gesture. "These flimsy robes are none too warm."

"Aye, and adding to the morning chill, there is a stiff cold breeze coming in off the river," Kemp complained as they made their way down the steps to the arched stone river gate. "I can feel the wind blowing straight up through the bottom of this pox-ridden robe."

"Well, 'twould not be the first time you had your pox-ridden privates waving in the breeze, now would it?" Speed said.

Kemp gave him a withering glare. "And how would *you* know, Bobby?"

"Oh! Stabbed to the quick!" Speed cried out, grabbing at his chest and staggering down the steps. "Sweet mercy, I am slain!"

They all burst out laughing as he "died" theatrically on the steps in a series of dramatic thrashings and convulsions. Even Kemp was moved to laugh, despite himself.

"Well worthy of a Caesar's death!" said Burbage, applauding. "Ned Alleyn himself could never have done better!"

"Aye, and he frequently did much worse," added Kemp, whose dislike for their late colleague, who had recently quit their company for their chief rivals, the Admiral's Men, was matched only by the legendary actor's profound distaste for him.

The mention of Alleyn's name momentarily broke their mood of levity, for aside from Kemp's dislike of him, Edward Alleyn was sorely missed. He was widely acknowledged as the finest actor of the day and if Kemp considered both his talent and his ego over-blown, Smythe knew it was because his feelings were motivated primarily by jealousy, for Alleyn's was the name that drew the audiences. They were of different schools, with Alleyn being the realistic dramatist and Kemp the capering clown who played directly to the audience and ad libbed whenever the mood struck him, or whenever he could not recall his lines, which he took little trouble to memorize in any case.

Unfortunately for Kemp, Smythe thought, his brand of broad, physical comedy seemed to be going out of style, just as Shakespeare had predicted, and Kemp seemed unwilling or unable to adapt. For all his grave portentousness and showy manner, Alleyn was now drawing significantly larger audiences at the Rose Theatre, and while the Queen's Men could still boast Her Royal Majesty as their patron, their reputation as the preeminent players of the day was on the wane. Their repertoire was somewhat shopworn and though Shakespeare had managed to improve several of their plays with rewrites, they badly needed something new to bring their audiences back. They were all too well aware of this, and the mention of Ned Alleyn's name merely served to underscore it.

"Well, come on now, Speed, bestir yourself," said Shakespeare, leaning down to give him a hand up. "You shall only soil your costume on these steps, aside from which, methinks I spy some boats drawing near."

Indeed, some small boats were approaching from the direction of the city, bearing the first arrivals of the day. After some brief discussion concerning the roles they were to play, they all decided simply to welcome the arriving guests as if they were citizens of Rome, coming to attend the wedding of Caesar and Cleopatra. It was decided that it would probably be for the best to avoid any reference to Calpurnia, or Mark Antony, for that matter, and that whatever they decided to call themselves as they improvised their way through their individual performances, the names of Casca, Cassius and Brutus might be a little inappropriate.

The players were not the only ones awaiting the arriving guests at the stone gate. As the boats drew up to the stone steps that came down to the water from the arched river gate, several of the household staff stood by to check their invitations, in order to make certain that no uninvited guests would be admitted. Rather cleverly, Will Kemp took it upon himself to receive the invitations from the men who checked them and then announce the guests as if they were arriving at an imperial court. It allowed him an opportunity to ham it up in front of some of London's most wealthy and influential citizens, while at the same time it kept him from having to keep going up and down the stairs to the house, as did all the others who escorted the arriving guests.

As the morning wore on and guests continued to arrive, Smythe remained by the gate with Kemp, playing subserviently to his character as if he were some ministerial aide and collecting all the invitations from him while paying particular attention to the noblemen who were arriving together with their grown and eligible sons. To his dismay, there turned out to be over a dozen of them. And then there were other sons of noble birth who arrived together with their fathers *and* their mothers, though it occurred to Smythe that he should not eliminate them from consideration simply because of that. A man who was bold enough to pose as the son of a nobleman in all this august company would certainly be resourceful enough to find a woman who could play the part of his mother, just as he had planned to have his co-conspirator pose as his wealthy, aristocratic father.

Unfortunately, thought Smythe, his background was not such that he would know any of these people. Some of their names might be familiar to him, but a lowly ostler and player such as himself did not move in such exalted circles, and so he therefore lacked the necessary knowledge to make any immediate determinations as to who was who. A good many of these people would naturally know one another, and would thus be better able to identify any strangers in their midst, but he could not simply approach noblemen and ask them to vouch for one another. Dick Burbage, perhaps, as one who had grown up in the city, would be better able to recognize many of these people, but more than anything else, Smythe wished that Sir William were here, so that he could consult with him. As a regular at court and a leader of London society, Sir William would certainly be able to help him narrow down the list of suspects.

However, in all likelihood, Sir William had accompanied the queen on her sojourn in the country, because whenever Her Majesty made her annual progresses through the countryside, her entire court would travel with her. It meant that whichever of her subjects she chose to stay with when she stopped would have to bear the expense of playing host not only to the queen, but to her entire court, as well. It would take a mansion such as Green Oaks or Middleton Manor to house them all and it would take a large retinue of servants to see to their needs. Why anyone would wish to put up with such a monumental inconvenience and expense, much less compete with others for the dubious privilege, was beyond Smythe, but compete for it they did, and this wedding festival at Middleton Manor was planned to serve that very purpose. Smythe understood, in essence, that playing for the queen's favor was important to those who wished to rise in rank and power, but he still found it difficult to understand why any of that would mean much to Sir William.

The first time they had met, Sir William had tried to rob him. Of course, he had not known it was Sir William at the time. The last thing Smythe would have expected to encounter on a country road while on his way to London was a knight of the realm dressed as a highwayman. It was not until much later that he discovered who the infamous Black Billy really was or why one of the wealthiest and most powerful men in London chose to lead a secret life as a legendary brigand. As master of the Sea Hawks, the privateers who had achieved everlasting fame and glory when, led by Sir Francis Drake, they had defeated and wrecked the Spanish Armada, Sir William had made his fortune as a shipwright. Though not personally a privateer, he liked to think of himself as something of a pirate, and in a sense, Smythe thought, he probably was. Though he had done his buccaneering with his purse strings rather than a cutlass, William Worley had been no less ruthless.

Smythe found it difficult to imagine how a man like Sir William could indulge in the sort of social jousting practiced by men like Godfrey Middleton and most of the queen's courtiers. It was rather like trying to imagine a hawk strutting with the chickens. It seemed both unlikely and absurd.

However, a friendship between a knight like Worley and a player like himself seemed equally unlikely and absurd, and yet despite that Sir William was his friend, though Smythe was under no illusions that they would possibly ever be equals. Aside from himself, Shakespeare was the only other person who knew that Sir William was Black Billy, at least to Smythe's knowledge. Sir Francis Walsingham undoubtedly knew, as well, though Smythe could only surmise that. Her Majesty's chief minister was reputedly a man of many secrets and Black Billy would be one of the best kept.

Without Sir William's presence, Smythe could only try to think what he would have done if he were here, and how he might have advised him to proceed. It was difficult for him to tell who the players were without a scorecard, but it occurred to him that anyone who was outside the general circle of London's high society should be immediately suspect. There were a number of foreign aristocrats in attendance, and they would need to be watched closely, as well as those nobles who came from beyond the environs of the city. Still, Smythe felt frustratingly handicapped by not knowing exactly who those people were.

What he needed, he realized, was Elizabeth's help. But would Elizabeth even speak to him after their last argument? She would probably be disposed to help safeguard her friend's sister from unscrupulous men, but how would he explain how he came by his information? He could just imagine her reaction if he told her that he had overheard two strangers plotting against Blanche Middleton because he had followed her out to the maze last night. No, he thought, that would never do.

He could, of course, simply choose to forget about the whole thing. After all, it did not really concern him personally. What was Blanche Middleton to him? He did not know her. He had not met her. He had never even seen her. His only connection to the Middletons was of a most tenuous nature, indeed. Elizabeth was Catherine's friend, and he cared about Elizabeth, who for all he knew no longer cared about him. He was disturbed at the idea of an innocent woman being duped and taken advantage of, but was it really any of his business? The whole thing was a pointless muddle, and it was giving him a headache, and perhaps he would do well just to forget about it all.

There was, however, the rather unsettling fact that they had tried to kill him, and might well do so again, if they discovered who he was. For that matter, it occurred to him that they might already *know* who he was. It was certainly possible that they could have come out of the maze before he did. If so, then they could easily have concealed themselves in the garden near the entrance to the maze and waited for him to come out, so they could mark him. After that, it would have been a simple enough matter to find out who he was. And even if he decided to avoid becoming involved, there was no way they would know that. The only way they could make certain that he could never give them away would be to kill him. It was not a reassuring thought.

He knew that he could count on Will to help him, but that would not be enough. Shakespeare had no more knowledge about London's upper crust than he did. Neither of them had been in the city very long. Without Sir William present, the only one who was in a position to help him was Elizabeth. And that brought him right back to the irksome problem of how he was to tell her what he knew and how he knew it. There seemed to be only one solution.

He would have to lie.

He recalled Sir William saying once that the best lies were those that kept closest to the truth, because they required the least embellishment and it was thereby easier to avoid making a slip. Therefore, he would stick to the truth as much as possible. He would say that he had overheard the two strangers plotting to take advantage of Blanche Middleton and her father. But then he would have to explain how it happened that he had heard them, but had never seen them. Once again, the simple truth would provide an easy and credible explanation, but what he wanted to avoid, if possible, was telling Elizabeth that he had overheard those men because he had followed her. And if he told her that it had happened last night, then even if he did not admit he followed her, she would realize that he had gone out to the maze at about the same time she did and she would doubtless guess the rest. So . . . the lie had to be concocted there.

It could not have happened any earlier than yesterday, he thought, for everybody knew when the players had arrived. But it could easily have happened several hours earlier, in the afternoon. There were several hours during which the Queen's Men had been settling in, getting their equipment put away, and preparing the stage for their performance. He would need no more pretext to say why he had gone out to the garden than to tell her that he had gone along with Shakespeare, to help him work out some last minute changes in the play.

With most of the visitors to the estate either in the house itself or at the fairgrounds, the garden, and in particular the maze, would seem like the perfect place to go to have some privacy and quiet in which to work. He would need only to tell Shakespeare of his plan, so that Will would know to say that he had been there with him. And because he had already discussed last night's events with him in detail, Will would not require any further briefing. He already knew as much as if he had been there himself.

Smythe nodded to himself with satisfaction. The plan at least seemed workable and he could see no flaw in it. It was also close enough to the truth to make it eminently practical. He would now have to try to find Elizabeth as soon as possible and tell her what he knew. In the face of this threat to the future of her friend's sister, surely, her earlier quarrel with him would be forgotten. That was almost worth an attempt upon his life.

An abrupt change in the manner of the two servants at his side alerted Smythe to pay closer attention to the next boat that was drawing up to the gate. It was a larger boat, better appointed, with a small mast and gaff-rigged sail. Even Kemp, who was not the most observant of individuals, noticed that the manner of the servants had changed somewhat. Their backs had stiffened noticeably and they began to check their costumes, brushing at them and making small adjustments.

"Look smartly now," said one of them. "Yonder boat bears Master Middleton and his younger daughter, with Sir Percival. Their arrival means that the wedding flotilla shall not be far behind."

Kemp drew himself up to his full height, which because he was not much taller than five feet had the comical effect of making him look like a bantam rooster trying to stretch itself into a game cock. The importance of making a good impression on their host, one of the richest men in London, was not lost on him, for Kemp had ambitions of his own that were no less lofty than Ned Alleyn's.

As the boat pulled up to the steps, Smythe marked Godfrey Middleton as he prepared to disembark. Smythe realized that he had seen this man before, when he had attended to his elaborate, black lacquered coach at the Theatre, though he had not known who he was. Now, he recognized him as Middleton stepped off the boat, assisted by his servants.

He was not a young man, by any means, though he was stout and barrel-chested, with thick legs that seemed a bit too short for his torso, so that he seemed to waddle slightly when he walked. His wide and round-cheeked face was ruddy and his prominent, bulbous nose was red, though whether from the chill upon the river or over-indulgence in fine wines, Smythe could not tell, though he could easily hazard a guess.

Godfrey Middleton had the appearance of a man who enjoyed all of the finer things in life and could easily afford them. His clothing was obviously expensive and exquisitely tailored. He wore a saffron ruff and his chestnut colored doublet was of the finest three-piled velvet, tailored in the French style, richly embroidered with gold and silver thread and sewn with jewels, puffed at the shoulders and slashed deeply at the sleeves, revealing bright glimpses of a marigold satin shirt beneath that must have been imported from Paris and probably cost more than Smythe could hope to make in a year. Middleton's galligaskins were deep scarlet and gartered with marigold silk ribbons that matched the silk rosettes upon his gold-buckled shoes. The striking ensemble was topped off with a long cloak in dark, chestnut-brown brocade with a matching floppy bonnet set off with marigold silk ribbons.

"There's a bright beplumaged bird," said Smythe.

"Softly, simpleton, else he shall hear you!" whispered Kemp, glancing at him sharply.

"I doubt it," Smythe replied, although he did lower his voice. "And methinks he would care little if he did. Look at him. He is positively green."

Indeed, Godfrey Middleton looked decidedly ill as he stepped unsteadily out of the boat, assisted by his servants. He appeared genuinely grateful to be on dry land once again. Even though it had been only a relatively short boat trip on the Thames, Middleton acted as if he had just barely survived an arduous transatlantic crossing.

"Zounds, what beastly weather!" he exclaimed to his companions as they disembarked. "That wretched wind! 'Twas a frightful chop out there, I tell you! I damn well nearly gave up breakfast!"

His voice was high-pitched and rather nasal and complemented his waddle perfectly. To Smythe, he sounded like a large, affronted goose, squawking with pompous indignation. The "frightful chop" that he referred to was, to Smythe's eyes, no more than a slight display of whitecaps on the water's surface, hardly what anyone would call rough sailing. It might be a bit of a rock in a small rowboat, perhaps, but it was only the Thames River, after all, not the English Channel. The breeze was brisk and cool, but it was a long way from being a "wretched wind." And Smythe thought that the only reasonable excuse that anyone would have for giving up their breakfast out there would be if they were pregnant.

"Well, 'twas a bit of an unpleasant journey, I'll agree, but 'tis over now and our feet are once again upon dry land," said one of Middleton's companions. "From now on, 'twill all be smooth sailing." The man chuckled at his own remark. "Eh? What? Smooth sailing? I say, that's jolly good, what?"

This gentleman turned out to be the groom. Sir Percival Pennington-Pugh was at least the same age as the bride's father, if not older, but there any similarity ended. Where Middleton was portly, thick-chested and short-legged, Sir Percival was thin as a hay-rake and practically all legs and elbows. And if Middleton brought to mind a puffed up goose, then Sir Percival looked like a spindly water fly, albeit one decked out in a costume so garish as to make Middleton's clothing look positively subdued.

For the occasion of his wedding, Sir Percival had donned a white ruff and a doublet of robin's egg blue silk with double rows of silver buttons set so close together that they touched. His sleeves were "pinked," or slashed to show a silk shirt in a newly fashionable color named "dead Spaniard," in honor of the sinking of the Armada. To Smythe, who did not have much of an eye for distinguishing fashionable subtleties of color, it simply looked dark purple. The groom's fashionable if rather impractical shoes were made of light blue silk, to match his doublet, and they were likewise pinked to show off his morbid Spanish hose. His baggy gaskins were made of velvet in a violet hue and he wore so many jeweled rings that merely lifting his long-fingered, bony hands seemed to take an effort. He wore a wide-linked silver chain, enameled as was currently the fashion in shades of black and purple, to match his high-crowned hat, and in keeping with the latest court fashion of matching one's tonsorial hues to one's haberdashery, he had dyed his hair and pointy beard a purple shade, as well. The servants approached him and helped him don a long, purple fringed robe over his ensemble and then exchanged his hat for an elaborate, Romanesque laurel wreath made of hammered gold. Smythe thought that the unlikely combination of the pleated ruff together with the Roman robe made him look rather like an ambulatory tablecloth surmounted by the head of John the Baptist sitting on a platter.

"God blind me!" he said softly, as the groom and the father of the bride began to climb the steps toward them. "Pity poor Catherine Middleton. With such a Caesar, would for her sake these were the Ides of March and not his wedding day!"

"*Shhh!*" hissed Kemp, elbowing him in the ribs. "Mock this Caesar at your peril, fool," he whispered. "They will club you down, stuff you in a weighted sack, and toss you in the river!"

Smythe fell silent, but not so much as a result of his companion's admonition as from the sight that greeted him as the next passenger lightly stepped off the boat and pulled back the hood of her long, dark blue velvet cloak with a languid, graceful gesture.

Blanche Middleton was all of sixteen, tall for her age, raven-haired, buxom and small-waisted, with grayish-blue eyes that looked like cracked diamonds. She wore a crimson velvet gown over a cartwheel farthingale, which could not have been very comfortable for sitting in a boat, and her puff-sleeved, black velvet bodice was heavily embroidered in gold and stiffened with a pointed stomacher that accentuated a very ample bosom that was displayed even more boldly than the current fashion dictated. She looked around and her gaze settled upon Smythe with such a frank, smouldering directness that it made him look around, thinking that she must have been looking at someone else behind him on the steps, someone quite familiar to her. But when he turned, he saw that there was no one there. When he looked back, her gaze met his once again and she smiled with a sultry, mocking sort of amusement. It struck Smythe that, unquestionably, she was looking straight at him, and he looked back with a frank, appraising stare to see if she would drop her gaze. But she did not.

She came straight up the steps towards him, her eyes never leaving his, save for one moment when they flicked briefly up and down, taking his measure with a boldness that Smythe had never before encountered in a girl.

"My, my," she said in a low and throaty voice, as she drew even with him. "You *are* a big one."

Feeling flustered and not quite knowing how else to respond, Smythe bowed slightly and said, "Your servant, ma'am."

"Indeed?" she replied, archly. "How lovely. I trust that you shall serve me well then."

"Come on, then, Blanche, stop dawdling!" her father called to her, from further up the steps. "We must hurry up and take our places. The flotilla is approaching!"

"Coming, Father!" she called, without taking her eyes off Smythe. And then she cleared her throat slightly, took a deep breath, enhancing her already ample cleavage, lowered her eyelids, and pursed her lips before continuing on her way up the steps with a lingering backward glance over her shoulder.

It took Smythe a moment to find his voice, and when he did, all he could say was, "Good God!"

"Neither God nor goodness has anything to do with *that*, my dear boy," said Kemp, dryly.

"Was I imagining things?" asked Smythe. "Kemp, did you *hear*? Did you *see*?"

"I have ears and I have eyes," Will Kemp replied. "And I have a very great concern for the integrity and preservation of my bones, which faculty I would most heartily commend to you, my lad. Yon saucy baggage is even more trouble than that Darcie wench. If that fire she has just ignited in your loins needs cooling, then may I suggest you jump into the river now and quench the flame post haste, before it burns you and all the rest of us, besides."

A crowd had gathered at the top of the steps behind them, drawn by the arrival of their host and their anticipation of the wedding flotilla bearing the bride. Many of the men were also doubtless drawn by the arrival of Blanche Middleton, who was certainly worth looking at and who seemed to delight in the effect she had on any male within viewing distance. Smythe noticed that all of the young aristocrats he had marked earlier were there, vying for her attention and trying to elbow one another out of the way. If this sort of thing kept up, he thought, there could well be trouble brewing before the day was through.

What concerned him more, however, was that he had as yet seen no sign of Elizabeth. Where could she be? Catherine was due to arrive at any moment. It puzzled Smythe that while Catherine Middleton had spent the night in London, at the residence her father maintained there, Elizabeth had been here, at Middleton Manor. Why? One would think that the logical place for her to have been was at her friend's side as she got ready for the wedding. And why was Elizabeth not part of the wedding party that was arriving on the barge?

The specter of suspicion rose up in his mind once more. There was no reason in the world that Smythe could think of why Elizabeth should not have been in London with Catherine, so that she could arrive with her on the "royal barge," unless of course, coming out early to Middleton Manor would have given her an opportunity to meet with someone. And that someone could only be another man. Nothing else made any sense. And as his thoughts returned to that once more, it again struck him how convenient it was that they had quarrelled the last time they had seen each other.

So . . . where, *was* Elizabeth? He knew where she had been last night. Where was she now? Why was she not here, with everybody else?

Someone called out that the wedding flotilla was approaching, and in moments, everyone was pointing and shouting excitedly. Indeed, the wedding party was approaching in a fleet of boats accompanying the royal barge, just as he had seen them rehearsing the previous day. This time, however, it all seemed to be going smoothly, and despite the "wretched wind" and "frightful chop" that Godfrey Middelton had complained of, the flotilla was approaching in perfect formation, albeit spaced out a bit more widely than before, no doubt in order to avoid the sort of collision that had occurred yesterday.

Smythe had to admit that it certainly looked impressive. The rivermen were an independent and often surly lot, but somehow Middleton's man had succeeded in getting them to work together and take direction in this waterborne pageant. The smaller boats stayed more or less in line and relatively equidistant from one another, forming an escort for the wedding barge that was being drawn by the larger boats in the center of the formation.

The crowd oohed and ahhed as the flotilla drew near and the details of the barge could now be seen. The elaborate, fringed purple canopy waved in the breeze, luffing and cracking like a sail as the "slave rowers" manned their oars, which were really more ornamental than functional. Some of them were actually dipping into the water, and perhaps providing some small amount of motive force, but most of the oars were simply waving in the air. On the flat deck of the barge, Egyptian maidens and high priests waved at the onlookers and tossed flower petals into the water from baskets. On the "upper deck," which was really no more than a wooden platform erected on the barge, Cleopatra sat regally upon her massive throne.

The rest of the Queen's Men now came back down the stairs so that they could finish playing their senatorial roles by greeting the queen of Egypt as she arrived.

"Well, at least they have not smashed into one another this time," Fleming said as the boats drew near.

"Pity," Speed replied. " 'Twas much more fun to watch, what with people shouting and falling overboard and such."

One of the servants overheard and gave him an irate look, which brought the irrepressible Speed an elbow in the ribs from Burbage.

As the barge came closer, they could see the details of the throne, which had been constructed especially for the occasion. It was made of wood, carved and painted to resemble gold and set with bits of colored glass to reflect the sunlight and make it look as if it were covered in jewels. The backrest was positively huge and resembled the prow of a ship. It was carved into the shape of a snake's head, meant to mimic the imperial Egyptian headdress that Catherine Middleton wore.

As the barge drew up to the river gate and the smaller boats held back, waiting for the bride and her party to disembark before they came up to discharge their passengers, all eyes were on the bride as she sat impressively upon her throne. She was dressed in a glittering white robe festooned with jewels and heavily embroidered with gold and silver. Her hair was covered by the imperial headdress, which was striped in black and white and held in place by a circlet of hammered gold, with a snake's head rising from it just over the forehead.

"I do not believe the queen herself ever made a grander entrance," Shakespeare said, as he came up to stand beside Smythe. "And I do not mean Cleopatra."

Indeed, Smythe thought, it was truly one of the grandest spectacles that he had ever seen and every bit worthy of a pageant put on for the queen. That was, of course, precisely what Godfrey Middleton had intended. It was so impressive that Smythe wondered whether the queen, when she heard accounts of it, might even feel resentful that she had missed the celebration. He wondered if perhaps Godfrey Middleton had not overplayed his hand by putting on such an elaborate celebration when the queen was out of town and could not possibly attend. On the other hand, perhaps not. Even if she felt piqued that she had missed it, Her Royal Majesty's appetite would certainly be whetted to see what sort of entertainment Middleton could stage for her if she gave him the opportunity. And after hearing about this, how could she not?

Part of the wedding party had disembarked and the high priests were now proceeding in line up the stone steps, carrying wooden staves with the heads of Egyptian gods upon them while two of the bridal maidens followed in their wake, strewing flowers as they went. The enthusiastic audience at the top of the steps applauded as they eagerly awaited the bride. But Queen Cleopatra had not moved. Catherine Middleton still remained seated on her throne.

" 'Tis what one might call royally milking an entrance," Kemp said with a smirk as they all waited for her to come down off her throne.

"Perhaps she is waiting for someone to help her down," said Burbage, with a slight frown. "That costume looks to be a bit cumbersome. Do you suppose that we were meant to go on board and welcome her, escort her? I cannot recall. Our directions did not seem very clear upon that point. I would hate to think that we have missed our cue!"

"She may only be experiencing the natural hesitation of a blushing bride," said Fleming, with a smile. "You know, having herself a bout of stage fright, as it were."

"When it comes to being married, fright is more often the natural condition of the groom," said Shakespeare. "Perhaps she is unwell. Do you think we should go and see if—"

At that moment, someone screamed. It was one of the bridesmaids still aboard the barge, and in moments, her scream was taken up by others. This, clearly, was not part of the script.

Except for a couple of servants, the players standing on the steps by the river gate were the closest to the barge. Smythe led the way as he ran down the remaining couple of steps and jumped onto the barge, where chaos and confusion now reigned. With Shakespeare and several of the others right behind him, he shouldered his way past the rowers, who had stood up from their benches and were now milling about in confusion. Several of the women were screaming hysterically up on the platform which formed the upper deck and one of the unfortunate girls either fell or else was accidentally knocked overboard into the river.

She started screaming that she could not swim and within moments, the weight of her soaked garments pulled her under. A couple of the rivermen jumped in to save her and fortunately managed to grab hold of her and pull her in towards shore, thus saving her life, but it seemed the bride was not so lucky. When Smythe reached her, one of the hysterical bridesmaids was sobbing and crying out, "She is dead! She is dead! Oh, God have mercy, she is dead!"

Indeed, Smythe found that Catherine Middleton felt cold to the touch, and did not seem to be breathing. Her eyes were closed and she looked quite peaceful, as if she had simply drifted off to sleep.

"Oh, heaven!" Burbage said, as Smythe bent over her. "Dead! Can it be true?"

Smythe put his ear to Catherine's chest. "I cannot hear her heart," he said.

"Oh, woeful day!" said Burbage.

"Injurious world!" said Fleming. "Poor girl! To die so young, and on her wedding day! Could anything ever be more tragic?"

"Perhaps it could," Shakespeare said.

They looked towards him. "What do you mean?" said Fleming. "What have you there?"

"A drinking flask," said Shakespeare, as he sniffed it contents.

"Lord, hand it here," said Kemp. "Methinks now we could all do with a drink!"

"I would be loath to have any of you drink from this," said

Shakespeare. "This potation might be of a potency not to your liking."

"What is it, Will?" Smythe asked.

" 'Tis known as brand," said Shakespeare. "Burnt wine, to some. A spiritous distillation from grape wine. Not a very common beverage, leastwise for the likes of us common folk. Our late, lamented Cleopatra had this flask lying right here at her feet."

"To keep her warm against the river chill, no doubt," said Burbage. "But what of it?"

"It does not smell right to me," said Shakespeare. "And mine, gentlemen, is a most educated nose. There has been something added to this flask that did not come from the vine."

"God shield us!" Burbage said. "Do you mean she has been *poisoned?*"

"Poisoned!" Kemp exclaimed.

The cry was taken up at once by everyone around them.

"I cannot say for certain," Shakespeare said, "but there is something rotten in Egypt. History repeats itself, for unless I miss my guess, Cleopatra has once more fallen to a deadly venom."

6

$\mathcal{T}$HE GUESTS WATCHING FROM THE plaza at the top of the steps knew something had gone wrong, but it was a while before word of what had happened reached them. They saw the commotion below them, where the wedding barge had pulled up to the river gate, and they heard the screaming and saw one of the bridesmaids fall into the river, which resulted in a burst of laughter breaking out among them, but within moments, they knew that something much more serious than a minor mishap had occurred.

When they saw the players rush onto the barge, accompanied by several of the servants, their merriment subsided into silence and the hush continued, stretching out uneasily as they saw the players gather around the bride. A few among the gathered guests began to whisper, wondering what had gone wrong, and then they heard the shouting. At first, they could not make out what was being shouted, and the whisperings among them grew into an anxious undertone that made the shouting down on the barge even more difficult to understand. Then, as people started running back up the steps, calling out what had happened, they finally learned the news of the bride's death.

Godfrey Middleton had stood among the wedding guests, together with his youngest daughter and the groom, impassively watching the spectacle below him. He had frowned angrily at first when the commotion broke out on the barge, doubtless thinking that something had gone amiss at the last moment in all the carefully rehearsed arrangements, but moments later, when it became apparent that something more serious had occurred, his angry frown became a look of consternation. And then the color drained out of his face when he saw Smythe coming slowly up the stairs, carrying the limp form of Catherine in his arms.

Instinctively, the people standing near him drew back, as if proximity could somehow infect them with his horror. Meanwhile, Godfrey Middleton stood absolutely motionless with Sir Percival and Blanche beside him, the three of them forming a sort of island in the sea of guests around them, guests invited to a wedding that was now clearly not going to take place.

The gravity of the situation had apparently not yet impressed itself upon Sir Percival, who seemed oblivious not only to Middleton's concern, but to the strained mood of the crowd around him, as well. "Dear me!" he said. "The poor girl looks to have swooned, eh, what? Bridal jitters, I daresay. Mere trifle. A few sips of wine and we shall have her right as rain, eh, what?"

"For God's sake, Sir Percival, shut up," said Blanche.

His eyebrows shot up and his jaw dropped. "*Well!* I never! The cheek! Godfrey! Good Lord, Godfrey, is this how you taught your daughter to address a gentleman?"

But Middleton moved away from him as if he hadn't even heard, and in all probability, he hadn't. His stricken gaze was riveted on Smythe as he came up the stairs, carrying Catherine in his arms. Blanche went to her father's side and took his arm, leaving the dithering groom standing alone, not quite knowing what to do with himself.

Middleton was pale as death as Smythe reached the top of the stairs and stopped before him. "Sir," Smythe said, haltingly, "oh, sir, I am so very sorry."

Middleton's lips began to tremble. He simply stood there for a moment, trying to find some way to accept the unacceptable. He looked up at Smythe, his eyes moist, holding an agonized expression. Somehow, he found his voice.

"Be so good as to take her into the house, young man," he said, his voice strained with his effort to control it.

"Of course, sir," Smythe replied.

The crowd parted before them silently as Smythe carried Catherine toward the house, with Middleton and Blanche following. As they passed Sir Percival, the groom stood there perplexed, with his mouth opening and closing like a fish.

"Is . . . is there to be no wedding, then?" he said.

Middleton stopped and turned to stare at him, aghast. "My God, sir," he said. "I knew you were a fool, but I did not suspect you were an utter, money-grubbing, inbred idiot." And with that, he turned and followed Smythe and Blanche into the house.

As Smythe was coming back downstairs, he saw Elizabeth at last, standing in the entrance hall with Shakespeare, in conversation with a gentleman who had apparently just arrived. He was still wearing his cloak and was in the act of pulling off his riding gloves while listening to Elizabeth intently. It was not until he removed his hat and cloak and handed them to a servant that Smythe saw to his surprised relief that it was Sir William Worley.

Accustomed as he was to seeing Sir William attired in subdued and somber colors, Smythe almost failed to recognize him resplendent in a gold embroidered, burgundy velvet doublet with generously puffed shoulders and gold buttons, with the wide sleeves slashed to reveal the crimson silk shirt he wore beneath it. His breeches matched his doublet and were tightly gartered and tucked into high, cuffed brown leather riding boots that made him look like one of the privateering captains who commanded his ships. His shoulder-length black hair hung loose, framing his chiseled, clean-shaven features.

He looked up at the sound of Smythe's approach. "Tuck!" he

said. "Elizabeth and Will were just telling me the dreadful news. 'Tis a sad, sad day, indeed."

Smythe came the rest of the way down the stairs and nodded. "Aye, milord. I have just carried Mistress Middleton upstairs to her room, where I have left her with her sister and her father."

Worley shook his head. "Poor Godfrey. I came to attend his daughter's wedding, and now it appears that I shall be attending her funeral, instead."

"And 'twould probably be best if 'twere attended to as soon as possible," Elizabeth said. "What with all the guests still here, their presence would doubtless be a comfort to Master Middleton in his time of grief. I should think 'twould be unbearable if he were to delay in laying her to rest til everybody left and then have to face making arrangements all over again."

"I quite agree," said Worley, nodding. " 'Tis a compassionate suggestion, and a very sensible one, as well. The sooner after death a body is interred, the better. Not only does it aid the bereaved in coming to grips with grief, but it lays the dead to rest before corruption can set in. I shall take the liberty of making certain his steward makes immediate arrangements to place Catherine in the family vault. It may be presumptuous, but under the circumstances, I suspect that I may be forgiven the presumption. Godfrey is doubtless devastated by what has happened. He shall need to have some help."

"I should go and see how he is bearing up," Elizabeth said. "And I should look to poor Blanche, as well."

"Indeed, you should," Worley agreed.

"Elizabeth . . ." Smythe began, but she interrupted him.

"We shall speak later, Tuck. For the present, I must go and try to comfort the Middletons."

"Of course. I understand."

As she hurried away up the stairs, Smythe turned to Shakespeare. "Have you told Sir William everything?"

"Not yet," Shakespeare replied. "Elizabeth was here. 'Twould have been a trifle awkward."

"What do you mean?" asked Worley. "What is awkward? What more is there to tell?"

"A great deal more, Sir William," Shakespeare said. "It has been a most unfortunate and trying day, a beastly trial for all concerned. And I, for one, could certainly use a drink."

He took out a small flask and unstoppered it, then started to raise it to his lips. In that instant, Smythe recognized the flask.

"*Will!*" He reached out and snatched it from him just before he drank. "For God's sake, man! The *poison!*"

Shakespeare paled. "Oh, sweet, merciful heavens! What in God's name was I thinking?"

"Poison?" said Sir William, with a frown. "What poison?"

"You had not told him?" Smythe said.

"I had not," Shakespeare replied, shaken by what he had almost done. He ran his fingers through his thinning hair distractedly. "Elizabeth did not seem to know and I did not wish to upset her any further, though it shall not be long before she hears about it, I am sure. The rumors are already flying among the guests. 'Tis entirely my fault, I fear. I should have been more discreet down at the barge, rather than blurt it out as I did." He put a hand up to his brow, as if he suddenly felt faint. "Odd's blood, I cannot believe I nearly drank the vile stuff!"

"Right," said Worley, grimly. "Come with me." He led them to the library in a brisk manner that made it clear he knew his way around the house. Once there, he closed the door behind them firmly and looked around to make sure they were alone. "Now . . . what is all this about poison?" he asked, frowning.

"Catherine Middleton was apparently drinking from this flask during her journey on the wedding barge," said Smythe, holding it up for Sir William to see. "Will found it lying stoppered at her feet."

"I opened it and sniffed to see what it contained," said Shakespeare. "And I knew at once that there was something wrong."

"Let me see it," Worley said.

Smythe handed it over. Worley unstoppered it and took a tentative sniff. He frowned. "Brand," he pronounced at once, identifying it correctly. "But for a surety, 'tis mixed with something else. There is a curious, uncommon, musty sort of odor."

"I thought so, too," said Shakespeare.

Worley sniffed the flask once more, frowned, then shook his head. "I cannot put a name to it. And you say Catherine was drinking from this?"

" 'Twould appear so," Smythe replied, "although we did not see it for ourselves."

"But Will found it lying stoppered at her feet, you said. If she were drinking from it, and 'twere poisoned, then would she not have dropped it while it was still open?"

"Perhaps," said Shakespeare. "But like one who has already had too much to drink and falls insensible in the act of raising the cup once more, if she had already drunk from it earlier and the poison was not very quick, then she may have been preparing to open the flask to take another drink when it finally took effect, causing her to drop the flask unopened."

Worley nodded. "That is certainly possible. And 'twould explain why the flask was still stoppered and unspilt. But though it may smell peculiar and raise a foul suspicion, we must nevertheless find out for certain if 'tis poison and, if possible, what the poison is. 'Twill take a skilled apothecary to make such a determination."

Smythe and Shakespeare exchanged glances and simultaneously replied, "Granny Meg."

"She is the cunning woman who had helped you once before, as I recall," said Worley.

"Aye," said Smythe. "She has an apothecary shop in the city."

"And she is possessed of uncommon skills," added Shakespeare.

"Her name is not unknown to me," said Worley. "But 'tis said she is a witch."

"If so, then she is an honest one," said Smythe. "And witch or no, she knows her herbs and potions. If anyone can tell us what manner of poison has been put into this wine, she is the one."

"So be it," Worley said, nodding. "Middleton has a light carriage in which you can make the journey with dispatch. In the meantime, I shall see to matters here and send word to Her Majesty that I shall not be rejoining her because of pressing matters that require my immediate attention."

"There is more, Sir William," Smythe said.

"What, *more*? Come on, then, out with it."

As quickly as he could, Smythe told him about what he had overheard the previous night in the maze, and how an attempt had been made upon his life to silence him.

"I see," Worley said, when he had finished. He fixed Smythe with a sharp look. "And how did it happen that you were in the maze to overhear this intrigue in the first place?"

Smythe hesitated awkwardly.

"Come on, Tuck, tell him, for God's sake," said Shakespeare. "There is no shame in it."

"I . . . was following Elizabeth," said Smythe, somewhat sheepishly. "We had quarrelled previously, some days ago, and I suspected that she was seeing someone else."

"And was she?"

"I never learned the truth of it," admitted Smythe. "I lost her in the maze, and then I heard the voices of those men, and you already know the rest. More than anything, I feared that they would stumble upon her and she would come to harm. Hence, I shouted out to warn her and to draw them off."

"Well, if 'twas ever any doubt that foul play was at hand, this certainly dispells it," Worley said. "Whoever those two plotters are, it seems evident from their attack on you that they will not stop at murder to achieve their goal. And now with Catherine's tragic death . . ." He grimaced and shook his head. "Catherine was, God rest her soul, a strong-minded young woman. Godfrey had been trying to get her married off for quite some time, but whether 'twas justified or not, she had a reputation as a shrew. Her sister seems to have a milder disposition, one most men would doubtless find preferable in a wife, but 'twas well known that Godfrey would never have consented to the betrothal of his younger daughter before the older one was married. And now Catherine is dead . . . 'out of the way,' as that miserable scoundrel put it."

"And with no sons to inherit Middleton's fortune, 'twould all go to Blanche now," Shakespeare said. "Or, more to the point, to whoever should become her husband."

"Indeed," said Worley. "And whoever marries Blanche will likely find her far more manageable than ever her sister would have been."

"I am not so sure of that," said Smythe, "but either way, me-thinks Master Middleton should know of this." He sighed heavily. "If I had only said something last night . . ." His voice trailed off.

" 'Twould have made no difference in the end, Tuck," said Shakespeare, gently. "Last night, as it turns out, Middleton was in London with his daughters. We did not know that then, yet even if we did, word could never have reached him in time to save Catherine. How were you to know that someone meant to kill her? And even if you knew, you could not have known she would be poisoned."

"Your friend speaks sensibly and truly," Worley said. "You are entirely blameless in the matter, Tuck. The guilt rests with the murderers. And we shall find them, have no fear. There cannot be many here who are not known to me. We shall look to Blanche's suitors for our suspects."

"But will they not be forewarned now?" Smythe asked.

"Perhaps," said Worley. "However, we have a number of things working in our favor. For one thing, they may not know who you are. And for another, even if they do, they can have no way of knowing that you have discussed with me the things you overheard last night. They shall have no reason to suspect any relationship between us, and we shall give them no reason to suspect one. For all they know, you are merely someone who may have overheard part of their conversation last night. They cannot know for certain what you may have heard, or whether you shall do anything about it, or even whether you shall make any connection between their plot to impersonate aristocrats and Catherine's death."

"But in either case," said Shakespeare, "would it not be in their interest to eliminate even the least possibility that their plot may be exposed?"

"To be sure," Worley agreed. "And they have already demonstrated their willingness to do so in their attack on Tuck. And if they did not hesitate to do so once, they shall not hesitate to try again. Remember that without Blanche Middleton, they have nothing. The entire success of their plan rests on their remaining here and seeing it through. And that is where they shall give themselves away."

Smythe sighed. "I fear I know where this is headed."

Worley clapped him on the shoulder. "Tuck, no one shall force you to take any risks you do not wish to take," he said. "But consider that one woman has already died and the welfare of another is at stake."

"I had already considered those things, Sir William," Smythe replied. "And there can be no question but that I must do whatever must be done. I am completely at your service."

"Good lad."

"I, too, stand ready to assist," said Shakespeare. "What would you have us do?"

"I knew that I could count on you both," Sir William said. "We shall have to move quickly, however. The more time that elapses, the more it favors the killers." He turned to Shakespeare. "Will, you must make all haste to London with this flask and see your Granny Meg. I shall have a carriage made ready for you at once."

"We shall change our clothes and leave immediately," said Smythe.

"Not you, Tuck," Worley said. "You shall be staying here. You have a different part to play."

"That of the Judas goat," said Smythe, dryly.

"Precisely. We must bait them into coming after you once more. Are you up to it?"

Smythe took a deep breath. "I am."

"Good. Now, the first order of business shall be to get Will on his way to Granny Meg's and then see to Catherine's funeral. I shall speak with Godfrey Middleton and fix him to our purpose. It shall not be difficult. He may appear foppish, but there is iron in his spine. I should not wish to have him as an enemy. Once he finds out that his daughter has been murdered, he shall not rest until he has seen her killers brought to justice. But at the same time, we must see to it that in his anger, he does not give our plan away."

"We have a plan, then?" Shakespeare asked.

"Aye," Smythe replied, "to put me into harm's way and see who tries to harm me."

"Ah. It sounds like a good plan to me."

"Oh, does it, indeed?" asked Smythe, wryly.

"Well, I much prefer it to putting myself into harm's way," the poet said, nonchalantly.

" 'Twould be an awful thing if the carriage hit a rut and dropped a wheel on its way to London, so that you fell out and broke your neck," said Smythe.

"Aye, and 'twould be terrible if someone stuck a rapier in your gizzard whilst I was not there to watch your back," Shakespeare riposted.

"If you two are finished fencing, there is more to be discussed," said Worley. "Now then, mark me well, here is what we shall do. . . ."

The journey back to London in Godfrey Middleton's light carriage took far less time than the trip out, but it was also far less comfortable. When they had set out for Middleton Manor, the Queen's Men had travelled by horseback and by wagon, but because their wagon was large and rather cumbersome and loaded with all of their gear, they had traveled slowly, those of them on horseback proceeding at an easy walk so as not to lose the wagon. This was Shakespeare's first ride in a gentleman's open carriage, and he was not especially enjoying the experience.

The well-padded, velvet-covered seats were certainly a vast improvement over a simple leather saddle or the hard, unupholstered wooden bench of a wagon, but the rate at which they travelled made the carriage bounce and jounce as they careened along the rutted road to London and each jarring impact was transmitted through the wooden wheels of the carriage to its frame, then through the seats, despite their padding, directly into the poet's bones. Every bump made his teeth click together sharply and at least twice he had almost bitten through his tongue. Sir William had directed the driver to waste no time in getting him to London and back, and the man was complying with disconcerting efficiency.

Shakespeare knew better than to ask the driver to slow down. The liveried servant had stared at him with thinly veiled contempt when he discovered whom he would be driving to the city and back. After all, he was a gentleman's driver. He had certain standards and a reputation to uphold. And Shakespeare knew that he did not even remotely resemble a gentleman.

Someday, he thought, it would be a fine thing to be able to call oneself a gentleman, with good clothes and a grand house and servants who would tug their forelocks at you. He imagined what it must be like to have his own coat-of-arms to display over his doorway and his mantlepiece, and have painted on the sides of a fine, black-lacquered coach. A coach whose driver he could order to drive *slowly*. He swore to himself as yet another jarring impact shot painfully through his tailbone into his spine. If this was how a gentleman was meant to travel, then he could damn well do without it. If I should ever become a gentleman, he thought, then I shall travel everywhere on horseback. At a walking pace.

It struck him suddenly how utterly ludicrous that thought was. That an actor should ever be regarded as a gentleman was simply ridiculous. An actor, he thought, had about as much chance of becoming a gentleman as he did of being knighted. Still, it was a lovely fantasy with which to pass the time.

It was not very long before the rutted road led to the outskirts of the city and then gave way to London's cobbled streets, which were no less gentle to the poet's fragile frame than they were to the stout, wooden frame of the carriage. Shakespeare swore softly to himself as he shifted uncomfortably in his seat. Carriages and coaches were a fairly recent addition to the traffic on the streets of London, but there were now so many of them vying for space with the wooden-wheeled carts and wagons of the farmers and trades-men, not to mention the horses and pedestrians, that the streets were more often than not hopelessly clogged. It was becoming insuffer-able and Shakespeare could not see it getting any better as more and more of the "new men" were infiltrating the ranks of the upper classes and buying carriages and coaches of their own.

The ditches that ran down the middle of each street trickled with a stinking quagmire of every sort of waste, including human and animal, raising a stench that was enough to take the starch out of a pleated ruff. And for those who could not navigate these streets from the relative safety of a carriage or a perch on horseback, it was a constant hazard to be splashed with the awful ooze, or to lose one's footing on the slippery cobbles. Not a few elegant suits of clothes in evidence on the streets were inelegantly bespattered, and those that were not bore testimony to the light-footedness of their owners.

At the same time, however, London was full to brimming with a sense of energy and purpose that Shakespeare found invigorating and even intoxicating. Unlike his sleepy home village of Stratford, this was a place where things were happening all the time. Here in these teeming streets, and behind those doors, fortunes were being made and lost and people struggled to survive, to live and love, sometimes with passion worthy of a poet's muse, and sometimes with a dull, rutting mindlessness that was nothing more than some primitive, instinctual affirmation of existence. It was all here, the base and the sublime, the endless drama of human character and existence that he found so endlessly fascinating and compelling. Just being here made him feel alive.

To him, *this* was the true theatre, whose machinations he wanted his more artificial theatre to reflect. There was an ongoing drama unfolding in these streets that was far more essential, far more basic, far more tragic, comedic, and uplifting than anything that was currently being acted on the stage. Compared to all of this, he thought, as his alert gaze swept the streets around him, how tawdry, how simple-minded and how utterly banal were the highjinks, jokes and caperings indulged in by the players of the day. All that petty posturing, all those silly, ribald songs, all those grandiloquent speeches said nothing at all about the piece of work man truly was. The ancient Greeks had understood something that men like Greene and his academic cronies seemed to have forgotten, and that was that the highest king could have at heart the motives of the basest peasant, and the meanest menial could possess nobility that would surpass that of the highest king.

The carriage had slowed considerably when they had entered the city and now, as it turned down a winding, narrow street, it slowed even more as the driver scanned the buildings carefully, unsure of his surroundings. Shakespeare called out to him, "Just a short way further on! Look for the sign of the mortar and the pestle!"

Moments later, the driver was reining in before a small apothecary shop on the ground floor of a small, two-story timbered house, crammed wall-to-wall in a row with other similar houses that lined the narrow, winding street. Above the heavy, planked front door hung a wooden sign with a mortar and a pestle painted on it, identifying the apothecary shop.

"Wait here," Shakespeare said to the driver, rather superfluously, for of course the man would wait. He had been ordered to take him there and back. The driver merely glanced at him with disdain and said nothing.

The shop was still open for business, so Shakespeare went straight in. The strong aroma of herbs filled the air inside the shop.

It was the same curious, yet somehow comforting mixture of rich smells he remembered from the first time he had visited the shop, together with Tuck Smythe, Dick Burbage, and Elizabeth Darcie. The door shut behind him with a loud, protracted creaking sound, accented by a soft tinkling of small bells tied to a cord. A profusion of herbs hung drying from the ceiling beams in bunches, dozens and dozens of them, giving the ceiling the appearance of a hanging garden. From one instant to the next, depending upon where he stood, different odors wafted over him, some familiar, like rosemary, fennel, thyme and basil, others strange and exotic. Wooden shelves from floor to ceiling lined all four walls, each shelf holding a wide assortment of earthenware jars of various sizes. In front of one row of shelves, to his left as he entered the shop, stood a long wooden counter upon which were spread cutting boards and mixing bowls, mortars and pestles, scales with weights and measures, scoops, funnels, scissors, knives and various other tools, some of which he could not even identify. For all the clutter, however, there was not a speck of dirt or dust anywhere in evidence.

A hanging cloth embroidered with the symbols of the zodiac was pushed aside and a tall, almost skeletal-looking man in a long black robe stepped out. His dark eyes were deeply set, giving them a hooded aspect, and his features were lined and gaunt. He had high, prominent cheekbones and a high forehead with long, wispy, snow white hair cascading down over his shoulders from beneath a woven skullcap. His face was set into what appeared to be a perpetual expression of somberness. Once again, Shakespeare thought that he looked like the very image of a sorcerer, only instead of having a dramatic name like Merlin Ambrosius or Asmodeus or some other suitably necromantic appellation, he bore the rather prosaic and innocuous name of Freddy.

"Good day to you, Master Shakespeare," Freddy said, greeting him with a slight bow.

" 'Allo, Freddy. I am pleased to see that you remembered me."

"Indeed, I do remember, sir. And if I had not, then Meg would have reminded me. She told me that we might be expecting you today."

"Did she?" The poet shook his head, smiling. "Your good wife continues to amaze me, Freddy. And did she also, by any chance, happen to tell you on what errand I would come?"

"A grave errand, Master Shakespeare."

The smile slipped from Shakespeare's face. "Aye. A grave errand, indeed. I trust that she will see me then?"

"But of course," said Freddy, standing aside and beckoning him through the doorway. "This way, sir."

The poet went through as Freddy held aside the hanging cloth and together they proceeded to the back of the dimly lit shop, towards a steep and narrow flight of stairs against the far wall. Shakespeare slowly climbed the creaky wooden stairs until he came out through the floor of the living quarters on the second story. It was a narrow, one-room apartment, longer than it was wide, with whitewashed walls and a planked wood floor that was, unlike the floor in the shop below, not covered with rushes, but swept bare and kept immaculately clean.

At the far end of the room was the only window, looking out over the street below. It was partially hidden by a free-standing wooden shelf that also functioned as a divider to screen off the sleeping area in the back. Nothing at all had changed since the last time he was here. The furnishings were still simple and rough-hewn, consisting of not much more than a couple of sturdy wooden chairs, several three-legged stools and a number of large, old-looking wooden chests. A rectangular wood-planked table similar to those that one might find in any tavern stood in the center of the room, before a fireplace.

Except in the homes of the wealthy, fireplaces on the second floor were simply unheard of. In thatch-roofed country homes, where the ceilings on the upper floors were usually just the dry thatch on the roof, the fire hazard would have been extreme, to say nothing of the flammability of the rushes strewn upon the floors.

However, there were no rushes scattered here, and the ceiling was planked and wood-beamed, not thatch. With the exception of a couple of candles, the flames from the hearth provided most of the light in the room, and there were several black cauldrons of various sizes hanging from iron hooks over the fire. In his mind's eye, the unbidden image of three witches came to him as they stood over the cauldrons, stirring the bubbling brew and cackling to themselves. He shook his head and smiled at his own foolishness, yet at the same time, his surroundings were very much conducive to that sort of vision.

Like the apothecary shop below, the walls were all but covered with wooden shelves crammed full of books and earthen jars, curious looking wooden carvings and small statuary made of stone, clay pots of every shape and size, necklaces and amulets of every description, little leather pouches suspended from thongs with who knew what sort of strange talismans contained therein . . . Shakespeare imagined eyes of newts and wings of bats and pulverized horn of unicorn. Everywhere he looked, there was something wonderfully different and strange to arrest his attention.

"Freddy, I was wondering . . ." he began as he turned around, then stopped abruptly when he saw that Freddy was not there. He frowned. He could have sworn that Freddy had come up the stairs right behind him. In fact, he was certain that he had. He made a wry grimace and shook his head. "The man moves like a ghost," he said to himself.

"Not all ghosts move quietly," said a soft, low voice from behind him.

He started when she spoke and turned around again to see Granny Meg standing by the table in front of the fireplace. It seemed as if she had simply appeared from out of nowhere. Clearly, she must have come from behind the screen at the far end of the room, by the window, but she was barefoot and had moved so quietly that he had not heard her footsteps. He tried to recall if Freddy had been barefoot also, but he had not noticed, and with his floor-length robe, it would have been difficult to tell, in any case.

Once again, he was struck by how ageless Granny Meg appeared. She was no longer young, but her skin was so fair and clear as to be almost translucent, without a single blemish or wrinkle. She was of average height, girlishly slim, and sharp-featured, with a pointed chin, high cheekbones, and a delicate, thin nose. Her thick, silvery-gray hair hung down to her waist. She had worn it loose the first time he had seen her, but now she had it plaited into one thick braid that hung down the left side of her chest and was held with simple rawhide thongs. She wore a simple homespun gown, lightly and delicately embroidered with green vines and flowers around the neckline. Her voice was low and mellifluous, memorable certainly, but not nearly so much as her eyes, which were an unusual, striking shade of pale grayish blue, so light that they seemed to absorb light and reflect it. And she seemed to be surrounded by a brightly glowing, pulsating aura.

Shakespeare blinked, taken aback, and then realized that it was but a momentary illusion of the firelight on the hearth behind her. He smiled, thinking of how easily his imagination ran away with him each time he came here. It was, after all, nothing more than an ordinary apothecary shop.

"I was thinking that surely no ghost could move as quietly as you, madame," Shakespeare said. "You gave me a bit of a start."

She smiled. "Forgive me. The floorboards here are stout, and these old bones are very light."

" 'Tis good to see you once more, Granny Meg. Good day to you. I am given to understand I was expected?"

She shrugged, a very spare and graceful gesture. "I had a strong presentiment that I would be seeing you today."

"And lo, here I am."

"There you are." She indicated one of the chairs at the table. "Please, be seated."

He took the chair and she sat down across from him.

"You are very troubled," she said.

"Indeed. You can divine that much already?"

"I can divine that simply by looking at your face," she replied, raising her eyebrows. "You wear a very troubled look."

"Ah. Well . . ." He nodded. "I am troubled, 'tis true. Very much troubled. Something has happened . . . something both unfortunate and terrible. There has been a murder . . . or at the very least, it seems very like a murder. A young woman is dead and it appears as if there may have been foul play. Indeed, we very much suspect so."

"We?" she asked.

"The esteemed Sir William Worley, Tuck Smythe, and my humble self," Shakespeare replied.

She nodded. "I have heard much of Sir William, and I remember Tuck, of course. Go on."

"Well . . ." He paused a moment, collecting his thoughts. "The poor, unfortunate girl . . . 'twas to be her wedding day, you see, and her father had prepared a most elaborate and lavish celebration at his estate outside the city. We players were to participate, which is why Tuck and I were there, of course, and Sir William was one of the illustrious invited guests. There was to be a fair, and a grand progress on the river with the bride in costume as Queen Cleopatra arriving on her royal barge. All went well, as had been planned, until the arrival of the bride, who tragically turned up dead upon her throne. And beside her body, I found this . . ." He took out the flask. " 'Twould appear that she was drinking from this flask to ward off the chill upon the river. 'Tis brand, burnt wine, but 'twas mixed with something else, methinks, some foreign matter. There is a curious sort of odor, one the girl no doubt could not discern, which would be no great surprise if she were not accustomed to the drink. I believe it may contain a deadly poison."

"And so you seek to have me confirm what you believe," Granny Meg said.

"Aye, 'twould prove that murder had been done," said Shakespeare, grimly. "And perhaps, if we knew the nature of the poison and where it might have been obtained, then 'tis possible we might learn who had obtained it. Sir William will see to it, of course, that your efforts in this matter are rewarded."

Granny Meg nodded. "Let me see the flask."

Shakespeare passed it to her across the table, but the moment her hand came in contact with the flask, Granny Meg stiffened and a frown crossed her features. Her grasp tightened on the flask. She closed her eyes and shook her head, as if to dispel whatever perception or sensation she had just experienced, or else deny it, then she unstoppered the flask and brought it up close to her lips, as if she were about to drink, only instead her nostrils flared delicately as she sniffed its contents once, and once only, whereupon she set the flask down and abruptly got up from the table.

Shakespeare could no longer contain himself. She knew what it was, that much seemed certain from her reaction. She had turned away from him and was staring intently into the flames upon the hearth. Clearly, she was greatly troubled.

"I can see that you recognized the odor," he said, softly. "I was right, was I not?"

Granny Meg kept staring into the flames as she slowly shook her head. "No. You were not."

He was completely taken aback by her reply. It did not seem possible. He had been so certain. " 'Tis *not* poison?" he said. "Are you certain?"

"I should think I ought to know," Granny Meg replied. "I had prepared it myself."

"*What?*" He stared at her, eyes wide with astonishment. "*You* prepared this flask?"

"Not the flask," she replied, "but 'twas I who mixed the potion that went into it. 'Tis an ancient blend of certain rare herbs and distillations, comingled with some common plants that can be found simply growing wild by the roadside. But the effect that it produces is not common at all."

"But . . . you just said 'twas not a poison," Shakespeare said. "And yet Catherine Middleton is dead!"

Granny Meg turned back towards him and shook her head. " 'Twas not the name she gave me, though I had a feeling that the name she gave was false. That alone might have dissuaded me from helping her, yet she came well recommended. If she was the bride of whom you speak, the one who drank this potion, then most assuredly it did not kill her."

Shakespeare pushed back his chair and stood. "Granny Meg, I was *there*! With my own eyes, I saw her lifeless body! She neither moved nor took a breath! Tuck listened at her chest and said her heart had ceased to beat! Odd's blood, if she came to you for some sort of tonic and by mishap you had made some dreadful error in the concoction that resulted in her death, why then . . . this terrible tragedy is *your* responsibility!"

"There has been no error, Master Shakespeare, I assure you," Granny Meg said calmly. "Hear me out before you rush to judgement of me. The potion I had mixed at the woman's own request has, by your own report, produced precisely the result that was desired."

"Good God!" he said. "Are you saying that Catherine Middleton *wanted* to kill herself?"

"No. Far from it. She had the best reason in the world to want to live. But she wanted to produce the illusion that she did not. She asked me if I could prepare a potion that could, for a certain length of time, produce the appearance of death, and yet not bring it about. I hesitated to perform the task she asked of me, and warned her that such a ruse was not without its dangers, but she and your friend who brought her to me both beseeched me, and said it was the only chance she had to avoid a life of hopeless misery."

"You said that a friend of mine had brought her to you?" Shakespeare said. "What do you mean? Which friend?"

"Why, the one you brought to see me once before," Granny Meg replied. "Young Mistress Darcie."

"Elizabeth?"

"Aye, she is the one who brought her to me."

"Then you mean to say that Catherine Middleton is not truly dead, but merely in a sort of morbid slumber?"

"Her heart still beats, but so weakly that one may not easily discern it," Granny Meg replied. "And she still breathes, but only barely, and to all outward appearances seems not to breathe at all. She will lie thus for at least a day or more, and then she will awake as if from an ordinary slumber, and should be no worse for wear."

"But . . . the funeral . . ." Shakespeare said.

"I was assured that there would be no burial," said Granny Meg, "but that she would be laid to rest within her family vault, where she could sleep in safety until the effects of the potion had worn off."

"Of course!" said Shakespeare. He remembered then Elizabeth's insistence that the funeral should take place as soon as possible, while the guests were still assembled, so that Catherine could be laid to rest inside the family vault, the better to ease her father's grief . . . and aid in the deception. "So there has been no murder after all!"

"And yet," said Granny Meg, as she reached out slowly and picked up the flask, "I have a strong presentiment of death." Her brow was deeply furrowed and her eyes had an unfocused, distant look. "Something is very wrong. I see death where there should be no death." She looked at him. "Go back," she said. "And ride with all due haste. Death comes; there is no time to waste."

7

THE NEWS OF THE BRIDE'S death had cast a pall over the festivities, but not quite to the extent that Smythe might have expected. For one thing, rather to his surprise, it had not brought the festivities to an end. Quite the contrary, it seemed to add a morbid stimulation to them. Instead of offering their condolences to their host, or at least sending them through servants and then leaving quietly, as Smythe had expected most of them to do, the guests had all, without exception, chosen to remain, no doubt out of curiosity to see what would develop and because there was still a fair they could attend, with the added spice of new rumors and gossip to exchange.

None of the merchants had packed up and left, mainly because no one had told them to go and the fair was still on so far as they were concerned. There were still good profits to be made and they continued to do a brisk business as the day wore on. When Godfrey Middleton's steward came out to announce formally that Catherine's funeral would be held that very afternoon, and that banqueting would follow for the guests, then anyone who might have considered leaving chose instead to stay. As Shakespeare had remarked wryly just before he left for London, " 'Tis thrift, Tuck, thrift. The baked meats of the wedding feast shall now coldly furnish forth the tables for the wake."

Smythe thought that was rather cold of his friend to make the observation in such bitter terms, yet he had to admit that it was accurate. His eldest daughter had just apparently been murdered on the very day of her wedding, and Godfrey Middleton, however distraught he might have felt, was nevertheless allowing the fair to continue. Was it because he had already made a commitment to the merchants, who had indeed gone to some trouble and expense to come out to Middleton Manor from London, or did he have more mercenary motives because he would, as owner of the grounds on which the fair was held, pocket a percentage of the merchants' profits?

"If 'twere my daughter," Smythe said to Sir William, "I would have shut down the fair and asked everyone to leave, albeit kindly, so that I could be left alone with my grief. Instead, the fair proceeds as planned, even with Catherine lying dead upstairs in the house." He shook his head. "I simply cannot see how Middleton can continue with it."

" 'Tis said the rich are different, Tuck," Sir William replied, "and having started out in life quite poor, I have seen both sides of fortune, good and ill. There is, indeed, a lot of truth to what they say. A poor man may not have a rich man's luxuries, but then neither does he have his obligations. And while 'tis true that money may beget more money, 'tis also true that it takes money to maintain money. Godfrey Middleton is a rich man, but his estate is frightfully expensive to keep up, as is his business and his home in London, too. All must be staffed, provisioned and supplied, and otherwise maintained. There are many people who depend upon him for their livelihoods. Just because a man is rich, Tuck, does not mean that he is without care or duty."

"I can see your point, Sir William," Smythe replied. "And yet, I still cannot help but think that there are times when a man can simply be past caring, and when duty can just be damned."

Worley nodded. "I can see your point, as well, lad. And 'tis well taken, too. For my own part, I have no children, so I cannot say for certain that I know how I would feel were I in Godfrey's place.

But I have known what it is to love, and then to lose that love, and if such pain can in any measure be akin to the pain of a lost child, then I believe that I would feel much the same as you."

Smythe glanced at Sir William briefly, but Worley seemed to be looking off into the distance somewhere. Smythe had never before heard Sir William speak of any romances in his past. Indeed, there was much about Sir William Worley's life he did not know—although in some respects, he knew a great deal more than most—and it would have been much too presumptuous of him to ask.

"Howsoever that may be," Worley continued, "it serves our purpose that the fair has not closed down and the guests have not been asked to leave, for we can now proceed to run our murderer to ground."

"Or murderers, if there be more than one," said Smythe, mindful of the two men whose plotting he had overheard.

"Indeed," said Worley. "And the first order of business shall be to inform Godfrey Middleton of how things stand. That, I fear, must be my sad duty to perform, as he is my friend and neighbor."

"And yet, he is your rival," Smythe observed.

"That, too. However, truth be told, 'tis a rivalry more keenly felt by him than me. I am aware of it, of course, but I do not pay it any mind. I know he envies me my privilege of playing host to Her Royal Majesty each year when she sets out for her progress through the country, but I shall tell you frankly—and in strict confidence, mind you—that 'tis a privilege I would gladly cede to him. Her Majesty alone can be a handful at the best of times, but together with her sycophantic pilot fish at court, she becomes much more of a vexation than a privilege. Each year, I play the gracious host to them and spend a small fortune on their entertainment. And each year after they have gone, it takes yet another small fortune to clean up the mess they leave behind. If Godfrey wishes to contend with that, believe me, he is more than welcome."

"Well, after what has happened, I should think there would be little chance that the queen would ever wish to lodge here."

Worley gave a snort. "After what has happened here, you could not beat the old girl off with a stick," he replied, in a manner rather more befitting his rough demeanor as Black Billy than the elegant Sir William. "There is no dish quite as piquant to the nobility as a good serving of scandal, and murder makes for the most savory morsel of them all. The queen is no exception. I love the old girl, and 'tis my honor and my duty both to serve her, but at heart she is as bloodthirsty as her father was before her. Godfrey wanted this to be a memorable occasion that all of London would talk about for months or even years to come. Well, he has paid a very high price for it, I fear, but he has gotten precisely what he wanted. Come on, then. Let us go and pay our respects to him."

"You wish me to go with you to see him?" Smythe said, with surprise.

"Of course," Worley replied. "He shall want to hear from you, in your own words, what you overheard those two men say out in the garden."

"But do you really think, that at such a time . . . that is, with his daughter's death as yet so fresh . . ."

"Godfrey Middleton is not a man who is ruled by sentiment, believe me," said Worley. "However grief-stricken he may be, he shall still want justice, rest assured. So let us go and speak with him."

They found Middleton alone in his own chambers, standing and staring impassively out the window at the river. They were admitted by his steward, Humphrey, who quietly withdrew, leaving them alone with him.

"Godfrey . . . I am so very sorry for your loss," said Worley.

Middleton slowly turned to face them. He nodded. "Thank you, Sir William. And my thanks to you for coming. I only wish that it were for my daughter's wedding rather than her funeral." His gaze settled upon Smythe. "You are the young man who brought my daughter up from the barge. Forgive me, but I do not believe I know your name."

"Tuck Smythe is one of the players, Godfrey," Worley said. "He is also my friend and protege."

Middleton's eyebrows went up. "Indeed?" He looked at Smythe with new interest. "That is not a claim that many men can make. It speaks very highly of you, young man."

"Thank you, sir."

" 'Tis I who should be thanking you for the service you performed," said Middleton, his voice flat and unemotional. "But forgive me, I am being rude. Please, be seated."

"I think that we should rather stand, for the bitter news that we have to impart," Worley told him.

Middleton stiffened. " 'Tis true, then, about the poison?"

"You knew?" asked Worley, frowning.

"My steward, Humphrey, told me that there was talk of poison among the guests, but he did not know if there was any truth to it." Middleton hesitated. The corner of his mouth twitched slightly. "Is there?"

"We do not yet know for certain," Worley replied, "but I have good reason to believe there is. She appeared to have been drinking from a flask to help keep warm upon the river. The flask was found and brought to me by William Shakespeare, another of the players, a young poet who is well known to me. I am nearly certain that the flask contained some sort of poison. I have sent Shakespeare to London with it, to have an apothecary analyze its contents so that we may know for certain. He will notify me of what was found as soon as he returns."

Middleton swallowed hard. "So then 'tis true. My daughter killed herself to spite me, rather than go through with a marriage that she did not want."

Worley frowned. "Good Lord, Godfrey! Is *that* what you thought?"

"What else should I think, damn you?" Middleton shot back, and then he suddenly caught his breath and paled as comprehension dawned. "Dear God in Heaven! Do you mean to tell me she was *murdered*?"

"I fear she was, Godfrey," Worley said. "Smythe, here, over-heard two men last night, plotting in the garden, and it very nearly cost him his life. I thought it best if he were to tell you what he heard in his own words."

Quickly, Smythe recounted the details of what had transpired in the maze the previous night. Middleton listened without saying a word, his features strained, his lips compressed into a tight grimace. When Smythe had finished, Middleton simply stood there, motion-less and silent, as if he could find no words to say.

At length, Sir William broke the awkward silence. "Godfrey . . . are you well? Perhaps you should sit down?"

Middleton blinked several times and looked at him. "My God," he said, hoarsely. He made a weak, waving sort of gesture towards the sideboard. "There is wine . . . in the decanter there. Help your-selves, please. I insist."

Smythe went to pour them all a drink. He handed a goblet to Middleton, one to Sir William, and then took one for himself.

"How is the groom taking it?" asked Worley.

Middleton snorted. "Sir Percival? He is out there somewhere, dithering and acting very put upon. One would think that Catherine died just to inconvenience him." He grimaced, then raised his goblet in a toast. "To my daughter, Catherine," he said, somberly. "May merciful Almighty God rest and protect her poor, unhappy and un-shriven soul."

"Amen," said Worley, softly.

They drank.

Middleton simply tossed the goblet aside onto the floor. "Now then," he said, grimly, "what are we going to do about this?"

"We are going to find the guilty parties, Godfrey," Worley said, "and then they shall hang."

"Not nearly punishment enough," said Middleton, with a hard

edge to his voice, "but as we are not Spaniards, I suppose that it shall have to do. What do you want from me?"

"Proceed with the funeral and hold the fair, as planned," said Worley. "Let it be known that it shall be held in Catherine's memory. In the meantime, we shall begin to ferret out our plotters by paying particular attention to your younger daughter's present suitors, especially those whose families we do not know. In this regard, Tuck Smythe here will assist us, as will young Shakespeare when he returns. They have assisted me before in a matter of great import and they have my fullest confidence."

Middleton nodded. "Then that is good enough for me. I shall see to it that they have whatever they require."

"Do so, but pray, do so with discretion," Worley cautioned him. "Our quarry shall be brought to ground more swiftly if they do not suspect that they are being hunted."

"It shall be done as you wish, Sir William," said Middleton. "I am in your debt."

"He who strikes out at my neighbor strikes at me," said Worley. "I am certain that you would do no less if you were in my place. Smythe and Shakespeare shall be our hounds in this regard. For the present, I fear that I must leave and rejoin Her Majesty, who shall be awaiting my return. However, I shall inform her of what has happened here and beg her leave to absent myself from court in order to pursue this matter to its swift conclusion. I feel confident that she shall not refuse me."

"You honor me in this," said Middleton.

"Murder does dishonor to us all," Worley replied. "Now, before I leave, let us sit down and put our heads together, so that Smythe may have the benefit of our common knowledge and proceed in my absence. . . ."

The funeral was held late that afternoon, when the performance of the play had originally been scheduled. Much to everyone's surprise, however, it was announced that the players would still perform on the afternoon of the following day. This news was as much of a surprise to the Queen's Men as to anybody else. They had fully expected that their performance would be cancelled because of the bride's death and were thus quite taken aback by the announcement. They had already returned the Roman togas they were given as costumes for the bride's arrival and had started packing up their gear to leave. Now, with this unexpected turn of events, it brought about a flurry of unpacking and new preparations.

A lively debate ensued among them about which play from their repertoire should be performed. Burbage was strongly of the opinion that Shakespeare's new play, being a broad and rather bawdy comedy, would now be completely unsuitable for the occasion, and most of the players agreed. Kemp, of course, was the notable exception, for any comedy with a good deal of physicality and broad humor played mostly to his strengths as a dancer and a clown. John Fleming argued that a tragedy should be performed instead, for that would be more in keeping with the funereal occasion.

Part of the problem was that with Shakespeare still away in London, the man who would be most adept at making any last minute alterations in any of their plays to render them more suitable was gone, and they could not seem to agree on which play should be performed or whether any changes should be made. The one thing they all seemed able to agree on was that, under the circumstances, the success of their performance would almost certainly be doomed from the beginning. However, they could not very well refuse to perform. It simply was not done, aside from which, they had already been paid; their audience would be an illustrious one; and their host was a good friend of one of their principal investors. It was a situation that none of them were pleased with and their mood was petulant and sullen.

After explaining that he and Shakespeare had both been directed by Sir William to perform some special tasks for their bereaved host, Smythe left them arguing amongst themselves. As he was not one of the principal actors, or even a significant supporting player, Smythe thought wryly that he would not truly be missed unless there was a need to move any heavy objects. It occurred to him, in passing, that here was probably the single greatest opportunity for him as a player to make a good impression on some of the most important people in the city, and it now looked as if he would not even be setting foot upon the stage. But then again, the few times that he *had* set foot upon it, he had not distinguished himself for anything save his maladroitness.

"Face it, Smythe," he mumbled to himself, as he left the others arguing in their quarters, "as a player, you make an admirable black-smith."

In the months since he had arrived in London together with Will Shakespeare, whom he had met upon the road, they had accomplished much together. They had managed to find jobs, for one thing, which in itself was a significant accomplishment, considering the vast numbers of people arriving in London every day from small towns and villages across the country. And not only had they found jobs, but they had found positions with one of the most illustrious companies of players in the land, which had been the dream they shared in common.

Granted, they had started out as ostlers, tending to the horses and carriages of playgoers, but Shakespeare had quickly demonstrated his value to the company as a poet and adapter of existing plays, while he, at least, had managed to move up to stagehand and occasional spear carrier, though he was still expected to perform his duties as an ostler when not otherwise engaged. And considering his appalling lack of talent as an actor and his disastrous clumsiness on stage, Smythe knew that he should consider himself fortunate not to have been summarily dismissed from the company. In all likelihood, he thought, he would have been let go already, were it not for Shakespeare, whose abilities were highly valued by the Queen's Men and for whose sake they had kept him on.

In all, Smythe knew that he had nothing to complain about.

There were many men and women in London who were jammed together in absolutely squalid quarters, a dozen to a room or more, barely able to eke out an existence by picking up odd jobs, or begging, or stealing, or selling themselves upon the streets. For many, their dreams of making a new life for themselves in the city would end up on the gibbet, or in prison, or perhaps worse still, in Bedlam, among the screaming lunatics. Yet, at odd moments, Smythe wondered what his life would have been like if he had remained in his small village in the Midlands and followed the trade to which he had been apprenticed.

He would have continued to work together with his Uncle Thomas at his forge, spending his days with the man who was more of a father to him than his own father ever was, and he would have pursued a trade at which he had some skill. Smythe knew he was a good smith, an excellent farrier, thanks to his natural way with horses, and he had a serviceable talent as a forger of blades which, under the skilled and gifted tutelage of his uncle, he could have developed into a separate trade of his own. In time, perhaps, he would have met a girl and married, and then had children and a home of his own. It would have been a good life, undoubtedly, better than most. From any practical standpoint, leaving home and coming instead to London to pursue a life in the theatre had been foolish beyond measure.

Yet, it had always been his dream. It was all he had wanted to do ever since he had seen his first play performed by the Queen's Men upon a makeshift stage in the courtyard of a village inn. Now, he had joined that very company, and was embarking upon his very first tour. True, the beginnings of the tour were certainly far from auspicious, and the players were already speaking with trepidation of the tour being ill-omened, but Smythe nevertheless felt buoyed by the knowledge that he was living out his dream.

Even the present circumstances could not dampen his enthusiasm. He was on the road with the Queen's Men and he was having an adventure. He could feel sympathy for Godfrey Middleton, and he certainly felt sorry for what had happened to his daughter, but then, he had never known her. It was not his tragedy and he could feel no grief. There was really only one dark cloud on his horizon . . . the possibility that Elizabeth had found somebody else.

Perhaps he was wrong for feeling jealous. After all, it was not as if Elizabeth were his lover. They had never been intimate; they did not have any sort of understanding between them and, indeed, they could not. Shakespeare was right when he pointed out that she was much too far above him. Her father was a wealthy man, a principal investor in the Burbage Theatre, and if Henry Darcie was not quite yet a member of the landed gentry, then the title of "gentleman" was certainly not very far beyond his reach. Henry Darcie often purchased dresses for his daughter that cost more than Smythe could make in several months. The thought that he could ever hope to meet with her on equal terms was ludicrous. Her father tolerated their friendship—rather grudgingly, it seemed—because of the service Smythe had rendered to his family, and because he knew that Sir William Worley had taken Smythe under his wing, but at the same time, Smythe knew it was a tolerance that would not bear much testing. Darcie still hoped to make a good, advantageous marriage for his daughter. He would not stand idly by and watch some randy young ostler spoil his plans.

Smythe knew and understood that, but still could not help the way he felt. And until recently, he had been certain that Elizabeth had felt something for him, too, something more than friendship. Now, he was no longer certain. Since the day they had argued in St. Paul's, Elizabeth had been avoiding him. She had barely even spoken to him, and the one time that she had, she had put him off. Granted, she had promised him that they would speak, and under the circumstances, it would have been the height of selfishness if he had expected her to put his needs above those of a grieving father, especially when the daughter he was grieving for had been Elizabeth's close friend. Smythe very much wanted to believe that was all it was. Yet, there was still the troublesome riddle of what Elizabeth had been doing in the garden maze that night.

It worried him throughout the funeral ceremony, which was mercifully short, doubtless because Godfrey Middleton would have found it unbearable to draw it out into an elaborate ritual, as he had intended to do with Catherine's wedding. The musicians who had been engaged to play for the wedding now played for the funeral instead, offering up sweet and solemn tunes which they played upon lutes, recorders, citterns, sackbutts, harps and psaltries, coaxing more than a few tears from the assembled guests, especially the women, many of whom joined in to sing several psalms for the procession to the family vault.

As it was a newly built estate, the vault was new as well, a small yet stately stone mausoleum which contained but one coffin, that of Catherine's mother. Now Catherine would sleep beside her, laid out in her wedding dress upon the slab until her own coffin could be prepared. It would doubtless be speedily arranged upon the morrow, if Middleton or, more likely, his steward did not already have a carpenter at the estate busily engaged upon the task. The procession gathered in the front courtyard of the house and then slowly and solemnly made its way across the grounds, in the opposite direction from the fair's pavillions, down a path that led along the riverside and through the woods to where the vault stood in a small clearing, surrounded by a stone wall with an iron gate set into it. It would, thought Smythe, be a very peaceful place to rest.

His thoughts and his attention were less upon the funeral, however, than upon those in attendance, in particular a certain few who had been the subject of discussion earlier between Godfrey Middleton, Sir William, and himself. Because of what he had overheard, their discussion had centered upon Blanche Middleton's suitors, in particular those who were not well known to either Middleton or Worley. Given that Blanche was quite a sultry beauty, and with a very wealthy father, there seemed to be no shortage of eager suitors for her hand in marriage. However, a good number of them were easily eliminated from consideration as suspects due to either Middleton or Worley being well acquainted with their families, if not with the young men themselves. That still left three or four who seemed quite worthy of suspicion.

One such was young Andrew Braithwaite, a baron's son who hailed from Lancashire. Or so he claimed. Middleton knew nothing of him and Worley had no knowledge of him, either. However, that did not necessarily mean Braithwaite was not who he said he was. Not all the members of England's nobility were regulars at court or sat among their peers in the House of Lords; some never even came to London. Consequently, they did not necessarily all know one another. Sir William had explained, primarily for Smythe's benefit, that presently there were three degrees of nobility in England, those of baron, viscount, and earl, in descending order. A duke would have been above a baron, of course, but at present, no one held that title.

As a country commoner with little formal education, Smythe did not know a great deal about the nobility, nor had he learned very much more since he came to London. He knew that a noble was created by the sovereign through a patent bearing the Great Seal of England and the title of that noble was thereupon passed down through the eldest son. He also knew that bishops, equal to the nobility in rank, were likewise appointed by the sovereign, and their offices were not hereditary. Below them were knights and gentlemen, with knighthood bestowed for special service or as a mark of favor by either the sovereign or a deputy empowered to act in the sovereign's name, such as a general or an admiral in time of war. As with a bishopric, a knighthood was not hereditary, and a gentleman could only properly call himself a gentleman when the College of Heralds saw fit to award him with a coat of arms. And that, essentially, was the limit of Smythe's knowledge.

Sir William was not sure exactly how many nobles there were in England at the present time. There were a dozen earls or so, he thought, a few viscounts, and probably more barons than any other degree of nobility, perhaps thirty or more. There were people at court, he said, who paid far more attention to that sort of thing than he did. Her Majesty, for one, would have more knowledge at her fingertips, as would her ministers and any of the heralds, for among their varied functions was the granting of coats of arms to gentlemen and the preservation of all records of England's noble families.

The heralds took their duties very seriously, Sir William had explained. Organized into a college, they were under the authority of the Earl Marshal, who was a court official. The three senior heralds held the titles of Garter King at Arms, Clarenceaux King at Arms, and Norry King at Arms. Below them were the heralds of York, Somerset, Lancaster, Richmond, Chester, and Windsor, with four pursuivants below them bearing the colorful titles of Rouge Dragon, Blue Mantle, Portcullis, and Rouge Croix. And while Her Majesty might conceivably lose track of a noble or two, Sir William said, especially if he were not in regular attendance at her court, it was unthinkable that a herald should do so, for one of their most important duties was to examine the claims of anyone, including foreign visitors, who claimed to be of noble or gentle birth. Regretably, there were no heralds handy, and with the royal court away from London, a bold imposter might easily believe that he could pass himself off as a nobleman and get away with it, at least for a while.

Young Braithwaite seemed modest to a fault, a quality which had initially impressed Middleton quite favorably, but that now made him suspicious. Braithwaite's apparent reticence in discussing his family had at first seemed like modest self-effacement, but now, given what Smythe had overheard from the two mysterious plotters, it could readily be perceived as guile. Moreover, there was something rather rakish about young Andrew Braithwaite, despite his outward display of manners. He was approximately the same age as Smythe, chestnut-haired, blue-eyed, clean-shaven and handsome in a rugged, provincial sort of way, but there was something in his manner that Smythe did not quite care for. He had a way of strutting when he walked, a sort of loose-hipped, rolling swagger that did not quite seem to match his seeming outward modesty. It was a small thing, perhaps, but it rubbed Smythe the wrong way.

The elder Braithwaite was not in attendance, which might have cast some doubt on the younger Braithwaite as a suspect, for the plan that Smythe had overheard involved one of the two men posing as the father. However, as Worley had pointed out, knowing that someone had overheard them, even if they did not know precisely who it was, could easily have brought about a change in the two scoundrels' plans. If they knew that someone might expect a nobleman and his son to be imposters, then it was possible that they might have decided to withhold the father, so to speak, and just advance the son, thus hoping to confuse anyone looking for a father *and* a son, while keeping the other man in reserve, standing by to perform whatever unsavory task might be required of him. That made sense to Smythe, therefore he did not dismiss the strutting Andrew Braithwaite out of hand. Nor did he miss the fact that Blanche very much seemed to enjoy the attention he was paying to her. But then, at the same time, she seemed more than willing to encourage the attentions of the chevalier Phillipe Dubois, as well.

Here, thought Smythe, was a different kettle of fish entirely, and he did not much care for how it smelled. One of the things he had discovered about the upper classes since coming to the city was that artifice was something that they often elevated to an art. They went to extraordinary lengths and expense to out-peacock one another, and an exaggerated sense of flamboyance — or at least so it seemed to Smythe, with his plain, country sensibilities — was usually the order of the day not only in fashion, but also in behavior. In this respect, Dubois excelled even in this company. True, the young Frenchman was not required, on this occasion, to compete with the more socially prominent and consequently more fashionably adept courtiers who were away from London with Her Majesty, but Worley had observed in passing, after only a brief glimpse of him, that Phillipe Dubois would have doubtless held his own with them, as well.

If Andrew Braithwaite could be considered handsome, Smythe thought, then Phillipe Dubois was very nearly beautiful to the point of femininity. Smythe had never before seen anyone quite like him. He could not have been very much older than twenty or so, but it was somewhat difficult to tell, for Dubois painted his face and wore a beauty mark, and his curled hair was so long that it hung almost to his waist. He clearly lavished a great deal of attention upon it and Smythe noticed not a few women gazing at his dark tresses with undisguised envy. Nor was envy the only emotion that Dubois seemed to engender in many of the ladies present.

He was tall, well-formed, and graceful to the point of being langorous. His slightest gesture seemed elegant, studied and deliberate, and his demeanor was the very epitome of cultured charm, which this French Huguenot supporter of Henry of Navarre wielded most adroitly and disarmingly.

Smythe had detested him on sight, in no small part because earlier he had observed Dubois walking with Elizabeth upon his arm, and Elizabeth seemed rather taken with him. It seemed unlikely, however, that this effete fop could be one of the plotters whom he had overheard, for those men both had English accents, and while Dubois spoke excellent English, his accent was unquestionably French. Nevertheless, Dubois had arrived together with his father, a French aristocrat who smiled at everyone, yet spoke to no one because, according to his son, he had gone completely deaf from some injury sustained upon the battlefield.

Then there was Hughe Camden of Pendennis, who had arrived at the estate with his father, Sir Richard. Smythe was not quite sure what to think of Sir Richard and his son. He supposed they could have been the men that he had overheard, although he could not say for certain. The white-bearded Sir Richard seemed rather aloof and close-mouthed, and acted as if he disdained the company that he was keeping. His short, curtly polite, yet somewhat irritable replies to any comments or questions that were addressed to him discouraged conversation. The general impression was that Sir Richard

Camden was a solitary gentleman of leisure, and no one was quite certain what he had done to merit a knighthood. Knights, said Worley, who spoke as one, were even harder to keep track of than barons, earls and viscounts. Indeed, there was concern among some of the nobility that the rank of knight was being diminished by the recent increase in the ranks of knighthood.

"In the old days," Sir William had said, "a mere merchant shipbuilder such as I would never have been knighted. But as I have done much to increase the royal coffers, so hath Her Majesty seen fit to increase my honor through my rank. 'Twas a generous offer, and one that I could scarcely refuse, you understand. But at the same time, neither did I campaign for it, as so many others have, and continue to do, often successfully. Why, if one were to throw a stone at some annoying dog in London these days, one would be just as liable to miss and strike a knight. So then, Sir Richard Camden may indeed be entitled to wear spurs, for all I know. And then again, he just as well may not be. For my part, I do not know him from Adam. He and his son, therefore, must remain suspect, at least until I can find out more about them."

For the present, it seemed somewhat easier to learn something of the younger Camden. Hughe was a slightly built, studious-looking young man in his mid-twenties, with a neatly-trimmed beard and moustache, and a thick shock of dark and curly hair that came just to his shoulders. He seemed as self-effacing in his dress as did Andrew Braithwaite in his manner, affecting somber hues of black and brown in his simple, unadorned doublet, breeches and hose with a plain, though well-made shoulder cloak. He was a student of the law, an inner barrister at the Inns of Court, and had a great fondness for poetry, which he had been observed to write in a fine Chancery hand well worthy of a scrivener. He seemed an amiable and pleasant enough fellow, and Middleton said he had applied for and been given a small stipend as Blanche's tutor in poetry and literature while they were at their home in London. He seemed clearly smitten with her and she, in turn, seemed not averse to his company, but at the same time, Smythe had the distinct impression that there were few males between the ages of eighteen and eighty to whose company Blanche Middleton might actually be averse.

Finally, that left Sir Roger Holland and his son, Daniel. Sir Roger had, apparently, won his knighthood on the field of battle in his younger days, had married well, sired a brood of children, and was now primarily devoted to managing his wife's fortune and her property in Lincolnshire. Beyond that, Middleton had said, he had not revealed very much of substance. He dressed reasonably well, if somewhat unfashionably, and had, in fairly short order, established himself as a crashing bore. He spoke of little else save hunting and his "sports"—the dogs he raised for fighting—and of those two subjects, he spoke almost incessantly. Middleton had said that regardless of what anyone tried to speak with him about, within moments Sir Roger would turn the conversation back to dog fighting or hunting and drone on with so much throat-clearing and hemming and hawing and harrumphing that one would be reminded of the sounds made by a pair of rutting hogs. Apparently, he did not seem to notice that anyone he struck up a conversation with thereafter tended to avoid him as if he had the pox. Or, perhaps that was his intent.

Daniel Holland seemed much more amiable than his father, and looked a few years older than both Braithwaite and Camden, and possibly Dubois, for the latter's age was not easy to determine and he had not volunteered it. However, what Daniel Holland may have lacked in youth, he made up for with a confident maturity that made him appear very self-possessed. Without saying so in so many words, he managed to give off the impression that he felt himself unquestionably superior to his rivals, and he positively smirked whenever his gaze fell upon the elegant Dubois. Blonde, bearded, green-eyed and good looking without quite being handsome, young Holland was of average height and stocky build. Being a gentleman of means, he had no need of a trade, although he claimed to know something of horses and their breeding. He stood to inherit a considerable amount of land and also spoke vaguely of some investments that he made in the New World.

Any of them, Smythe thought, could be the plotters he had overheard in the maze, though some seemed more likely candidates than others. There seemed to be no way, at least for the present, to verify their true status or their claims, and Smythe was certainly in no position to question their veracity. To his immense frustration, he was not able to recognize any of their voices. Dubois' voice seemed the most unlike those that he had overheard, as did his accent, but then again, the accent could be something he was faking, although if he was, he was certainly convincing, and his father spoke not at all, which Smythe found a bit suspicious. Of the remaining three, Daniel Holland seemed, perhaps, the least likely to be one of the plotters, as both Worley and Middleton had thought, as well. He neither looked nor acted like a rogue, and if Smythe were casting for the part, Daniel Holland would probably have been the last one that he would pick. He *looked* like a student at the Inns of Court, and he seemed very well educated. He quoted poetry and wrote it. Yet since Sir William had departed, Smythe had noticed something else about young Holland that had given him some pause.

Most well-dressed gentlemen went armed, and the guests at Middleton Manor were no exception, especially the young, fashionable men who vied for Blanche Middleton's attention. Dubois, as might be expected of a French chevalier, had a very showy blade, a rapier with a curvaceous basket hilt and jewelled crossguards. It seemed quite well made, though Smythe was unable to make a close inspection. However, it made sense that a man who could afford the sort of elegant clothing Dubois wore would also be able to afford a first-class blade. Whether or not he knew how to use it was another matter entirely. He wore it in a rakish hanger, but beyond that, Smythe had his doubts that the blade had ever been drawn in practice, much less combat. Likewise, Braithwaite and Camden both wore blades, and if they were not as showy and expensive looking as the Frenchman's, they were nevertheless quite handsome. Daniel Holland, on the other hand, who looked as if wearing a blade would suit him about as well as a silk dressing gown would suit a horse, wore a rather plain-looking rapier with a cup hilt and hooked cross-guards. It was of Spanish design, and it was most certainly not the blade of a courtier or fop or roaring boy. It was the purposeful blade of a duelist. It was, of course, quite possible that Holland had purchased it cheaply in the city from some down-on-his-luck soldier and had no more idea how to use it than Smythe had of writing poetry. But Smythe found it interesting, just the same.

Until he knew more, Smythe could not eliminate any of them from consideration. Sir William had the best chance of uncovering any possible deception with a few inquiries at court, but until he could return, Smythe was on his own. The trouble was he did not know what, if anything, he could accomplish. He wished that Shakespeare would return from London soon, for the poet had a clever way of thinking through things and looking at situations from all sides that doubtless came from plotting out his plays. His mind was quite adept at doing that. However, as the day wore on towards evening and Shakespeare still did not return, Smythe could but observe the suspects from a distance and attempt to guess which, if any of them, had tried to kill him in the maze.

At the same time, he could not help but notice that Elizabeth kept right on avoiding him. At the funeral, she had wept openly and unashamedly, and was more demonstrative in her grief than anyone, even Blanche, who dabbed daintily at her eyes with a handkerchief and kept her gaze downcast. Elizabeth had been escorted by her father, who had left for London shortly thereafter, promising to send a carriage for her on the following day, for she had seemed much too distraught to travel. Since then, Smythe had not even seen her. He told himself that she had every reason to feel upset and had probably retired to one of the upstairs rooms. But something told him there was more to it than that.

Elizabeth simply did not seem herself, and some instinct told him there was more to it than grief over a murdered friend, however unlikely that may have seemed. He simply could not shake the feeling. He had learned to trust his instincts. Therefore, when he saw Elizabeth come furtively down the stairs that evening as the sun was going down and head outside, he followed her once more.

8

HE WAS COLD AND WET and there was mud all over his clothing from helping the coachman wrestle with the wheel of the carriage in the pouring rain. The fool had been as reckless with his breakneck speed on the return trip as he had been going out to London, but this time, instead of worrying about a wreck, Shakespeare had urged him to go even faster.

Shortly after they set out, it began to rain and he had held on for dear life, gritting his teeth and trying to ignore the way the light carriage careened and bounced along the rutted road. He could think of nothing else but what Granny Meg had told him and he knew he had to get back to Middleton Manor as soon as humanly possible. And so, of course, they had a wreck.

The wheel had come off after the carriage had bounced up and come down particularly hard, and Shakespeare was very nearly thrown from the seat. He and the driver had both somehow managed to hang on as the carriage slewed to a stop, further damage prevented only by the fact that the road had completely turned to mud where a creek had overflowed its banks and washed across their way, thereby softening the surface. Fortunately, the wheel had not been damaged and together they were able to replace it, effecting a barely workable repair. However, that was not until they had sworn and shouted at each other and pretty much exhausted their entire repertoire of epithets, at which point the driver, exasperated to the point of sheer blind fury, had launched himself at Shakespeare and together they tumbled down into the mud, where they grappled and pummelled one another until the utter absurdity of their situation struck them and they had started laughing, which ended the fight and induced a spirit of mutual cooperation in the face of adversity.

"Come on, now, Ian, God blind you," Shakespeare urged the coachman, from his seat beside him, "can you not go any faster?"

"Not unless you want that poxed wheel to come off again," Ian replied. "Now sit still, damn you, and stop pestering me!"

" 'Tis growing dark," said Shakespeare, with concern. "How much farther?"

"*God!*" Ian rolled his eyes. "Not far. Only a few miles. Have patience!"

"We wasted too much time back there."

"Well now, whose fault was that, eh?"

"You dissentious scoundrel! You dare suggest 'twas mine? The reins were in *your* hands!"

"Aye, but you distracted me!"

"Odd's blood, you were *born* distracted, you simpleton!"

"Sod off!"

"You bloody well sod off!"

"One more word and God be my judge, 'tis walking back ye'll be!"

The carriage lurched suddenly and skewed sharply to the left, coming down with a jarring impact and skidding to a halt as the hoses neighed and reared in protest.

"Oh, Hell's spite! The poxed wheel's come off again!" said Ian, throwing down the reins in disgust. "Now it looks like we shall both be walking."

"The devil you say!" Shakespeare replied. "Unhitch the horses."

"What? And leave the carriage? Master Middleton would strip the hide straight off me if I was to abandon it."

"I promise you, he will do much more than that if we are de-

layed much longer," Shakespeare said. "Now unhitch them, damn
you! We must reach Middleton Manor before nightfall!"

It had begun to rain and Smythe cursed himself for not having the
foresight to bring along a cloak, as Elizabeth had. Unlike most of
the guests at the estate, whose sense of fashion had demanded that
they bring enough suits of clothing with them to change at least
several times a day, he owned but one cloak, two doublets, two pair
of breeches, two shirts, two pair of hose—both threadbare—and but
one pair of shoes, which were well worn. On one hand, it made
packing fairly simple. On the other, it meant that ruining one suit
of clothes left him with only one to wear. There would have been
no time to run and get his cloak, for he would have lost track of
Elizabeth. Therefore, he was forced to go dressed as he was, which
meant getting cold and wet as he pursued Elizabeth outside. However, mindful of what had happened the last time he had followed
her, he hesitated only long enough to grab a rapier off the wall in
the great hall, where it had been displayed along with its companion
and a buckler. He was pleased to note that it was a good Sheffield
blade, not ostentatious, but quite servicable.

He gave Elizabeth some leadway, so that she would not suspect
that she was being followed. She had been furtive in her movements
as she went outside, glancing around several times, as if to make
certain no one saw her. Several times Smythe had to duck back out
of sight in order to prevent her spotting him, but now she seemed
far more intent upon her destination than upon making sure she was
not followed. Once more, Smythe thought, she was going out alone
at night, in a manner that was most suspicious. If she were not going
to meet a man, then what else could she possibly be doing?

He had expected her to circle back around the house and head
out towards the maze again, on the other side. Instead, she kept on
going straight, away from the house and the fairgrounds, down a
path leading towards the river. It struck him that she was taking the

same path that the funeral procession had followed to the Middleton family vault.

It started raining harder as Elizabeth disappeared from sight, heading down the slope and towards the woods. Smythe gave her a moment's lead, then ran across the open courtyard on the river side of the house, towards the path leading down into the trees. He could not see Elizabeth as he came running down the slope, following the pathway, but as he reached the trees, he caught a glimpse of her dark cloak, disappearing round a bend, into the woods. He paused to let her get a little more ahead of him, lest the sounds of his running footsteps give him away. He waited for a moment, catching his breath as he leaned back against a tree.

It sounded quiet and peaceful, just the steady, trickling sounds of raindrops pattering down and dripping from the leaves and the calls of a few birds. Then there was a sudden, sharp, whistling sound followed by a soft *thunk* as a crossbow bolt embedded itself deeply in the tree trunk merely an inch away from Smythe's right ear.

It was a sound that he was all too familiar with from the time a hidden archer had attacked him on the road while he had been on his way to London. Smythe knew what it was at once, even before he saw the bolt sticking in the tree, and he ducked down and scuttled back into the brush alongside the path, the rapier held ready in his hand. He knew that a good archer with a longbow could loose several shafts in just the space of a breath, but a crossbow could not be shot as quickly. It would take more time to wind back the powerful steel spring with the handle and then insert another bolt and aim. He peered out through the brush, but could not see very far in such conditions, what with the rain and the failing light. There was no following shot, nor was there any sign of the archer. However, he heard running footsteps in the distance, spashing in the puddles on the pathway. It sounded as if whoever it was had run back towards the house.

There were two possiblities that immediately occurred to him. The first and most obvious explanation was that the archer had been one of the two plotters he had overheard, which would mean, of course, that they knew who he was. He had never seen them leave the maze, which must have meant that they had gotten out before him and had seen him when he came out, then later recognized him at the house. And the second possibility was that whoever Elizabeth was on her way to meet had noticed that she was being followed and had followed him in turn, either to make an attempt upon his life or else to scare him off. In either case, it had been only the narrowest of escapes, and Smythe felt his anger boiling up within him. The time was past for niceties. Whether she liked it or not, he was going to confront Elizabeth right now and find out what she was up to. One mystery on his hands was quite enough. He had no time for two.

Cautiously, he stepped back out onto the path and resumed following Elizabeth, keeping a close watch out for anyone who might come up behind him. He made certain to avoid the open and keep as close to the trees as possible, moving in a weaving sort of pattern so that if the archer happened to return, he could not "lead" him with the bow. He moved quickly, anxious to catch up with Elizabeth. Before long, he reached the clearing where the vault stood.

The iron gate was open. He quickly glanced around, then crossed the clearing at a run and came up to the gate. He saw Elizabeth standing by the door to the crypt . . . and beside her stood a young man in a dark cloak.

The first thing he did was check to see if the young man was carrying a crossbow, though logic told him there was no way he could have shot that bolt and then run back to circle through the woods and reach the vault ahead of him. There would never have been enough time. Still, he thought, there had been *two* of them. . . . He shook his head. No, it could not be possible. He could not imagine Elizabeth involved with anything like that. Catherine was her friend. And yet, incredibly, Elizabeth was apparently going to have an assignation with a lover in the very crypt where her close friend had only just been laid to rest! The very idea horrified him. He stepped through the gate and confronted them.

"*Elizabeth!* What the devil are you doing?"

She turned towards him and gasped with surprise. At the same time, the young man she was with saw the rapier Smythe was holding and at once threw back his cloak and drew his own.

"John, *no!*" Elizabeth cried out, but the young man was already rushing forward with his blade raised.

Smythe met his rush and parried his stroke, then quickly riposted. The young man was surprised by his speed and barely managed a parry of his own, then quickly backed away to get some room. Smythe would not allow it. He kept after him, sensing that this was no experienced swordsman. His attack had been clumsy and his defensive parry had been more luck than skill. Their blades clashed against each other as the young man fought off Smythe's furious attack.

"*Stop it, Tuck! Stop it!*" Elizabeth cried out. "For God's sake, *stop!* I beg you!"

Smythe hesitated, allowing the young man some room, but he held his rapier at the ready. "Tell him to throw down his blade!"

"And be run through for my trouble? I think not!" the young man replied. He was trying to sound confident, but his hard swallow and his rapid, shallow breathing betrayed his alarm.

"Stop it, both of you!" Elizabeth said. "Tuck, what in God's name are you doing here?"

"I might well ask you the same thing!" said Smythe. He gestured with his rapier towards the door to the crypt. "In the name of Heaven, is *this* how you show respect to your dear, departed friend? By meeting with your lover *here,* within mere hours of her funeral?"

Elizabeth's eyes grew wide. "My *lover?* Are you mad?"

"Oh, Lord!" the young man said. "I see now what he thinks!"

"Tuck, I *swear* to you that John is *not* my lover." said Elizabeth.

"Well, who in blazes *is* he, then?"

"He is Catherine's lover."

Smythe blinked. "What?"

"John is *Catherine's* lover!" Elizabeth repeated.

The young man shook his head. His shoulders slumped and he sighed. " 'Tis all over," he said, with resignation. "We are undone."

Smythe simply stood there, bewildered, the rain dripping off him, his hair matted to his forehead, his rapier lowered til the point nearly touched the ground. He stared at them both with complete incomprehension.

"Did you say *Catherine's* lover?" he said, not certain that he had heard correctly.

"You misjudge the lady, sir," the young man said. "I assure you, 'twas not Elizabeth I came to meet, but Catherine."

"Have you both lost your senses? Or do you take me for an utter fool?" Smythe said. "Catherine Middleton is dead, for God's sake!" He gestured toward the vault with his rapier. "We have just been to her funeral! That is her corpse that rests within!"

"No," Elizabeth said. "She is *not* dead. She merely sleeps."

"What addle-pated prattle is this? Elizabeth, 'twas *I* who lifted her up and carried her from the barge up to the house and then laid her down upon her bed before her grieving father. And I tell you that her sleep is eternal, one from which she shall nevermore awake. Catherine Middleton is *dead*."

"No, Tuck," Elizabeth insisted. " 'Tis but the clever counterfeit of death, brought on by a potion she had taken in her wine."

"A potion? 'Twas poison in the flask we found," said Smythe. "Will has taken it to London, to Granny Meg, in the hope that she may tell us what sort of vile concoction it may be."

"Then he shall bear out my tale when he returns," Elizabeth replied, "for 'twas Granny Meg herself who had prepared it."

Smythe stared at her with astonishment. "What? *Granny Meg* prepared the poison?"

"The *potion*, not the poison, you fool!"

"Tell him all of it," the young man said. "It makes no difference now. The game is up. We are undone. 'Twas all for nothing."

"No, John," Elizabeth said, " 'twas not for nothing. Tuck is my friend. My very dear friend. He shall not betray us."

Smythe felt hopelessly confused. He glanced from one to the other, staring at them as if they were speaking in tongues. "What are you saying? What is there to betray? I understand none of this! 'Tis madness!"

"Then 'tis a madness that you, Tuck, of all men, should comprehend," Elizabeth told him. "By arrangement, Catherine was to wed Sir Percival, as you know. But Catherine did not *want* the marriage. She did not love him. Nor could she ever come to love him. How could she? You saw him; he is an imbecile, a foolish, prattling old man whose only care in life is for the cut of his silk doublets. But when Catherine protested that she did not wish to marry, her father would not hear it. The match was made, and Catherine was to do as she was told. She was to do her duty, as a daughter should. Does that sound familiar to you?"

Smythe nodded. It had been exactly so with Elizabeth, when her father had tried to force her to marry against her will. It was not uncommon for parents to arrange their children's marriages for mutual advantage, unless they were poor, of course, in which case their children had the luxury of being free to marry for love. It was, perhaps, one of the very few advantages of being poor. He could see why Elizabeth had felt so sympathetic to Catherine's situation.

"Well, Catherine has always been a strong-willed and clever girl," Elizabeth continued, "and she had absolutely no intention of marrying Sir Percy, since she was already in love . . . with John Mason, here. Only there was no chance of her father's approving of anyone like John, for John is not a gentleman, you see. In truth, John's station in life is very much like yours, Tuck. He is a groom at Green Oaks."

"Do you mean *Sir William's* estate?" said Smythe.

John Mason nodded. "I have served Sir William since I was a mere boy," he said. "My father serves him, too, as groundskeeper." He grimaced and shook his head. "There was no question of my ever asking for Catherine's hand in marriage. 'Twould have been outrageous, presumptuous, and ridiculous. And yet, we were in love. We had met while out riding in the countryside. Catherine loves to ride, and 'tis among my regular duties to exercise Sir William's horses. Thus we encountered one another, and from the very first, we fell in love. We both knew it was hopeless, but there was no helping it, you see. Neither of us could conceive of life without the other. And so, we planned to run away."

"Only Catherine knew that her father would spare no expense to track them down and bring her back," Elizabeth said. "She was afraid for John, as well, of what would happen to him if they ran away together and were caught. On the other hand, if she were *dead* . . ."

"The plan was insane," said Mason. "I should never have consented to it."

"You had no choice," Elizabeth replied. "Catherine was going through with it with or without your consent, because she realized that there was no other way."

"So she came to you with this preposterous idea and you took her to see Granny Meg," said Smythe.

"I knew that if anyone could help us, then she would be the one," Elizabeth replied. "We told her what was needed—a potion that would produce the semblance of death, yet without bringing it about. Something that would cause Catherine to fall into a deathlike sleep, and yet awaken without harm after a day or two."

"And Granny Meg actually *agreed* to this mad idea?" said Smythe.

"Not at first. She did not wish to do it. She said it would be very dangerous. There would be risks involved of the sort that no apothecary nor even a skilled cunning woman could predict. But we both pleaded with her. And we also paid her very well."

"I see," said Smythe. "Well, this truly passes all understanding and strains credulity to the very limit. So what you mean to tell me, if I have heard aright, is that Catherine is not really dead, but merely in some sort of deep, enchanted sleep that mimics death, and that when the effects of this potion wear off, she will simply awake as if nothing had happened?"

"That was the plan, in its entirety," Elizabeth said. "And then she and John can have a chance for happiness at last. They can go away together, and with her father believing her dead, no one shall go looking for them. I was to be their go-between, who would help them in the final stages of the plan. Once Catherine had gone to London, I was to carry messages to John."

"Then that was why you had gone out to the maze the other night?"

"So that *was* you shouting! I *thought* the voice sounded familiar! You followed me!"

"Aye, because I thought that you were going to meet another man. When I lost you in the maze, I shouted out to warn you that there were others present who might—"

"*You were jealous!*"

"Never mind that. 'Tis of no consequence now. What matters most is that there are things that you and Catherine have overlooked, things that have cast this entire, unfortunate situation in a most disastrous light."

"True," she admitted, "it did not all turn out quite as we had intended. We had planned for it to look as if Catherine had simply died. We did not count upon Will finding the flask nor anyone thinking it was poisoned. She was supposed to toss it overboard. I can only guess that the potion must have taken effect far more quickly than she had anticipated."

"And what of the carpenter whose instructions are to make the casket? What do you suppose shall happen when he comes to place Catherine's shrouded corpse within it, only to find her gone?"

"He has been richly bribed," Elizabeth said. "He shall place stones within the coffin and then seal it up, and none shall be the wiser. Then not long thereafter, he shall depart the estate and with what he has earned for aiding us in this deception, he shall be able to set himself up in trade somewhere. Thus, his future depends upon his silence. No one else shall ever know that Catherine is not dead. And all you need do to ensure that, Tuck, is keep silent and tell no one what you have learned tonight. If not for Catherine's sake, then at least for mine. Surely, 'tis not asking for so very much, is it?"

She gazed at him with intense entreaty in her eyes and Smythe was not unsympathetic. He also realized that what Elizabeth had come very close to admitting, without actually saying it in so many words, was that John and Catherine's situation was very much like theirs. They were two people from different social classes, different worlds, who had been drawn together by their love for one another, in spite of all the obstacles that stood between them. It was as close as Elizabeth had ever come to openly acknowledging that there was something more than friendship between them. He felt ashamed for having suspected her of infidelity . . . as if fidelity were anything she even owed him. Yet, though he felt moved by her plea, he still felt torn.

"Elizabeth . . . I do not know what to tell you," he said. " 'Tis not all as simple as you think. For one thing, you have entirely forgotten about Will. He has gone to London on the instructions of Sir William, and he should have returned by now. And unless Granny Meg has chosen to deceive him, which I think most unlikely considering the circumstances, then even as we speak, he may already be at the house, giving out what he has learned. If not, then he shall reveal the truth as soon as he returns."

"Then you must stop him!" said Elizabeth.

"It may already be too late. And if not, then there is still Sir William to consider. He has taken a personal interest in this and there are few men in England with more influence or power. Aside from that, I owe him a great deal, as, indeed, do you. The problem is that everyone believes that Catherine has been murdered. The hunt for her killer shall not cease if Will and I choose to keep silent. What if it befalls that someone innocent is blamed? Should Will and I and Granny Meg and the carpenter and even you and John and

Catherine keep silent while someone innocent of guilt is hanged for a crime that never was committed?"

"But that is all mere supposition!" cried Elizabeth. "No one has been blamed for Catherine's death because no one has killed her! So what if they shall seek a murderer? They shall never find him, because he does not exist! How can someone who has done no wrong be found guilty of a crime that has never been committed?"

Smythe sighed. "Oh, Elizabeth, how little you know of the inequities of life! There are men who are thrown into prison every day for offenses no greater than stealing a mere loaf of bread. When the daughter of a rich man with powerful friends is killed—or falsely believed to have been killed—then they shall never stop looking for a killer til they find one."

"He is right, Elizabeth," said Mason, who had listened to their conversation with a look of utter helplessness. "When no murderer is found, then they will find instead some hapless wretch and beat a confession out of him rather than admit that they have failed. 'Twould not be the first time a man was hanged for a crime that he did not commit. The plan had risks enough when it entailed merely the pretense that Catherine had died. Now that they believe it to be murder, how could we ever live in peace, knowing that our happiness may have been bought at the price of an innocent man's life?" He shook his head emphatically. "Even the possibility of that would be enough to ruin any chance of happiness that we could ever have. 'Twould destroy us in the end."

Elizabeth looked desperate. "So what would you have us do instead, John? Confess the fraud and have all the pains that we have gone to be for naught? And do you suppose that there would be no consequences for what we have done?"

"Your part in it need never be revealed," John replied. "No purpose would be served in that. I cannot believe that Catherine's father would be too severe with her. After all, a daughter he thought dead would be suddenly restored. Surely, 'twould be welcome news that would mitigate his anger. For my own part, I would endeavor to bear whatever consequences should be meted out with manly fortitude."

"A brave speech and well spoken," Smythe said. "And I can find no flaw in your character for it save a slight lack of practical consideration. For a certainty, you shall be made the scapegoat for this entire melancholy situation, and to use your own words, no purpose would be served in that, either."

"What would you have me do, run off like some craven coward?"

"You have already proven that you are no coward," Smythe said. "You know that, and now I know it, Elizabeth knows it, and I am certain Catherine knew it from the start. Others may not, but does their opinion truly matter?"

"And what of my family?" Mason asked. "Would you have me run away and leave them in disgrace?"

Smythe sighed. "I see your point, and have no counter to it. But there must be some other solution to this unfortunate dilemma. Perhaps if I spoke with Sir William—"

"Wait," Elizabeth said, suddenly. "What if it turned out that Catherine had killed herself?"

"*What?*" said Mason.

"Hear me out," Elizabeth said, intently. "I have just had an idea that could provide us with the solution that we seek! What if Catherine had obtained the so-called poison knowingly, and drank it so that she might end her life rather than condemn herself to living with a man she did not love?"

"Oh, for God's sake, Elizabeth!" said Mason. "Why would anyone believe that?"

"Why would they *not* believe it, if a note were found, written in Catherine's own hand, explaining all? She could write it herself, as soon as she awoke!"

"Again, you have forgotten about Will," said Smythe. "He shall return from London with a very different tale."

"But if you were to intercept him afore he spoke to anyone,"

Elizabeth persisted, "and told him to say it *had* been poison, then could it not still work?"

Smythe frowned. "What of the flask?"

"What of it? He could say that the contents had to be poured out and subjected to some sort of arcane, alchemical procedure to determine the ingredients. We could make something up. Or else we could simply say that no exact determination could be made, though it was proven to be deadly. . . ."

"And what of Granny Meg?" asked Smythe.

"What reason would anyone have to question her about the matter?" said Elizabeth. "Will would already have brought back her report!"

"Another mad notion born of desperation!" Mason said.

"Perhaps," said Smythe, frowning as he looked for flaws in the idea. "But on the face of it, at least, it does sound plausible."

"It *could* work, could it not?" Elizabeth asked, hopefully.

They all stood there in the rain, which was thankfully starting to let up, but they were still dripping wet. Smythe could feel the cold chilling him through as he considered Elizabeth's idea. They looked more like three drowned cats than desperate plotters, but the situation seemed to call for desperate measures. Smythe wondered how he had become caught up in it. It was Elizabeth, of course. Once more, Elizabeth had found herself squarely in the midst of an intrigue, and she had been drawn into it because she cared about her friend. Now he had become involved because he cared about Elizabeth and it seemed that Will would be pulled into it as well . . . assuming he agreed to do it out of friendship for him.

However, he could scarcely blame Will if he were to refuse. From any reasonable standpoint, refusing to go along with such a byzantine deception seemed the only rational thing to do. Shakespeare had nothing at all to gain by going along with it and everything to lose. His career in the theatre was only just beginning and he had already made a very promising start. He also had a family back in Stratford to consider. He did not seem to care much for his wife, but he took his obligations seriously.

"I do not know," Smythe said. "It all seems to depend on Will. 'Tis getting late, and if he has not returned by now, then doubtless he has chosen to remain in the city rather than risk the road at night, which means that he shall surely start out first thing in the morning. If I can get to him and convince him to go along with this before he speaks to anyone, then 'tis possible it just might work."

"Why should your friend wish to help us?" Mason asked.

"I do not know that he shall," replied Smythe. " 'Tis asking a great deal. But if he does, then he shall do it for friendship's sake."

"As you do it for Elizabeth's sake," said Mason, as if echoing Smythe's earlier thoughts. "Already, too many people are involved in this. Too many share the risk. It has gone beyond the pale."

"Yet now there is no stopping it," Elizabeth said. "Win or lose, we must be strong and see it through, John. We must do it for Catherine."

"Aye," said Mason, "I have had no peace these past two nights, thinking of her in London with that witch's potion, mustering up the courage to drink it down and dance with death. I have been at my wit's end with worry. God, Elizabeth, what if she does not awake? I could not live with that!"

"She *shall* awake," Elizabeth insisted. "I have complete faith in Granny Meg."

"Would that I shared your confidence," said Mason. The strain was obviously telling on him. His last reserves of energy seemed to be draining out of him even as he spoke. "I must know how she fares. You promised that she was to awake tonight."

"Granny Meg said that there was no way of determining the time for certain. She had measured everything with great exactitude, but she warned us there were risks."

"We must get inside," said Mason, moving towards the door. "I *must* see her! I cannot bear the uncertainty. I shall not stray from her side til she awakes!"

"Wait," said Smythe.

"*Wait?* I am done with waiting! 'Tis a simple thing for you to say—"

"Be still!" Smythe said, turning around. "*Someone is coming!*"

Elizabeth stiffened, turned, and froze, like a startled deer, eyes wide and peering into the night. Over the faint pattering of raindrops, they heard the unmistakable sounds of voices in the distance. And a moment later, they could see the bobbing light of torches coming towards them.

"God's body! Death and damnation to them all!" cried John, and he threw his shoulder against the door with all his might.

9

$\mathcal{S}$HAKESPEARE HAD GROWN UP IN the country and knew how to ride bareback, but then he had not done so since he was a boy. Nor, he quickly realized, was he even remotely nostalgic for the experience. He had always liked horses and counted himself a decent rider, but he had been spoiled by saddles. Riding bareback at the gallop, which he had done so often in his childhood, was now a punishing experience.

The coachman had not wanted to abandon the expensive carriage and had argued that they should try to get the wheel back on once more. Shakespeare had insisted that they had no time to lose and the horses had to be unhitched and ridden bareback. They had argued and Shakespeare said that he would take one of the horses and ride back no matter what, come Hell or high water. They had nearly come to blows over it, and the argument was settled finally when they noticed that the wheel had cracked and the axle had been damaged. There was nothing for it but to abandon the carriage in the road and ride the horses home.

They had quickly modified the harnesses, shortened the reins and gotten on their way, by which time their already muddy clothes were reduced to little more than torn and sodden rags, but nightfall had caught up to them and they lacked a clear sky and a full moon by which to see. The rain had let up somewhat, but the roads were still puddled and quite soft in places. With Shakespeare insisting on riding at the gallop, the going was treacherous, to say the least.

By the time they reached Middleton Manor, Shakespeare was roundly cursing every mare that ever foaled. They came splashing up the road leading to the house, skidded on the wet cobblestones of the courtyard and nearly went down in a tangle, but somehow, miraculously, their mounts managed to retain their footing and they reined in without further incident. Their noisy arrival, however, had alerted some within the house, for many of the guests had not retired early and were still participating in the wake. A few of them might even have remembered whom the wake was for.

Humphrey, the ever-efficient steward, was one of the first upon the scene as they came staggering up to the front door, looking for all the world like two weary and embattled soldiers freshly returned from the wars.

"Good God!" he said, when he beheld their grim and grimey appearance. "What happened, for mercy's sake? Have the two of you been set upon by brigands?"

"The carriage broke down on the road from London, but never mind that now," Shakespeare said, trying to catch his breath. "Damn me, but I need a drink! Is Sir William here?"

"Sir William had departed hours ago," said Humphrey, as the hall behind him began to fill up with curious onlookers. "You look like Death! What is the matter?"

"Get the master of the house at once!" said Shakespeare. "And get Tuck Smythe. And get me a drink, while you are at it."

"I shall do no such thing!" Humphrey replied, in an affronted tone. "Master Middleton has retired. This day has been a terrible trial for him, as you must surely know. He is grief-stricken and exhausted. His daughter's funeral has been a horrible ordeal for him."

"Well, then wake up the old bugger and we shall crack open the tomb and raise her up again! And God damn it, get me a tupping *drink!*"

The crowd behind Humphrey gasped collectively. But a few

were enough past the point of caring that they chuckled at Shakespeare's irreverent remarks. Humphrey tossed them an acid gaze over his shoulder, then turned the full force of his basilisk glare on Shakespeare and the hapless coachman, who simply stood there helpless, not knowing what to say or do.

"You must be drunk!" said Humphrey, with outrage. "I shall have you thrashed and driven off the property!"

"Then you shall answer to Sir William Worley," Shakespeare replied, shoving past the incredulous steward and making his way toward the tables. "And you shall likewise answer to your master, who shall not take kindly, I assure you, to being deprived of his eldest daughter for yet a second time!" He picked up a goblet and filled it, then quaffed it in one breath.

By now, more people had gathered round and everyone was talking at once. Humphrey was sputtering with outrage and turning purple with apoplexy, but Shakespeare did not care. He refilled the goblet and drank it down again, spilling some of the wine down his already thoroughly drenched and muddy doublet. It was ruined and it had been one of only two he owned, and the second one was threadbare, whereas some of the guests around him thought nothing of wearing at least three different doublets in one afternoon. He was tired; he was sore; he was cold and he was wet. He was a poet, not some post rider, and he felt resentful of the entire company around him. He had come to stage a play, and instead had played a part in one, the part of errand boy. Worse still, the whole situation had been nothing but a sham.

"Now see here—" Humphrey began, but Shakespeare merely shoved him away roughly without even a glance at him or a break in drinking.

"What in Heaven's name is all this row?" Godfrey Middleton's voice cut through the conversation. He stood up in the gallery, wearing a velvet dressing gown and looking down on the assemblage with cold fury. His gaze settled on Shakespeare as the obvious center of it all. "For the love of God, sir, have you no respect? No decency? My eldest daughter has just been laid to rest!"

"Well, mark my word, Master Middleton, she shan't be resting long," Shakespeare replied.

"This is an outrage!" Middleton said.

"I shall have the servants throw the vile villain out at once!" Humphrey said, finding his voice at last. "I shall set the dogs upon the pestilential rascal!"

Middleton suddenly seemed to recognize Shakepeare for the first time. "You are the man Sir William sent to London, are you not?"

"I am that very man," Shakespeare replied. "Or what is left of him after the foul journey I have made. Your carriage, by the way, lies broken on the road some miles hence, I cannot say how far or where, precisely. We had tried to fix it once, but the damned wheel came off again a few miles down the road and cracked, and there was an end to it. By now, 'tis likely kindling for some rufflers. We unhitched the horses and rode back like red Indians in the pouring rain, your coachman and I, and we are tired men and chilled straight through to the bone, but by God, we have brought fascinating tidings! To wit, sir . . ." He took another long drink from the goblet, ". . . your daughter is not dead, because there was no poison in that flask from which she drank. 'Twas instead a potion merely meant to lull her for a time into the arms of Morpheus and only make it seem as if she slept eternally with Hades. So go back to your bed and rest you well, sir, if you wish, but know that when you wake upon the morrow, you shall find that Catherine had awoke afore you and absconded with her lover."

He ignored the stunned reactions of the guests around him, turned his back on Middleton, and reached across the table for a cold and greasy drumstick that looked more appetizing to him now than any dish that he had ever seen. As he bit into it, he turned back and looked up towards the gallery. Middleton was gone. Shakespeare glanced at Ian, the coachman, who was staring at him with absolute astonishment, and shrugged.

"Well, I suppose that woke him up, eh, Ian?" he said. He held out the drumstick. "D'you fancy a bite?"

He did not have very much time to eat. Middleton came down almost at once, having paused only long enough to pull on a pair of boots and throw a cloak over his dressing gown. He barked out sharp orders to Humphrey, calling for torches and men, then put on his hat and turned a baleful eye on Shakespeare.

"Young man, you had best be telling me the truth, for if this is your gruesome idea of a prank, then you shall answer to me! I shall have you whipped until your eyes bleed. Now come with me!"

"I should answer quite well to a whipping," Shakespeare mumbled, taking another quick swallow of wine before following his host.

Phillipe Dubois worked his way through the crowd to Shakespeare's side. "Prithee, *mon ami*, do you mean to tell me that Mademoiselle Catherine is not truly dead?" he asked, as they went back outside, herded along by the press of people behind them.

"No, milord, I had meant to tell Master Middleton that Catherine is not truly dead," Shakespeare replied. 'Strewth, I had not meant to tell you anything."

"You have great cheek for a vagabond," said Dubois, somewhat stiffly.

"And you lisp and wear strange suits."

"I say, small wonder you players have such a scandalous and lowly reputation," Ian said, as they left Dubois gaping with astonishment behind them. "You really are insufferably rude."

"And you really are an amazing prig for a mere coachman, Ian."

"I happen to be a liveried servant to a gentleman!"

"You are a glorified bootblack, Ian, so go stuff your hubris. Or you can actually be useful and go find my friend, Tuck Smythe, and let him know what has transpired, for your master seems intent upon marching us all into the dripping wood when we should all be drinking sensibly inside. I am beginning to envy Catherine. At least she has had an opportunity to lie down for a while."

"A word with you, sir, if I may?" Hughe Camden called as he hurried to catch up with them. Ian the coachman stopped and fell behind as Camden took his place at Shakespeare's side.

"And lo, another suitor. The kites begin to flock," mumbled Shakespeare to himself.

"I beg your pardon?" Camden said.

"And you shall have it, sir. I am feeling positively popish to-night. Tell me your sin and I shall grant you absolution."

"I see you are impertinent."

"Impertinent and insufferable, as well. Add intemperate and you can compass me with alliteration."

"I believe you are drunk, sir."

"Not yet, but on such a night as this, 'tis a course well worth pursuing. How may I serve you, sir? Something to do with the lately lamented Lady Catherine, no doubt?"

"I was listening when you spoke just now," said Camden, as they continued down the path in the wake of Middleton and his torch-bearers. "You said something about Catherine planning this astonishing deception so that she might run off with a lover?"

"Aye, quite so."

"Sir, I must say that I find this tale very hard to credit. 'Tis a harsh thing to defame the dead. I cannot believe that she would have done anything like what you propose. I have heard that Catherine could be somewhat shrewish on occasion, but at heart, she was a good woman."

"Well, we might have a good woman born before every blazing star or at an earthquake," Shakespeare said, "but I would not look for such a singular event with any greater frequency."

"You have, it seems, a rather bilious and spiteful view of women, sir."

"I am a married man, sir. My view is unobstructed."

"Who is this lover you allege Catherine of having?"

"Ah, there I cannot answer you, for I have no knowledge of his name."

"How, then, do you know that he exists? Or do you merely surmise?"

"Surmise, allege, tales hard to credit . . . I gather you must be the lawyer."

"I have the honor to attend the Inns of Court. My name is Hughe Camden. You may know my father."

"May I? Well then, so I shall, if you decide to introduce him. In the meantime, learned sir, know that whilst I cannot bear witness to the alleged lover's name, I can vouchsafe his existence by the testimony of the lady herself, who spoke of running off with him."

"You have *heard* her say this?"

"Not with mine own ears, but earlier today, I spoke with one who did hear the lady say so."

"Hearsay, sir. 'Twas a lie, I'll warrant."

Shakespeare shrugged. "Well, we shall find out soon enough."

"I am not at all sure what you have to gain by raising all this fuss," said Camden, looking at him as if trying to gauge his motives.

"I have nothing at all to gain, sir," Shakespeare said, "and only time to lose. You, on the other hand, would stand to gain a great deal more, I should think, if Catherine were truly dead. That would increase her sister's worth considerably, would it not?"

"I do not care for your tone, sir."

"I do not much care for yours, either. I have played penny whistles that have made less grating noise."

"What is your name, sir?" asked Camden, stiffly.

"Marlowe," Shakespeare said. "Christopher Marlowe, at your service."

"Marlowe." Camden nodded. "I shall make a point to remember that name."

"Suit yourself. I have already forgotten yours."

Camden fell behind as Shakespeare increased his stride and hurried on ahead. He had almost caught up to Middleton, at the head of the procession, when yet another of Blanche's suitors came up beside him and introduced himself.

"Sir, my name is Andrew Braithwaite. Might I have a word with you?"

"Have three, as you are the third to ask."

"Indeed, I did see Dubois and Camden speaking with you just now. Did they say anything of interest?"

"No, not really. I rather hope you shall do better."

Braithwaite smiled. "I fear, then, that you are doomed to disappointment. I doubt I can be much more interesting, for I am neither a great wit nor a learned scholar."

"Then you at least appear to be an honest man, which in itself makes you more interesting. A plain bird would stand out 'mongst all this plummage."

Braithwaite chuckled. "You do not care much for this company, I see. And yet, here where each man competes with every other, you have seized everyone's attention. You stand centerstage, and yet seem to regard it as an imposition."

"It amuses you?" asked Shakespeare, glancing at Braithwaite to see if he was being mocked. But it seemed that he was not.

"If I can say so without giving offense, aye, it does amuse me. But the amusement, I hasten to add, is not at your expense."

"I am not offended then."

"Good."

Shakespeare glanced at him with interest. "Most people, especially in this vaunted company, would not concern themselves overmuch about giving offense to a mere player."

"Well, I try not to be careless about whom I may offend," Braithwaite replied. "That way, I can husband my offenses for those who most deserve them."

"Well said."

"Thank you."

"You are welcome, sir. What would you have of me?"

"Why, nothing in particular," Braithwaite replied.

"What, not even after my singular announcement at the wake?"

" 'Twas, indeed, singular," Braithwaite said. "Quite astonishing, in fact."

"And in light of it, you have nothing more you wish to ask?"

"Not at present. I suppose if what you said proves to be the truth . . . well, frankly, I have absolutely no idea what will occasion then. It should prove quite fascinating. But if what you said turns out to be false, I have a rather better idea of what will occur. Godfrey Middleton will have you whipped for your impertinence and then see you thrown off his estate. That is, assuming you survive the whipping."

"Which would you prefer to see, I wonder, Catherine alive or me whipped?"

"Oh, I would much prefer to see Catherine alive. The ensuing scandal would be absolutely marvelous. And you seem much too fine a fellow to be whipped."

"Odd's blood, Master Braithwaite, 'tis entirely too likeable for a knight's son, you are. I may be in danger of aspiring to have a friend above my station."

"Never fear, I have no shortage of friends below mine. And those friends call me Andrew." He offered his hand and Shakespeare took it.

"Will Shakespeare is my name."

"I heard you tell Camden that your name was Marlowe."

"I lied."

"I knew that. Among those lowly friends of mine is a certain poet by the name of Marlowe. Camden's father has considerable influence. You may have caused Chris some annoyance."

"Well . . . he deserves it."

"Aye, he does, at that. He is a scoundrel. But then, I seem to like scoundrels. I generally find them much more entertaining than this lot. We are nearly there, I think. 'Tis hard to tell. At night, things often neither look nor sound the same."

"Indeed. I do not see young Master Holland."

"I have not seen him myself since the funeral. But as we are all

rivals for Blanche Middleton's affections, we do not enjoy a particular camaraderie. Perhaps he had retired early and thus missed your
dramatic entrance and your speech. If so, then he shall doubtless
miss whatever happens next, for we have arrived."

They were just behind Middleton and the torchbearers at the
head of the procession, and ahead of them they could dimly make
out the white stone structure in the clearing that was the Middleton
family vault. As they approached it, however, a piercing scream
sounded and, for a moment, froze everybody in their tracks. It had
been, unmistakably, a woman's voice.

"Good God!" Braithwaite exclaimed. "*Did that issue from within
the crypt?*"

Shakespeare did not respond, however. He was already running
towards the door, for he saw that it stood open. Braithwaite was
right on his heels, having had enough presence of mind to pause
only long enough to grab a torch from one of the servants. They
ran past Middleton, who stood rooted to the spot with the others
in the vanguard, and Shakespeare was almost to the door when he
felt his arm seized from behind.

"Wait, Will!" Braithwaite said. "Have a care!" He handed him
the torch and drew his rapier. "You are unarmed. Stay close behind
me."

Shakespeare hesitated, then followed him through the door.

The scene that greeted them within the vault was startling, to
say the least. There stood Smythe, holding Elizabeth in his arms.
She was sobbing against his chest as he held her close and tried to
comfort her. Next to the carved stone pedestal where Catherine's
shrouded body had been placed, awaiting the completion of the
coffin, stood a young man Shakespeare had never seen before. He
appeared to be about the same age as Smythe, but of a slighter build,
cleanshaven, with blonde hair and strong, handsome features that
were contorted with misery as he bent over Catherine's now un-
shrouded body, holding it in his arms as he wept unashamedly. But
as dramatic a sight as that presented, even more striking was the

stark red blood all over Catherine's snow white gown and the dagger protruding from her chest.

"Tuck!" said Shakespeare, as soon as he recovered from his initial shock and found his voice. "Angels and ministers of grace defend us! What deviltry is this?"

"Treachery and murder, Will," Smythe said, looking shaken. "Murder most foul."

Braithwaite stood there with rapier drawn and held ready, looking both stunned and uncertain. Behind them, Middleton and several others came into the chamber.

"God's mercy!" Middleton exclaimed, as he beheld the startling tableau before him. "What foul, horrible and loathesome desecration is this ! *Seize that man!*"

Several of the servants rushed forward and grabbed hold of the young man, prying him away from Catherine's body. For a moment, he resisted them, holding onto her corpse as if with desperation, then he seemed to resign himself and simply went limp, allowing them to pull him away.

Middleton's eyes widened even further as he recognized Elizabeth, who had turned around at the sound of Shakespeare's voice and now stared at them all with desolation, her ashen face streaked with tears. "*Elizabeth!* Dear God in Heaven, what are *you* doing in here?"

Her mouth opened as if she were about to reply, but no sound issued forth. It was as if she had lost the power of speech. She could simply find no words.

"We came in and found her thus," said Smythe, indicating Catherine's body, which now lay sprawled at an awkward angle, her head hanging down, the dagger protruding starkly. " 'Twas Elizabeth who screamed. Catherine was already dead."

"Is this some ill-conceived notion of a joke?" asked Middleton, his face pale and drawn. "My God, man, what else should she be but dead in her own tomb?"

"That dagger was not there when she was laid to rest earlier this day," said Smythe.

"Of course that dagger was not there, you imbecile!" said Middleton, his voice trembling with fury. "Because this . . . this . . . foul, perfidious, evil fiend has violated both her tomb and body and thus desecrated my poor dead girl by plunging it within! Oh, horrors! Horrors! What manner of vile beast would mutilate the dead?"

"Methinks that was not what happened here," said Braithwaite slowly, gazing at the body curiously. He put away his rapier and approached Catherine's corpse. "I truly mean no disrespect by what I am about to say, Master Middleton, but as any hunter would readily attest, blood does not gush forth from a carcass as 'twould from a body freshly slain. And what we have here, I would hazard from my experience at tracking, is blood that seems but freshly spilled within the hour. 'Twould seem Will Shakespeare spoke the truth in what he told us all tonight. Without a doubt, your daughter was still alive when she was stabbed."

"Can this be possible?" said Middleton, his voice strained. "Am I to bury the same daughter twice within the same day? Oh, Heaven! Oh, monstrous spite! Then this foul villain has slain her!"

"No!" Elizabeth shouted. "No, 'tis not true! He loved her!"

"Then from whence came that dagger buried in her breast?" Middleteon demanded.

" 'Tis mine," Mason said, dully.

"John, no!" Elizabeth shouted.

"There! You see? Convicted out of his own mouth!" cried Middleton, pointing at him. "Venomous wretch! Who are you, that you would visit such vile treachery upon me? What is your name, villain? Speak!"

"My name is John Mason," he replied, emptily. "I am . . . or I have been a groom at Green Oaks. Now . . . now I am nothing."

"A groom! A *groom*, by God! And at good Sir William's estate! Incredible! And you . . . ." He turned his wrathful gaze on Elizabeth. "My best friend's daughter, and I had treated you as if you were my own! Thus do you repay my kindness towards you, by conspiring with this deceitful rogue to seduce my poor daughter and lead her to her ruin! You are as guilty of her death as he is!"

"Oh, that was base!" Elizabeth said, flushing red with anger. "In your spiteful eagerness to place the blame, you put it everywhere save where it belongs, squarely upon your own shoulders! Had you not tried to force her into a farcical and loveless marriage intended solely to advance your own ambitions, there would have been no need for Catherine to resort to the deception that has led to this sad end! John Mason is no murderer. Look at him! See his face! So utterly undone is he by Catherine's death that he will not even speak out to defend himself! He did not do this awful thing! If you have him arrested for this crime, then the *true* criminal shall go free! And God Himself shall judge you for it!"

"Enough!" said Middleton. "You go too far! This is what comes of too much tolerance and too soft a hand with children! You have said quite enough, Elizabeth! Had you been born a man, so help me, I would seek my satisfaction, but as you are a woman, I will leave you to your father. Let him decide what is to be done with you. Henceforth, you are no longer welcome in my house. You may stay the night, until your father comes for you in the morning, but I shall suffer neither your impertinence nor your presence any longer. Now get out of my sight!"

"Tuck," she said, trying hard to keep her voice from breaking, "would you be so kind as to escort me?"

"Of course," said Smythe. He glanced at Shakespeare. "Will?"

Shakespeare nodded and started to walk out with them.

"Get out, all of you!" shouted Middleton to the others. "Jackals! Get out and let my poor daughter rest in peace!"

Elizabeth walked quickly with her head held high and Smythe hurried to catch up with her. Shakespeare paused to take a torch from one of the servants, then trotted after them. They quickly outdistanced all the others, who slowly made their way back up the path.

"Elizabeth . . ." Smythe said.

"I am all right," she replied, although her voice was strained. "I am more afraid for John. What shall they do to him?"

"I do not think they shall do anything, for the present," Smythe replied. "Middleton will likely have him locked up somewhere, until he can be delivered to the authorities in London."

"I would agree," said Shakespeare. " 'Tis likely that he shall turn him over to Sir William, since he is his servant, and let Sir William make proper dispensation of his fate."

"But John is innocent!" Elizabeth said. "You know he did not do it, Tuck."

"In truth, Elizabeth, I do *not* know it for a certainty. And he did admit the dagger was his own. How else should it have gotten there?"

"Because he left it there for her! He was concerned that she might be defenseless in the tomb and so we arranged to leave it hidden there for her in case she should awake and feel frightened, or in the event that robbers should come to steal her jewelry."

"Then why did he not say so?" Shakespeare asked.

"Because he no longer cares what may become of him!" Elizabeth replied. "He loved Catherine with all his heart! He hated the whole idea of this plan, despised it and said 'twas much too dangerous. He wanted simply to run away with her, instead. And now he blames himself. You saw him! A part of him died along with her! But you know he did not do this, Tuck! You were there with us!"

"Aye, for a time," said Smythe. "Because I had followed you, I know when *you* met him at the vault, but I cannot say when *he* got there. 'Tis possible that he had come there earlier, which means that he could have found Catherine when she awoke, and then slain her for some reason that we do not know."

"You cannot believe that, surely!"

"Elizabeth, I do not know John Mason. I have never before laid eyes on him until this night. But while I admit 'tis possible he may have killed her, I do not believe he did."

"What reasons have you for thinking so?" asked Shakespeare.

"Several," Smythe replied. "For one thing, I am inclined to believe Elizabeth. While I did not have much speech with Mason, he struck me as a decent sort. I do not think he is a killer. And I have no doubt that he loved Catherine."

" 'Twould not be the first time a love had led to murder," Shakespeare said.

"Perhaps not," said Smythe, "but there would have to be some reason for it and there is none here that I can see. The whole plan was designed so that Catherine and he could safely go away together and never be pursued. If his love were so intense and feverish that he might have gone mad if she were to change her mind at the last moment, then I suppose 'tis possible he might have killed her. Yet, if Catherine were to change her mind, for whatever reason, the time to do so would have been *before* she took the potion. Otherwise, why take the risk?"

"Why, indeed?" said Shakespeare. "Your reasoning is sound. Well done. And I agree completely."

"And there is one more thing that makes me doubt his guilt," said Smythe.

"And what is that?"

"The fact that someone tried to kill me tonight while I was following Elizabeth to the vault."

"*What?*" Elizabeth exclaimed. "And you never said a thing about it!"

" 'Twas not the time, I thought. And I wanted to see what would occur between you two."

"What do you mean someone tried to kill you?" Shakespeare asked, with concern. "How?"

"With a crossbow," Smythe replied. "And whoever shot that bolt damn near put it through my eye."

"Good Lord!" said Shakespeare.

"Nearly killed!" Elizabeth exclaimed. "And you said nothing!"

"There seemed no reason to say anything about it then. I had thought he saw an opportunity to strike and followed me out from the house, for I heard someone running back toward it after the bolt was shot. Now, however, it occurs to me that whoever shot at me may have been coming back to the house from the tomb, instead."

"Then would I have not seen him on the path?" Elizabeth asked.

"Not if he heard you coming and hid until you had passed."

"I do not understand," Elizabeth said. "Why would someone wish to kill you?"

"Because I had overheard their plot," said Smythe.

"*What* plot? What on Earth are you talking about?"

"Elizabeth, do you remember when I told you that 'twas I who shouted out to warn you there were others present in the maze that night? There were two men . . . unfortunately, I never saw them, for there was a hedge between us, but I had overheard them plotting. One of them said to the other that with Catherine out of the way, he would be free to make his move. The plot, it seems, was to impersonate a nobleman and his son, then seek to secure Middleton's consent for Blanche's hand in marriage. The prize would be Blanche, herself, and of course, her dowry, which would likely be considerable, especially if Middleton believed that he were dealing with a nobleman. I heard no further, for I had made some noise and gave myself away, whereupon they tried to run me through with their rapiers right through the hedge."

Elizabeth gave a gasp and stopped, staring at him with alarm. "Then *twice* someone has tried to kill you!"

Smythe took her arm and moved her along, not wishing any of the others to catch up and overhear them. "True, they have tried twice, and they may yet try thrice if I cannot unmask them. But . . . here is my point. I know they were in the maze that night. And now I also know they must have seen me, for they now know who I am, which puts me at a considerable disadvantage. What if they had also overheard what you discussed with Mason? Then they would have known about the plan you made with Catherine. And they would have known that Catherine was not truly dead."

"But if everyone believed that she were dead, and she was going away with John, then what purpose would be served in killing her?" Elizabeth asked.

"To divert attention and suspicion from themselves," said Shakespeare.

"Precisely," Smythe agreed. "We are clearly dealing with cold-blooded men who shall stop at nothing to achieve their ends."

"You must tell Godfrey Middleton about this!"

"He already knows, Elizabeth. As does Sir William. We have told them both about it and have their charge to do anything we can to help get to the bottom of it."

"He *knows* about it?" she replied, with amazement. "Then why in God's name does he blame John?"

"Because he is distraught, Elizabeth. Give the poor man some consideration. He has had a daughter murdered twice in the same day. And then there is his outrage over John being her lover, and worse yet, being a lowly groom."

"A neighbor's groom," said Shakespeare. "A neighbor with whom he fancies himself to be in competition."

"And do not forget John admitted that the dagger stuck in Catherine's breast was his," added Smythe. "Under the circumstances, can anyone blame Middleton for reaching the conclusion that he did? In time, when he has had a chance to recover from this heavy blow, then Middleton shall no doubt see reason and reach the same conclusions that we have. But in the meantime, we must do what we can to find the real killer."

"And, with any luck, do so without being killed ourselves," Shakespeare added, wryly. "God's wounds, but this has been a day to try a man's soul! Just when I think that things cannot possibly get any worse, they promptly do!"

"You seem to have had quite a time of it," said Smythe. "You look a sight. What happened?"

"That fool of a driver wrecked the carriage," Shakespeare replied.

"And some of your best clothes, it seems."

"Aye, but that is of no consequence. What plagues me beyond all measure is that if Braithwaite was right, then if the wheel had not come off the carriage and delayed me, I could have returned in time to save Catherine's life."

"Oh, no, Will! Do not blame yourself for that!" Elizabeth said.

"Elizabeth is right, Will," said Smythe. "You are no more at fault than she is for helping Catherine, despite what Middleton has said. 'Twas Catherine's own choice to do what she did, as 'twas the killer's choice to murder her. We should not hold ourselves responsible for what others choose to do of their own free will. We can but be responsible for our own actions. Each of us must suffer the slings and arrows of his own outrageous fortune."

"Gad, Tuck, that was well put! I wish I had said that."

"Never fear, I am sure you will."

"Zounds! You dare unpack your wit at my expense? I have half a mind to pay you back in kind!"

"That would make you a halfwit, then."

"Villain!"

"Clod!"

"Scurvy knave!"

"Steaming turd!"

"Rustic mountebank!"

"Bad poet!"

"Oh, that was base! Where is my rapier?"

"You do not own one."

"Right. I must make amends at once and buy one at the fair so that I can call you out."

"You might buy some clothes first, so that you are fit to go out."

Elizabeth laughed, and then brought her hands up to her head. "Oh, Heaven, that I should find myself able to laugh at such a time as this! How vile must I be?"

"Without laughter, Elizabeth, we have no saving grace at all and must perforce go mad," said Shakespeare.

"Thank you, Will. You are a kind soul."

"I am a damned weary soul. This has been a very long and very trying day."

"And I have been sent packing, to leave upon the morrow," said Elizabeth. " 'Tis a sad thing to be no longer welcome in this house, and yet, 'tis a house that no longer holds any pleasant memories for me. What do you suppose will happen now?"

Smythe shook his head. "I am not sure, Elizabeth. A great deal will depend on Middleton and what he chooses to do. And then do not forget that we still have not heard from Sir William, who does not yet know the full story of all that has transpired."

"The fair was to last three days," said Shakespeare. "Under the circumstances, however, I do not think that anyone would blame our host if he were to cancel the remainder of it."

"True," Smythe said, "but at the same time, in a peculiar sort of way, nothing has really changed since we first spoke with Master Middleton, has it? I mean that at the time, we had all, except Elizabeth, of course, believed Catherine to be dead. Well, she was not, but now, she is. We also believed her to have been murdered. She was not, but now, she has been. Middleton was grieving for his daughter, yet wanted to see justice done. And now, he is still grieving for his daugher, so . . . what has changed?"

"Hmm, I see what you mean," said Shakespeare. " 'Tis a curious situation, indeed. Our expectations of the situation were unfounded, yet now, we have found them to be true. Most strange. I cannot imagine how I would respond in Middleton's place. Would I wish to continue with my original plan to find the murderer and get justice, or would I fold under the weight of this new blow and wish to banish everybody from my sight?"

"Well, only Middleton can answer that," said Smythe. "Elizabeth, you know him best. What do you think he will do now?"

She shook her head. "Godfrey Middelton, for all his stout and doughy looks, is a strong-minded and most ambitious man. In many respects, Catherine took after him. Their similarity of character was the source of many of their clashes. They were both strong-willed and stubborn. Once she had made up her mind, Catherine would not easily be dissuaded. Her father is no different. He is not the sort of man who would forgive a slight. I cannot imagine that he could forgive the murder of his own daughter."

"So you believe that he shall stay the course, then, and do everything possible to find the killer?" Smythe said.

"I cannot think he would do otherwise."

They were approaching the house now. They glanced behind them and saw torches on the path not far away. The others were returning.

"There are still things we need to speak of before you must leave in the morning," Smythe said to Elizabeth. "The rain has stopped. Will you walk with us awhile in the garden?"

"Of course. I am far from eager to retire. I do not think that I shall sleep at all tonight. And I do not really want to be alone right now."

They reached the courtyard and turned to go around the house, to the opposite side where the garden was, with the maze, thought Smythe, where it all began for him.

"What of Blanche?" Smythe asked. "What can you tell us about her?"

Elizabeth sniffed with disapproval. "She is as strong-willed as Catherine, in her way. A very different way."

"What sort of way?" asked Shakespeare.

"Well, Blanche wants what she desires, and desires what she wants. And one way or another, she always contrives somehow to get it."

"Spoiled, in other words," said Shakespeare. "Her father indulges her?"

"Very much so," Elizabeth replied. "And she plays upon him like the virginals. She is much more subtle than Catherine. At least, with him."

"And not with other men?" asked Smythe, remembering his first impression of her.

"Not with any other men, so far as I have seen."

"You disapprove of her?" said Shakespeare.

" 'Tis not for me to approve nor disapprove," Elizabeth replied. "I simply do not like her."

"She does not seem to want for suitors," Smythe said.

"No. She is very beautiful, as I am sure you have remarked," she added dryly.

"Aye, beautiful . . . and rather bold, I thought."

Elizabeth raised her eyebrows. "Oh? I was not aware that you had spoken with her."

"Only briefly, when she arrived together with the wedding party," Smythe replied.

"Indeed? And pray tell, what did she say to you?"

"I do not recall precisely. Nothing of substance, I am sure."

"And yet you do recall that she was bold."

"Well, doubtless, 'twas more in the nature of her manner than anything she said."

"Do tell. And what *was* her manner towards you?"

Shakespeare chuckled. "You have found, Tuck, both the greatest fault and greatest virtue of all women. They listen."

"Bestill yourself, you clever quillmaster," Elizabeth said, sharply. " 'Twas not you that I was asking!"

"Mum's the word, ma'am. I shall take my cue from womankind and be all ears."

"And I shall box those ears for you if you do not have a care!"

Smythe laughed.

"Laugh all you like," Elizabeth said, "but when you are done, I shall still be waiting for my answer. I am not distracted."

"Well . . . she said . . ." Smythe shrugged with exasperation. "In all truth, Elizabeth, I cannot recall now what she said, only that what she said seemed very bold. If I had not known better, I might have thought that she had set her cap at me."

"Blanche has set her cap at men so many times that it has grown quite threadbare," Elizabeth replied, dryly.

"A woman's wit is never quite so sharp as when it pricks another woman," Shakespeare said.

"Provoke me more and you shall find that it can prick a poet, too! Besides, I speak naught but the truth. And there are others, I am sure, who can bear witness to it. Her flaws are plain for all but men to see, who see them not for being blinded by her beauty."

"And yet 'twas Catherine who had the worse reputation of the two," said Smythe.

"Aye, for being a shrew," Elizabeth replied. "For that is what men call a woman who dares to speak her mind. But if she should speak with other parts of her anatomy, then men will think with other parts of theirs, as well."

"Which part would that be, pray tell?" Shakespeare asked, innocently.

"In your case, I have no doubt 'twould be the smallest."

Smythe laughed. " 'Twould seem she *can* box a poet's ears!"

" 'Twere not my ears that she defamed," Shakespeare replied, with a grimace. And then his expression softened. "Why, Elizabeth, you are crying."

" 'Tis for Catherine," she replied, her voice quavering. "Oh, I do not know how I can stand it! My heart is breaking!"

"There now," Shakespeare said. "No shame in tears for a departed friend."

He offered her his handkerchief. Unfortunately, the kindly intention of the gesture was overwhelmed by the sheer filthiness of the grimey handkerchief, which he had earlier used to wipe away some of the mud with which his face was still besmirched. Elizabeth simply stared at the muddy rag for a moment, then started to laugh, despite herself. Smythe and Shakespeare both joined in, and she put her arms around their waists as they staggered together around the house, toward the other side, helpless with laughter.

"Thank you," Elizabeth said, as the wave of laughter subsided. "Thank you both for being such good friends."

"Well, in truth, Elizabeth," Shakespeare replied, "I fear I cannot claim that I was always a good friend to you."

"How so? And why not?"

"I must admit that upon more than one occasion, I had told Tuck here that you would only bring him trouble."

"And so I have," Elizabeth replied.

"Do not say that, Elizabeth," Smythe protested.

" 'Tis naught but the truth, Tuck," she replied, with a sigh. "From the day we first met at the theatre, I have only brought you trouble. And Will, too. I cannot forget that he was nearly killed on my account."

" 'Tis true that I was very nearly killed," said Shakespeare, "but 'twas not on your account, Elizabeth."

"I know," she said, "but neither you nor Tuck would ever have found yourselves placed in harm's way had you not chosen to befriend and aid me. And now it has happened once again. You might have been killed or badly injured in that wreck, and twice now Tuck was nearly killed. And all on my account!"

"Well . . . when you put it that way, it does seem as if all the fault is yours," said Shakespeare.

"*Will*! For God's sake, she feels badly enough as things stand!"

"I spoke in jest," Shakespeare replied. "So far as I can see, Elizabeth, if you were at fault in anything, 'twas in going along with Catherine in this hare-brained scheme, but then you were only trying to help a friend and I cannot fault you in that. I would do no less for Tuck, nor Tuck for me. That misfortune has befallen is in some part, doubtless, due to Fate, but in part due also to the intervention of others. 'Tis there the true blame lies, and 'tis there that we must seek to place it."

"I agree," said Tuck, emphatically. "We know that two of the guests here are impostors, and that those two are likely to be found among Blanche's suitors. Some we have already managed to eliminate from our consideration, but that still leaves Braithwaite, Camden, Holland, and Dubois, and their respective 'fathers,' if fathers they truly be."

"Aye," said Shakespeare. "And I am somewhat disposed towards eliminating Braithwaite from our list of suspects, too."

"Why?" asked Smythe.

"Well . . . he seems a very decent sort of fellow," Shakespeare said. "And I have a good feeling about him."

"I see. So you wish to eliminate him from consideration merely because you happen to like him?"

"Not entirely. He is the one suspect who does not have a father present, and we are looking for *two* men. Although I do admit I like him. He is a very likeable young man."

"That very quality makes for a good cozener," said Smythe.

"What, are you suggesting that I could be easily taken by some sharp cozener?"

"Will, anyone could be taken by a cozener, especially a sharp one," Smythe replied. "Do you think you are immune because, as a poet, you are a great observer of human nature and its foibles? Well, with all due respect, by comparison, you are but an apprentice at the art of observation. A good cozener is a *master* of observing human nature and its foibles. If I have learned nothing else since I have arrived in London, I have at the very least learned that!"

"I suppose you have a point," said Shakespeare, "although my instincts still tell me that he is no more and no less than what he represents himself to be. What do you know of him, Elizabeth?"

"No more than you," she replied. "He seems like a nice young man, and he has good manners. 'Twould seem that he has breeding. Beyond that, I can tell you nothing more. I have not had much to do with him."

"Well, what of Dubois?" asked Smythe. "You seemed to have had rather more to do with him," he added, and immediately regretted it. Still, he could not prevent himself from going on. "You seemed quite taken with him when I saw the two of you out walking."

Elizabeth smiled. "Monsieur Dubois is very charming. His manners are exquiste and his sense of fashion is impeccable. He is capable of learned discourse on such things as poetry and history and philosophy. I cannot imagine that he could be some sort of criminal."

"I find it even more difficult to imagine that he could be searching for a wife," said Smythe.

"The ladies here all seem to find him very handsome," said Elizabeth.

"And how do you suppose he finds the ladies? Or does he even bother looking?"

"Such pettiness does not become you," said Elizabeth. "You could do well to emulate Monsieur Dubois."

"I do not think I could quite manage the walk," said Smythe, dryly.

"Oh, but I should like to see you try," said Shakespeare.

"I think that you are both being very rude," Elizabeth said. "Phillipe Dubois is a gentleman in every sense of the word."

"Well, be that as it may," said Smythe, "I think we can probably agree that Dubois is not a very likely suspect. Still, one never knows. I should like to see what Sir William makes of him, but regretably, he has not returned. What about Camden?"

"I do not like him," Shakespeare said.

"Excellent," said Smythe. "We shall hang him on the strength of that. The crime is solved. We may now get on with our tour."

"Spare me your sarcasm," Shakespeare said. "There seems to be no pleasing you tonight. You criticize me for liking one man and then mock me for disliking another. What would you have of me? We know next to nothing of these people. Well, we know enough of Dubois, at least, to know that he can at least impress a lady with his manners and his erudition. But then, he is French, and a Frenchman learns to impress women from the time he learns his hornbook.

Do you have any opinion of young Camden, Elizabeth, that you would like to share?"

"The barrister? He seems amiable, but rather full of himself," she replied. "But then if that were a crime, they would doubtless have to arrest at least half the men in England. I know he was tutoring Blanche in poetry and literature. Beyond that, I have scarcely spoken with him. Blanche's suitors, for the most part, seem to have had eyes only for Blanche, which should not be surprising."

"That leaves Daniel Holland, then," Smythe said.

"Which one is he?" asked Shakespeare.

"Sir Roger's son, blond, bearded, stocky, handsome, but a bit of a dullard—talks of little else save breeding horses."

"I have not seen him tonight."

"Nor have I, come to think of it. I have not laid eyes upon him since the funeral," said Smythe.

"Did he attend the funeral?" asked Shakespeare.

"Aye, he did," said Smythe. "But he has been conspicuous by his absence since you have returned. I wonder why. It seemed as if almost everyone had gathered at the tomb tonight. And yet, I did not see him."

"Nor did I," Elizabeth said, shaking her head.

They had reached the stairs leading down to the garden and the maze. Elizabeth walked between them, holding onto their arms as they descended. Their torch had sputtered out by now and the stone steps were wet, so they went slowly in the darkness, watching where they walked.

"Are you thinking what I am thinking?" Smythe asked Shakespeare.

"He could have been the one who took a shot at you tonight," said Shakespeare.

"And whilst everyone else was at the wake up at the house," said Smythe, "he could easily have gone back to the tomb and murdered Catherine."

They felt Elizabeth tense between them.

"Forgive us, Elizabeth," Smythe said. "If this is upsetting to you, then we could escort you back to the house."

"No, I would rather stay with you," she said. "I wish to do anything I can to help."

"You are quite certain?" Shakespeare said. "I can see how this could be difficult and painful for you."

"Do not worry about me. Go on."

"Well, that is just the point," said Smythe. "Where *do* we go from here? The murderer could be any one of them."

"Aye, it could, indeed, but the more I think on it, the more I am troubled by the motivation," said Shakespeare.

Smythe frowned. "How so?"

"Well, 'twould seem to me to be taking a significantly greater risk in order to divert attention from a much smaller one. Our impostor and his confederate, whoever they may be, are thoroughly unscrupulous men. That much, we already know. What you had overheard them planning was a brazen bit of cozenage, indeed, one that would require fortitude, quick-thinking, and an appalling lack of shame and conscience. Men such as that would easily be capable of murder, I suppose."

"Indeed," Smythe said. "They have already tried to kill me twice in order to safeguard their plan. So why should they hesitate to kill another?"

"Why, indeed?" said Shakespeare. "Save only that it does not seem to have been truly necessary. Everyone already *believed* Catherine was dead. That her death had been intended as a ruse was known only to Catherine, Elizabeth, John Mason and Granny Meg, if I am not mistaken. There was not anyone else who knew about the planned deception, was there? At least, not until I had returned from London and revealed it?"

"No, there was not," Elizabeth said. "Catherine was most adamant that the secret be kept strictly between ourselves. John disliked the plan, but he loved Catherine and would never have told anyone about it. Indeed, if he had told anyone, he would have revealed the truth about their love, which he knew he could not do. And as for Granny Meg, I find it difficult to believe that she could have betrayed us."

"As do I," said Shakespeare. "She told me the truth of it only when she learned everyone believed that Catherine had been poisoned. And in so doing, she placed herself at considerable risk, I might add. Godfrey Middleton is a very wealthy and influential man. He could make things quite unpleasant for her if he wished to. She most certainly did not have to tell me that she was the one who had mixed the potion. She could easily have pretended to examine the contents of the flask and then revealed her findings to me without ever revealing the part that she had played in the deception. She could have kept the secret, save that she knew if everyone believed it to be murder, then a murderer would be sought. 'Tis one thing to concoct a potion that would enable a girl to escape a loveless marriage and run off with the man she truly loved, and 'tis yet another thing entirely to keep silent about a murder that was not a murder."

"I agree," said Smythe. "Granny Meg is not a woman without scruples, whatever anyone else may say of her. I know there are many who fear witches and believe them to be evil, but the truth is that a witch will not knowingly do harm, for she believes that 'twill return to her thricefold."

"Well, then, we are agreed upon that score," said Shakespeare. "Yet there is still something that gnaws at me about all this, some small detail, something that it seems we are overlooking. . . ."

"The *carpenter*!" said Smythe, snapping his fingers.

"Odd's blood! Of course!" said Shakespeare. "Elizabeth, you had forgotten all about the carpenter!"

She bit her lower lip. "Indeed, I had. But then he was richly paid to keep his silence."

"Aye, which only goes to prove he could be bribed," said Shakespeare.

"An excellent point," said Smythe. "And if the man could be bribed once, then why not twice?"

"But then his own part in the deception would have been revealed," said Elizabeth. "He could not betray us without leaving himself vulnerable, too. 'Twas why Catherine and I felt certain that we had securely bought his silence."

"Ah, but suppose that he betrayed you to someone who did not care about his part in it and could profit from the information, thus posing no threat to him?" asked Shakespeare.

"Who?" Elizabeth asked, frowning.

"What say we go and ask him?" Smythe suggested.

"You mean . . . right now?" Elizabeth asked.

"Why not?" asked Shakespeare. " 'Tis a capital idea! We shall all three go and confront him and find out what he has to say for himself. I think we should go at once."

Suddenly, Smythe pulled them both off the garden path and back into the wet shrubbery. Elizabeth gasped and started to cry out, but Smythe quickly clapped his hand over her mouth.

"What in—"

"Hush, Will! Be still!" said Smythe, softly, but with urgency. "Look over there, by the maze!"

Their eyes, by now, had grown accustomed to the darkness, but at a distance, it was still difficult to make anything out. However, after a moment, they could perceive some movement near the entrance to the maze. A dark figure became evident as it moved away from the hedges and came out into the open, on the path, moving quickly and furtively.

"Do you think he saw us?" Shakespeare whispered, as they watched from their hiding place in the shrubs.

Smythe shook his head. "I do not believe so," he replied, very softly.

"Who *is* it?" whispered Elizabeth.

"I cannot tell," said Smythe. "Be very still. We shall find out in a moment. He is coming this way. . . ."

10

✳

A S THE DARK FIGURE CAME closer, they all crouched behind
the shrubbery and kept very still. Clearly, whoever it was had
not seen them, for he kept coming directly towards them on the
path, moving briskly. As he came closer, they still could not see who
it was, for the figure was wearing a dark cloak and a hat and his face
was in shadow. As he drew even with them, and they still could not
discern his features, Smythe surprised both Shakespeare and Elizabeth by suddenly lunging out from their hiding place and throwing
himself upon the dark figure, seizing him around the waist and
bringing him down upon the ground.

The man grunted as Smythe brought him down, but otherwise
did not cry out. However, he fought back fiercely, struggling in
Smythe's powerful grasp as they rolled around on the ground.

"Hold him, Tuck!" said Shakespeare, rushing to his aid.

At the same time, Smythe's antagonist brought up his knee
sharply and Smythe wheezed with pain as the blow struck his groin.
He let go and the stranger rolled away, but Shakespeare leaped upon
him before he could rise back to his feet.

"Aha! I have you now!"

"Shakespeare, let go of me, you damned fool!"

"What . . . Good Lord! *Sir William!*"

Worley pushed him off and got to his feet. He was dressed all
in dark clothing, a stark contrast to the resplendent suit he had worn

earlier. He bent over Smythe, solicitously. "Tuck . . . are you injured?"

Smythe made a gasping, wheezing sort of sound and nodded weakly.

"Hell and damnation. Come on, then, shake it off. Give me your hand. . . . Help me, Will, he weighs more than a bloody ox."

Together, they helped Smythe to his feet.

"Forgive me, Tuck," Sir William said. "Are you badly hurt?"

"I . . . I shall live . . . I think," Smythe managed, his voice strained and constricted.

"Sir William, we had not realized 'twas you," said Shakespeare. "We thought you might have been the killer! Whatever were you doing out here at this time of night?"

"I might well ask you lot the same thing," Worley replied.

"We were attempting to deduce who murdered Catherine tonight," said Shakespeare.

"You mean this morning," Worley said.

"No, I mean tonight," said Shakespeare. "She was stabbed to death sometime this evening in her tomb."

"A moment," Worley said, frowning. "I could have sworn that you just said she was stabbed to death this evening in her tomb."

"Aye, she was slain within her tomb, milord," said Smythe.

"Presumably, one must already be dead before one is laid to rest within a tomb," said Worley. "I mean, 'tis customary, is it not?"

"Under ordinary circumstances, 'twould indeed be so," Smythe replied, "but in this case, things were far from ordinary. Catherine was not dead when she was laid to rest within her tomb, you see, but merely drugged with a potion so as to feign death."

"You see, milord, 'twas all a plot conceived by Catherine and Elizabeth," Shakespeare added, "to enable Catherine to escape the marriage to Sir Percival and instead run off with John Mason."

"John Mason? It so happens I have a young groom by that name."

"And it so happens Catherine had a young lover by that name," said Shakespeare.

" 'Twas the very same man, milord," said Smythe.

"My *groom* was Catherine's lover?" Worley glanced from Smythe to Shakespeare to Elizabeth. "Can this be true?"

"Aye, Sir William," she replied. " 'Tis true."

"Zounds! Where is he now?"

"Middleton has him locked away somewhere, presumably," said Shakespeare. He quickly brought Sir William up to date on what had happened.

"Astonishing!" said Worley, when the poet had finished. He shook his head. "What a terrible and tragic twist of fate. The poor, unfortunate girl."

Smythe had, by now, largely recovered from the effects of the blow, though he still stood a bit bent over. "We were going to question the carpenter, Sir William. We think the killer might have been young Holland. No one has seen him since the funeral, it seems."

Worley shook his head. "Not so. Holland was surely not the killer," he said. "I, for one, have seen him."

"When, milord? And where?" asked Smythe.

"Just now, back there," said Worley, jerking a thumb back toward the maze.

"In the *maze*?" Elizabeth said, with surprise. "Why, whatever would he be doing in there?"

"Blanche Middleton," said Worley, dryly, "with apologies for my indelicacy, milady. But within moments after I returned, I saw young Holland skulking about suspiciously and so decided to follow him. The two of them met within the maze, in an arbor at its center, and were still . . . actively engaged . . . when I departed. Needless to say, they did not see me. They were quite preoccupied."

"Well, thus is my report of Blanche's character borne out, as you can see," Elizabeth said, with distaste. "And by no less impeccable a witness than Sir William. That she could so disgracefully disport herself on the very day of her own sister's funeral . . . Heavens, need any more be said?"

"I take it, then, that her behavior in this instance does not come as a complete surprise to you?" said Worley.

"I fear not, milord," Elizabeth replied. "Whoever barters for that baggage will be getting goods well used."

"I see," said Worley. "I would assume, then, that her father would be unaware of her proclivities in this regard."

"We are informed that she plays upon him like the virginals . . . while being not quite virginal herself," said Shakespeare.

"How very unfortunate," said Worley.

"Forgive me, milord."

"I meant the circumstances, Shakespeare, not the pun," said Worley. "However, your apology remains no less deserved, thus I accept it. But this failing in the young lady's character is a fortunate thing for Holland in more ways than one, as things turn out, for it now provides him with an alibi. He could not have murdered Catherine while deflowering her sister."

"Those petals dropped quite some time ago, I fear," Elizabeth said, wryly.

"Well, could he not have murdered Catherine and then still had time to get back here and meet with Blanche?" asked Smythe.

"What, you mean kill one sister and within the very hour make love to the other? Egad, that would be cold-blooded, indeed," said Worley. "Such a man would be the very devil, and I do not believe that Daniel Holland answers to that description. What is more, I have ascertained that he is no imposter, but exactly who he claims to be. His father, Sir Roger Holland, whilst not a regular at court, is nevertheless well known to the queen. Thus, while young Holland may lack in judgement and discretion, he does not lack in pedigree, at least."

"So then Holland is not our man," said Smythe. "That still leaves us with the other three."

"And of those three, Hughe Camden, our young inner barrister, is also who he claims to be," said Worley. "The Earl of Oxford recalled him from the Inns of Court, where he once saw him performing in a play by Greene and thus made his acquaintance. Edward described the young man to me in some detail and I am satisified that Hughe Camden is the man whom he had met. Likewise, his father, Sir Richard, was known to several of the heralds."

"So then they are not imposters, either," Shakespeare said. He frowned. "Well, that brings us down to Braithwaite and the Frenchman. Everyone else seems to have been accounted for."

"And we have already agreed that 'tis quite unlikely for the imposter to be Dubois," said Smythe.

Shakespeare sighed. "I know. It just seems hard to credit," he said. "Braithwaite truly seemed like a good fellow."

"Perhaps he is, for all we know," said Worley, "for as it happens, I have been unable to establish anything about our friend Dubois. No one at court seems to know a thing about him . . . or his self-effacing, silent father. I have arranged for the heralds to investigate his claims, but then that will take some time, I fear."

"What of Andrew Braithwaite?" Smythe asked.

"I have had no luck there, either," Worley replied. "I have men investigating his claims, as well, but I was unable to immediately confirm his identity with anyone at court. A number of people said they might recall his father, but that was hardly reliable evidence and no one could give any stronger testimony. Once again, it will take some time to establish whether or not he is an imposter."

"Time is a commodity we may only have in short supply," said Smythe.

"Not necessarily," Worley replied. "Consider what has already been accomplished. We know that we are seeking two men, one of whom seems to be the principal motivating force behind this deviltry, whilst the other works as his confederate. Both may already be upon the scene as imposters, or else one is here amongst us openly whilst the other waits somewhere nearby, perhaps among the merchants at the fair, held in reserve. We have already managed to eliminate most of the guests from consideration as suspects. We appear to be down to only two."

"Only the fair is drawing to a close," said Shakespeare.

"True, but 'tis no cause for alarm," said Worley. "Remember that in order for the plot to succeed, the prize must be secured. And the prize, in this instance, is Blanche Middleton. More specifically, her dowry. And once that prize is secured, Blanche then becomes disposable."

"Goodness!" said Elizabeth, shivering involuntarily.

"Forgive me, milady," Worley said, "but the truth of the matter is that we are dealing with desperate and evil men, or at the very least, with one man who is the evil genius of this plot and another who merely allows himself to be led. Either way, the sort of character who would hatch a devilish plot like this is not a man who would be squeamish or would frighten easily. He knows that you, Tuck, have overheard something of his plan, but he cannot know for certain how *much* you may have overheard. Thus, methinks that he will likely be disposed to gamble."

"How so, milord?" asked Smythe.

"Well, it takes an old corsair to know how another pirate thinks," said Worley. "And whilst our man may be a landlubber, he is nevertheless quite the buccaneer in the way he sails straight into danger with every inch of canvas up. He knows that at least in part, his plan has been exposed, and yet he also knows that if his true identity were known, he would have been in chains by now. Since he is not, he has made the logical assumption that his masquerade still remains intact. We do not know who he is. Therefore, he perseveres. There is still considerable risk involved, but then he knew that from the very start. The risk has now increased, of course, but to such a man, 'twould only add spice to the adventure."

"As with one who plays at dice or cards, the thrill is in the risk," said Shakespeare.

"Verily," Worley said, nodding in agreement. "And our man knows that the greatest risk to him at present is our friend, Tuck, here. He is the one who overheard the plot, or at the very least a part of it, and thus he is the one who may yet recognize one or both of the voices he had heard. Thus, Tuck is the obvious risk to be eliminated."

"And our man has tried that twice already," Smythe said, grimly.

"Doubtless, he shall try again," Worley replied. "You may depend on it, so watch your back. However, here is what our quarry does *not* know. He does not know about *me*. He assumes that because the queen has left the city with her court, that anyone of consequence among the nobility will be traveling with her, as indeed, most of them are. He has also assumed that because Middleton is not, himself, a peer or a prominent fixture in court society, though he has ambitions in that regard, that the guests at his daughter's wedding celebration will not be among the upper crust, but rather the topmost layer beneath it, if you will. In other words, primarily the wealthy new men of the middle class and, perhaps, a few rather minor members of the nobility. He knows that there is still a chance his masquerade might be exposed, but the risk of that is not so great as 'twould have been were any courtiers present, for they have little else to do but keep track of one another and their respective standing in the pecking order. Thus, our man puts on a bold face and proceeds as planned. But he does not know that I am here, or that I have been alerted to his villainy and have already made inquiries which have enabled us to narrow down our list of suspects to just two. As a result, the degree of risk for him has now become quite high . . . only he does not yet know that."

"But he shall surely know it as soon as he becomes aware of your presence here, milord," Elizabeth said.

"Which is precisely why he shall *not* become aware of it," said Worley. "Save for the three of you, no one else knows I have returned. Therefore, let us keep it that way. Do not mention my return to anyone, and if anyone should ask, feign ignorance."

"But . . . where shall you be, milord?" Elizabeth asked. "Even if you intend to conceal yourself in the upstairs rooms, the servants will become aware of you and they will surely spread the word."

Worley smiled. "Never fear. Not even Godfrey Middleton will know I have returned. I have already made preparations in anticipation of this."

"But . . . where will you be, milord?" asked Shakespeare.

"Hiding in plain sight," said Worley, with a smile. But before he could continue, a sharp cry echoed suddenly across the grounds.

"Goodness! What was that?" Elizabeth said, clutching at Smythe instinctively.

"I think it came from over there," said Shakespeare, pointing.

"The maze!" said Worley. He started running towards the entrance.

"Elizabeth, get back to the house," said Smythe.

"No, I am going with you."

"Elizabeth, for God's sake!"

"I feel much safer with you," she insisted. "Do not bother to argue, for I am not going back!"

"What if I go back?" said Shakespeare.

"Oh, Hell's bells! Come on, both of you! We must catch up with Sir William!"

Smythe quickly realized that was more easily said than done, for Sir William's long legs had given him a considerable head start and he was running very quickly. If Smythe had not known about his secret life as the outlaw, Black Billy, he might have been surprised at how fit Sir William was for a supposedly indolent aristocrat, but he knew that Worley was in truth anything but that. By the time they reached the entrance to the maze, Sir William had already gone inside.

Their eyes were well accustomed to the night by now, but it was nearly pitch dark inside the maze. Smythe still had his sword, and he now drew it, holding it before him as they proceeded, for although it was difficult to see, what they *heard* gave them due cause for caution.

Somewhere within the labyrinthine hedges of the maze, a furious fight was taking place. They could hear the rapid clanging of blades ringing out in the darkness somewhere nearby, and judging by the sounds of the combat, it was in deadly earnest. Smythe knew enough of swordsmanship to tell, just by the sounds of blade on blade, that the men engaged were both skilled swordsmen.

"Elizabeth, which way?" he said, tensely.

"To the right," she said, keeping close behind him.

"Odd's blood, I do not like this one bit," said Shakespeare, glancing around uneasily. "I can scarcely see in this infernal shrubbery!"

"Now to the left," Elizabeth said, directing them from memory as they proceeded. "Oh, I do hope Sir William is all right!"

"Sir William can take care of himself, never fear," said Smythe. "He is an accomplished swordsman."

"Well, he may be, but I am not," said Shakespeare, "so if there is any fighting to be done, it is my devout wish that he shall be the one to do it, for I lack not only swordmanship, I lack a sword, as well!"

"You should have worn one," Smythe said.

"And this from the man who forgets to wear one half the time himself," Shakespeare replied. "For all the use a sword would be to me, I might just as well wear a farthingale."

"And very fetching you would look in one, methinks," said Smythe. He paused. "I do not hear anything now. Do you?"

"Not a thing," Shakespeare replied.

"Should we call out?" Elizabeth asked, softly.

"And give away Sir William's presence?" Smythe said. "He is somewhere ahead of us. If he needs help—"

"Will! Tuck! Come quickly!" Worley called out. He sounded very close.

A moment later, as they made another turn, they came upon him, standing stooped over what appeared to be a pile of leaves upon the ground. He dropped to one knee as they approached, stretching out his hand, and Smythe abruptly realized that it was not a pile of leaves at all, but a body lying on the ground.

"Good Lord!" said Shakespeare. "Is that . . . ?"

" 'Tis Holland," Worley replied. "Or 'twas Holland, I should say. He has been run through, clean through the heart. There is also a wound here, high in the left shoulder."

"Oh, God!" Elizabeth said, drawing back. "And what of Blanche?"

"Not a sign of her," said Worley.

"You do not think . . ." Elizabeth's voice trailed off as she brought her knuckle up to her mouth and bit down on it, as if to stifle a cry.

"I do not yet know what to think, milady," he said, frowning.

"Well, I suppose this definitely removes young Holland from our list of suspects," Shakespeare said.

"Here, Smythe," said Worley, tossing him a gauntlet. "Strike him for me, will you?"

Smythe caught the glove and smacked Shakespeare on the shoulder with it.

"Sorry," Shakespeare said, lamely.

"You ought to be."

"I know 'twas rather bad form, but I could not help myself. This whole thing is beginning to take on the aspect of a Greek tragedy."

"Elizabeth, there is more than one way out of this maze, is there not?" asked Worley.

"There are three," she replied, "counting the way we came in."

"As I thought," he said. "That explains why we did not encounter anyone as we came in. Blanche and the killer must have left by another way."

"So then he has her?" Smythe said.

"Not necessarily," Worley replied. "We did not hear her cry out. And Holland here was fully dressed and on his way out from the center of the maze, heading back the way he came. Blanche must have left by another way."

"Aye, that would make sense," said Smythe. " 'Twould ensure

they were not seen together. So whoever killed Holland caught him as he was on his way out. He struck, and Holland cried out in alarm, then drew his blade."

"That is what I think," Worley agreed. "This wound here, in the shoulder, must have been the first touch, before Holland had time to draw steel. He must have twisted away at the last moment, else this would have been the fatal touch. The combat was fast and furious, but very brief. The killer had already fled when I arrived and found Holland slain. The question is, why?"

"Good question," Shakespeare said. "What say we go back to the house, have a drink and mull it over within the safety of four walls and a well lit room?"

"He is eliminating his rivals," Smythe said.

Worley glanced at him as he stood up from the body. "Aye, a sensible deduction," he said, nodding. "Our man must feel very secure in his deception."

"Then why his attempts to kill Tuck?" asked Elizabeth.

"The same reason he has just killed Holland, I should think," Smythe replied. "He wishes to improve his chances."

"But does he not place himself even more at risk by this?" asked Elizabeth.

"Perhaps," said Smythe, "but if he is the sort of man we judge him to be, one who thrives upon the thrill of risk—a gambler, in other words—then this second slaying is nothing more than a playing of the odds."

"Nothing *more*?" Elizabeth said, shocked.

"Well, to his mind, Elizabeth, not ours," Smythe hastened to explain. "Clearly, he has no scruples about the taking of life. It does not trouble his conscience, if he even has one. He must have observed Blanche and Holland together earlier and seen some evidence of a mutual attraction, then followed Holland to their rendezvous and killed him."

"Wait," said Worley, "your reasoning is sound, save for one

thing. If the killer had followed Holland, then why would he not have encountered me? Or any of you?"

"Indeed, he likely would have," Smythe corrected himself, "which means he must have followed Blanche, instead. We have already deduced that she must have left the maze by another way, so then it follows that she came by that way, also. That would explain why none of us had seen them."

"Of course," said Shakespeare, somewhat mollified now that he felt reasonably sure the murderer had fled the scene and was not lurking somewhere nearby. "And now that Holland has been eliminated, the competition has been reduced by one, but we should keep in mind that 'tis the field of *suitors* that has been reduced, and not the list of suspects."

"Whatever do you mean?" asked Worley, with a puzzled frown. "How can the list of suspects not have been reduced?" He indicated Holland's body. "Yonder is one less!"

"Aye, milord," said Shakespeare. "But only to *us*. For us, 'tis one less suspect, from a list we have already narrowed down to two likely candidates. However, the killer does not know that, as you have already pointed out. We must think like the killer if we are to comprehend the motives for his actions. From the *killer's* point of view, he has merely reduced the field of suitors by one, that one being an individual who clearly had a leg up . . . so to speak . . . on the others. Since the killer does not know that you are here, milord, he therefore cannot know that through your knowledge of the nobility and court society, as well as through inquires, you have already eliminated most of Blanche's suitors from our list of suspects. Consequently, he believes that he stands well hidden in a forest, when in truth, unbeknownst to him, most of the trees have already been cut down around him. Thus, he does not realize the extent of his exposure, and so this killing, from his point of view, does not seem so great a risk."

"You have a most interesting faculty, Shakespeare," said Worley. "You have the ability to put yourself into another's shoes, assume his character, and then reason not only from his point of view, but with his emotions and morality, as well. 'Tis a talent that should serve you well upon the stage, but if you are not careful, it could bring you to grief in the real world."

"If this be the real world, methinks that I shall take the stage, milord," said Shakespeare, wryly. "At least when one dies upon the stage, one generally revives in time for the next performance."

"Elizabeth," said Smythe, "are you all right?"

She was staring at the body with a strange expression on her face, a look somewhere between alarm and desolation. " 'Tis the third time now that I have seen somebody slain. First Anthony Gresham, struck in the back by a thrown knife before my very eyes. Then within the span of but a few months, Catherine is stabbed to death, and now poor Daniel Holland is run through with a sword." She took a deep breath and let it out in a heavy sigh. "I gaze down on his body and I feel sadness and regret that his young life should have been snuffed out so suddenly and cruelly, and yet . . . I do not scream with terror. I am not horrified into near insensibility by the sight. I do not feel my gorge rising at the sight, nor do tears come coursing down my cheeks. I wonder what has become of me that I can look so calmly upon death?"

"Familiarity doth breed contempt, milady," Worley replied. "With repeated exposure, one can grow accustomed to almost anything. Else one would go mad. 'Tis a lesson learned by each and every soldier on the battlefield, and each and every sailor on the sea. I am saddened that a young lady like yourself should learn it, also. Would that it were not so." He turned to Smythe and Shakespeare. "You two should take up Holland's body and bring it to the house. When you are asked what happened, tell the truth . . . just take care that you do not tell it all. Say no more than what you know and what you yourselves have witnessed. Say nothing of Holland's tryst with Blanche. You were out walking in the garden and you heard a cry. You responded, and you found him slain. Say nothing of my presence. 'Twould be best were I not seen. Remember . . . I am *not* here."

"But how shall we find you if we need you, milord?" asked Smythe.

"Never fear, I shall find you. Now go on. Take Holland back. Let us stir up a hornet's nest and watch what happens next."

As Shakespeare said when they returned to the house, "The specter of death appears to have brought new life to the festivities." Indeed, thought Smythe, it was strangely and unsettlingly all too true. The house was ablaze with lights when they returned, and even the fairgrounds were weirdly illuminated with flickering torchlight and campfires. Having earlier closed up their stalls and colorful pavillions, the merchants had opened them up once again to take advantage of the situation as the guests stayed up and wandered through the house and fairgrounds. It seemed that no one slept, as they were all eager to hear or else impart the latest bit of gossip.

Catherine's dramatic resurrection and murder already had everyone abuzz, and anyone who had retired for the night had been awakened by the uproar of people running through the halls and calling out the news or else banging upon doors to awaken their friends. When Shakespeare and Smythe, accompanied by Elizabeth, returned to the house, bearing between them the limp body of Daniel Holland, the news exploded through the estate like a petard.

The stricken Sir Roger was desolated by the news of his son's death, but his grief was mixed with righteous fury as he announced to one and all that he would pay a thousand crowns to whoever brought his son's murderer before him. Not to be outdone, Godfrey Middleton immediately doubled the amount.

"This outrage against justice and all humanity shall not be tolerated!" he cried out to the assembled guests. "We shall never submit to it! We shall not suffer damned, bloodthirsty assassins to walk amongst us unmolested! I hereby swear before Almighty God that our children's foul murders shall be avenged!"

"Oh, damn, where did I leave my pen?" muttered Shakespeare,

as he listened raptly to Middleton's address. "This is great stuff!"

"Really, Will!" said Elizabeth, taken aback by his response.

"Forget it, Elizabeth," Smythe said to her, shaking his head. " 'Tis hopeless. He cannot help himself. He is a poet, and to a poet, all the world's a stage and all the people in it merely players."

Shakespeare cocked an eyebrow at him, but said nothing.

They were questioned at length by everyone, it seemed, until both Smythe and Shakespeare had grown nearly hoarse from telling the story over and over again. To escape all the attention, Elizabeth finally retired to her room to pack her things. Middleton had said nothing about rescinding his order for her departure, and though she was not eager to leave now that things had reached a fever pitch of excitement, she did not seem to have much choice.

"What a perverse creature I have become," she said to Smythe, before she went back upstairs. "All sensibility and logic dictates that I should make all haste to leave this place, and yet, I find myself longing to remain and see how it all turns out. I cannot reconcile my feelings. I am both repelled and fascinated."

"I know just how you feel," Smythe told her. "I felt much the same when first I set foot on London Bridge and beheld the severed heads of criminals set upon the spikes there. I had never seen anything like that at home, in my small village, and when I first beheld the birds feasting on the rotting flesh of those gruesome, severed heads, I was nearly sickened by the sight. I was appalled by it, and yet, I could not look away. Now, when I pass by them on the bridge or by the law courts, I scarcely even notice them."

"Have we become so callous then," she asked, "that the sight of violent death touches us so little, or even not at all?"

"It does, indeed, touch us," Shakespeare said, "else we would not be speaking of it so. 'Tis when we stop speaking of it that we must feel concern about our very souls. Ask yourself, Tuck, about those very heads of which you speak. Is it truly that you scarcely notice them because you do not find them remarkable in any way at all, or because despite having become accustomed to their presence, you nevertheless prefer to look away and not dwell upon the sight? If we see a beggar on the street, scrofulous and ragged, do we gaze at him directly, with honest curiosity, or do we not look away? And if we look away, is it because we are not touched by his sad plight, or because we fear we may be touched too much? Those severed heads are not placed there on the spikes in order to inure us to the sight, but quite the opposite. They are put there to horrify, as an object lesson, intended to touch us with its violence."

"And yet there are those who are not touched at all," said Smythe.

"Aye," said Shakespeare. "And 'tis their heads that are placed upon the spikes to remind us of the consequences."

"Well, I, for one, shall pray that whosoever murdered Catherine and Daniel shall suffer those selfsame consequences," said Elizabeth. She looked around. "This celebration has become a festival of death and we are all specters at this wedding. 'Tis meet that I should leave, lest I begin to enjoy myself too much."

"Methinks the lady thinks too much," said Shakespeare, as he watched her walk away. " 'Twill make her life most cumbersome."

"Hmm," said Smythe. "And then again, some men have found life cumbersome because they thought too little."

Shakespeare smiled a bit ruefully. "I do believe the lad has scored a touch. Methinks you like her more than just a little. You are a caring soul, Tuck. Take care you do not care too much."

"We have had this conversation."

"Indeed, we have. Point made and taken. Let us proceed then to another matter close at hand. Namely, our two remaining suspects. What shall we do about them, do you think?"

Smythe shook his head. "I am not sure. Sir William was not very clear in his instructions."

"Well, he did say we should stir up a hornet's nest," said Shakespeare. "Yonder comes the Frenchman, making straight for us. Let us poke him just a bit and see how he responds."

11

✳

*M*ON DIEU, I HAVE ONLY just heard the terrible news!" Dubois said, as he came rushing up to them. He looked as if he just got out of bed and had dressed hastily. He seemed quite agitated and his French accent was a bit more pronounced. Smythe noticed that although his command of English was excellent, as before, he seemed to hesitate slightly, as if in his excitement he was flustered in his attempt to choose the precise words. "*Monsieur* Holland is slain? How . . . how did this happen?"

Smythe sighed wearily as he prepared to tell the story yet again, but Shakespeare spoke before he could begin.

"One of Blanche Middleton's suitors, it seems, was intent on removing a rival . . . permanently," he said.

Dubois frowned. "That is a most serious accusation, *monsieur*," he said. "But unless you were present, how can you know this to be true?"

" 'Tis obvious to anyone who is capable of reason," Shakespeare replied. "One need only ask, what was a respectable young gentleman like Daniel Holland doing in the maze at such a time of night, alone? What possible reason could he have had for going there? Why, the only reason any respectable young gentleman could have in such a circumstance, no doubt . . . a romantic rendezvous with a young lady."

Dubois' nostrils flared slightly. "Indeed, *monsieur*, what you suggest does not seem entirely implausible, and yet it is also quite possible there was some other explanation, *n'est çe pas?*"

"Well, I suppose that many things are possible," Shakespeare replied, with a shrug. "He might have been seized with a sudden impulse to trim some hedges in the middle of the night, perhaps. Or else he may have simply been out walking when he saw a stag go into the maze and followed, so that he might do a bit of hunting on the spur of the moment, as it were. Or else, perhaps—"

"You have made your point, *monsieur*," Dubois said, tightly. "It is not needful . . . nor is it very wise . . . to resort to mockery."

"*Mockery?*" Shakespeare exclaimed, as if shocked by the suggestion. "God save me, would I do such a thing? 'Twould be sheer folly, *Chevalier* Dubois. Never would I risk offending a gentleman of your stature, sir, under any circumstances! You wear the handsome rapier of a true swordsman, while I . . ." he spread out his arms to show he was unarmed. ". . . I would not know how to use a blade even if I had one!"

Dubois pursed his lips tightly while his fingers toyed absently with the pommel of his sword. "So," he said, after a moment, "perhaps I had misunderstood, *monsieur*. There are subtleties of language one cannot always follow, as a foreigner. I perceive now that you meant no offense."

"Oh, good heavens, no!" said Shakespeare, stepping back. "Forgive me, 'twas all my fault, I am quite certain. To be sure, I am an abject fool. I misspoke, or else expressed myself quite badly. I . . . I am not an educated man, I say the wrong thing often, very often . . ."

"*La!*" Dubois said. "Enough, *monsieur*. It was a minor misunderstanding, nothing more. I assure you, the matter is entirely forgotten. You have clearly had a very trying night, what with discovering the body of that most unfortunate young gentleman."

"Indeed," said Smythe, "that maze seems to be bad luck for anyone who goes there, if you ask me. From now on, I intend to avoid it at all costs! The last thing I would wish was to be run through in there!"

"It would seem that it was, indeed, a most unlucky place for *Monsieur* Holland," said Dubois. "A man would be wise to avoid any place where such unfortunate things happened. It was a terrible thing, terrible. Poor Sir Roger. I must go and express my condolences. *Bonsoir.*"

"Hmm," said Shakespeare, as they watched him walk away. "For a moment there, he was positively threatening."

"Bluff and bluster, nothing more," Smythe said, with a grimace.

"You think so? Well, I am not so sure. He did seem to take umbrage quite readily when I tweaked him. The way he looked at me and placed his hand upon his sword, I almost thought that he was going to run me through."

Smythe snorted. "If that fop ever ran through anything more substantial than an hors d'oeuvre, I shall eat my hat. It takes no bravery to play the bravo when your opponent is unarmed. 'Twas the superiority of his class that he was counting on to intimidate you, not his skill with a sword, you may be sure."

"You are unquestionably the expert when it comes to judging blades," said Shakespeare, "but that sword of his looked like a quality piece of work to me."

"Would you expect someone in his position to purchase something second rate?" asked Smythe. He shrugged. "I could not give it a close inspection, of course, but it seemed quite the showy piece, all bejeweled flash and dazzle. To my mind, 'tis not the sort of weapon a serious swordsman would wear."

"So you do not see him as the killer, then?"

"He hardly seems the lethal sort, Will."

"Then that leaves us with Braithwaite."

"I suppose it does," said Smythe.

Shakespeare shook his head. " 'Tis only that he seems so *unlike* a killer. He seems so . . . amiable."

"Where is it writ that a murderer cannot be amiable?"

"Would that villainy were clearly written on the countenance," said Shakespeare, sourly. " 'Twould make our task ever so much simpler."

"You like the fellow."

"I suppose I do. He is not without his charm. He has wit and is the sort that grows upon you."

"The sort that makes for the most dangerous kind of cozener and scoundrel," Smythe said. "The sort who may smile and smile and yet still be a villain."

"Well put. You argue well and soundly. I can say but little in the way of dispute."

"I find I do not share your favorable opinion of him," Smythe replied, dryly. "He strikes me as a cocky sort, like the roaring boys who often cause mischief at the theatre. He swaggers when he walks and I suppose he thinks himself a young Apollo. Where *is* Braithwaite, anyway? I have not seen him."

"I do not know," Shakespeare responded. "I have not seen him since we all left the tomb."

"And what of Camden?"

"I have not seen him, either."

"Well, let us hope for his sake that Blanche does not next choose to favor him with her attentions," Smythe said. "That could bode ill for his chances of living to a ripe old age."

"Two of our original suspects left," Shakespeare said. "One of whom Sir William vouches for, at least in terms of being who he says he is, the other still an unknown quantity. And both seem unaccounted for as of this time. Do you want to see if we can find them?"

"Aye," Smythe replied. "Let us see how they respond to the news of Holland's murder. And let us also see if either of them have any witnesses who can vouch for where they were when Holland died."

They decided to make a quick tour of the lower floor, but saw no sign of either Braithwaite or Camden, which suggested that either both had retired to their rooms for the night and had heard nothing of Holland's murder or else had gone out to the fairgrounds, as had many of the guests—in which case, they would undoubtedly soon learn what had transpired as word spread.

Rather alarmingly, many of the guests had obtained torches and gone out to the garden to visit the maze, presumably to see if they could find the spot where the murder had taken place. Smythe thought it quite macabre, imagining them wandering about in there, looking down at the ground and holding their torches low to see if they could spy any traces of spilled blood, but Shakespeare did not find it at all surprising or unusual.

"We are bloodthirsty creatures, Tuck," he said, as they walked down the great hall of the mansion, past portraits of Godfrey Middleton's ancestors and illustrious figures from England's history, including, of course, the queen. It would not do at all for her to visit at some point and not see a portrait of herself in a place of honor in the great hall. "We think of ourselves as being a civilized people, and yet, in truth, we are still little more than savages. We all flock to a good hanging or a drawing and quartering, and the more the unfortunate victim screams and blubbers, the more we seem to like it."

"I thought you said before that such sights were meant to horrify and caution us," Smythe replied.

"Oh, indeed they are," said Shakespeare. "But even so, there is some savage part of us that hearkens back to those ancient times when we painted our bums blue and smashed one another's heads in with stone axes, and 'tis that part which finds the horror curiously stimulating. We discover that it thrills the blood and invigorates the humors. If we should see a carriage wrecked up by the roadside as we ride by, what do we do? Why, we slow down to a walk, thus the better to observe the carnage. And if we happen by when two men are fighting in the street, pummeling each other into bloody pulp, why then we stop and watch, we pick a favorite and cheer him on, perhaps even lay wagers. Our own mortality is sport to us and

we play it with a vengeance. Thus, the ground upon which a murder
victim falls becomes a sort of playing field."

"I must say, you see things in a curious way sometimes," said
Smythe, looking around the long hall as they went.

" 'Tis because I observe people," replied Shakespeare, "and people are often very curious."

As they walked, Smythe noticed their surroundings. They had
the great hall almost entirely to themselves. There were a few guests
promenading up and down, talking amongst themselves, and every
few moments a servant would hustle by with an annoyed expression,
because of the lateness of the hour. Night had turned into day at
the Middleton estate, and while some of the guests were sleeping,
most were still up, though by now they had moved out to the torch-
lit fairgrounds to gather round the stalls or at the campfires and
discuss the day's events. The festival had taken a dark turn and no
one wanted to miss out on hearing any gossip or miss seeing anything else that might occur.

Smythe had not been to many rich people's homes. This was
only the second one he'd seen. He had been honored to have been
invited to Sir William's handsome and sprawling estate, Green Oaks,
on several occasions and he could tell that Godfrey Middleton had
taken pains to see that Middleton Manor did not suffer greatly by
comparison.

As at Green Oaks, the great hall of Middleton Manor was built
with a long gallery, and the walls were panelled with imported
woods. The ceilings were an intricate pattern of shallow plaster ribs
in geometrical forms, ornamented with arabesques and figures of
birds and fishes and beasts, as well as flowers and scrollworks of
vines. The staircases were ornate, with solid oak block steps and
landings with massive hand rails and newel posts that were all elab-
orately carved and ornamented with small statues. No expense was
spared anywhere in the construction of this house.

Likewise, the decorations in the hall were all expensive and ornate. Several gleaming and enamelled suits of armor stood about,

every one of them apparently brand new and doubtless never worn, and there were various weapons hanging on the walls in display arrangements, among them broadswords, rapiers, maces and hal-breds, battle axes and, Smythe especially noted, several crossbows with pouches full of bolts.

There were large, richly woven tapestries, with not a painted cloth among them, and of course, large, gilt-framed ancestral por-traits and paintings of historical personages. It was these which had caught Smythe's eye as they walked. There was something curious about them, somehow, something which had troubled him vaguely, and for a while he could not quite put his finger on it, but abruptly, it occurred to him exactly what it was.

"Speaking of observing people, have you noticed anything strange about these portraits?" Smythe asked.

"Strange?" Shakespeare frowned. He had not been paying atten-tion to them. "The portraits? How so?"

"Well . . . have you not noticed that there are no signs of age on any of them?" Smythe paused and approached one of the paint-ings, examining it more closely. He stretched out a finger and gently touched the canvas. "The canvas is still quite taut, stretched tight as a drum, and the colors are all so fresh and vivid, they look as if they have scarcely had the time to dry. Most of these portraits have only been painted fairly recently, unless I miss my guess."

Shakespeare shrugged. "And so what of it? The house is still relatively new, is it not? 'Tis no more than a few years old. So Mid-dleton had commissioned a few score portraits to hang upon his walls. I suppose he could have purchased older paintings, but then why not commission new ones? After all, he can certainly afford them."

"Oh, I do not dispute that," Smythe replied. " 'Twas not my point, Will. Middleton is very rich, I grant you that. 'Tis just that I was thinking . . . if most of these paintings are supposed to be por-traits of his ancestors, then do you not find it curious that they were only painted recently?"

"Perhaps he merely had some older portraits copied," Shakespeare said.

"But why would anyone do that?" persisted Smythe. "A portrait of an ancestor becomes more valued and more meaningful with age. It conveys a sense of history, of lineage. Making copies of old portraits so that new ones could be hung would be rather like opening a cask of fine, aged wine and spilling it all out, only to refill it with juice from newly ripened grapes. It simply makes no sense."

"No . . . I suppose not," said Shakespeare, with a puzzled look. "I had not considered it that way. In truth, I had not considered it at all. I was, in fact, considering the murders that took place at this house, not the paintings that are hung within it."

"Well, I am not sure why it struck my notice, only that it did," said Smythe. "Does it not make you wonder how genuine the likenesses may be?"

"What are you going *on* about?" asked Shakespeare, frowning. "We have two murders we must solve! What *is* all this about the blasted paintings? What have they to do with anything?"

"I am not certain," Smythe replied. "Perhaps nothing at all." He shook his head. "I cannot say why I notice such things, only that I do, you see. You observe people closely, I suppose because you write about them and thus need to understand them better. I simply observe *things*, perhaps because I have been taught to make them well. I notice if a sword is crafted well or if 'tis simply flashy, ornamented to no purpose save to disguise the fact that the blade is not made very well. The blade the Frenchman carries, for example, seems to be a fairly good one from what little I could see of it, and young Holland carried a simple, albeit first-class duelist's rapier. What was more, he knew how to use it. If we were to make inquiries, I would wager we would find that he had studied with a fencing master."

"Well, whoever killed him must have studied harder," Shakespeare said, wryly.

"Precisely," Smythe replied. "You may jest, but I could tell from the cadence of the strokes that both combatants knew what they were about. That it went so quickly also tells me that the killer was either very lucky or else he was a first-rate swordsman. Holland had skill, yet despite that, he never stood a chance. For my money, our man is the very devil with a blade."

"All the more reason we should avoid making his close acquaintance," Shakespeare said.

"I thought you just said that you wanted to solve these murders," Smythe replied.

"I do, insofar as 'tis an exercise intended as a challenge to the mind, only I would prefer to do so at a safe distance. I find it interesting to puzzle out a killer's motives and attempt to deduce who he might be, but when it comes to chasing him about with swords and things, I find that my enthusiasm wanes."

Smythe stopped. "Well, we have now made a complete circuit of the hall and all the lower rooms," he said. "If Braithwaite and Camden are not outside on the fairgrounds, they must be upstairs, asleep."

"Perhaps we should follow their example," Shakespeare said.

"What, and miss all the excitement? I should think that scarcely anyone will sleep this night."

"I would make a liar of you in an instant."

"Oh, come on, Will! You have spent many a night at The Toad and Badger, carousing until dawn. Are you going to start yawning on me now?"

"The very mention of it tempts me."

"Well, fine then. Go sleep, if you must. I shall carry on alone."

"And catch a dagger or an arrow in your back without me there to watch it for you? I should never sleep a wink again. Your ghost would haunt me, I am certain."

"Aye, my shade would stand over your bed each night, all horrible and bloody, and would wail piteously until dawn. 'Willlllllllll . . . Willlllllllll . . . 'twas all your fault! 'Twas all your fault!' "

"You know, I do believe that you would do just that, to spite me."

"I would."

"You, sir, are a bounder and a scoundrel."

"And you, sir, are a lily-livered goose."

A muffled high-pitched giggle stopped them as they went past the library. The door stood slightly ajar. Shakespeare glanced at Smythe. "Surely, you do not suppose . . . ?"

"Two of the guests, perhaps, emboldened by the night's events?"

"Should we make sure, you think?"

"Perhaps not. 'Tis really none of our concern . . ."

They opened the doors to the library together. Hughe Camden scrambled to his feet from the floor as if he had been stung. Blanche Middleton, on the other hand, remained lying where she was, in a tangle of silks and taffeta, revealing a great deal more shapely feminine leg than Smythe had ever seen before, and looking up at them with insolent amusement.

"Uh . . . we were . . . uh . . . just talking and . . . uh . . . the lady fell," said Camden, hastily, his face beet red. "Aye, she fell . . . that is to say . . . she swooned, doubtless from the strain of all tonight's events. . . ."

"No doubt," said Shakespeare, with a perfectly straight face. "With all of the activity tonight, it must have been quite a strain for her."

"To be sure, to be sure," said Camden, hastily, regaining some of his composure. "I was merely trying to help her up, you see, and I misjudged her weight . . ."

"I *beg* your pardon!" Blanche said, from the floor.

"That is to say, the angle, you see, I misjudged the *angle*, and we both fell, and so now . . ."

"Now you are back up again," said Shakespeare.

"Um, precisely. Well. Well, then." He turned back to Blanche and bent over slightly, holding out his hand to help her up. "Milady . . ."

She simply gazed up at him, wide-eyed, saying nothing. She made no move to take his hand. "Perhaps these two gentlemen could assist me," she said, her voice dripping with sarcasm. "I am sure that between the two of them, they could certainly manage the weight."

Camden straightened up and cleared his throat, awkwardly. "Ah, well, to be sure, if milady would prefer . . ." He bit his lower lip, flustered, searching for the proper exit line. "Well, uh . . ."

Blanche saved him, after a fashion. "Thank you, Master Camden, for your concern and your attentions."

"My pleasure, milady. Uh . . . that is to say . . . you are most welcome. Most welcome, indeed." He cleared his throat once more. "Gentlemen . . ."

Shakespeare gave him a small bow and Smythe followed his example. Camden made haste to leave the room.

"I think perhaps I should go after him," said Shakespeare, "and see if he has heard the news."

"Aye, perhaps you should," said Smythe. "I shall be along shortly."

"No hurry," Shakespeare said, pursing his lips and raising his eyebrows. He turned and left the room.

"May I assist you, milady?" Smythe said, offering his hand to Blanche, trying not to be distracted by the fetching sight of all that leg.

"Thank you, good sir," she said, taking his hand. He gently helped her to her feet and she quickly readjusted her clothing, brushing herself off. "I am really not sure what came over me," she said. "I suddenly felt so faint, I must indeed have swooned."

"It must have been a very trying day for you, milady. You should get some rest."

"I think you are right," she replied. "If you would be so kind as to lend me your arm and escort me up the stairs? I fear that I might swoon again and lose my footing."

"Of course," said Smythe. He offered her his arm. "Tuck Smythe, milady, at your service."

She took his arm, her fingertips resting lightly on the back of his hand. She smiled at him as they left the library and headed towards the stairs. The hall was deserted now and quiet.

"What news was your friend speaking of just now?" she asked, as they approached the stairway.

"Oh, uh . . . well, perhaps now is not the time," said Smythe. "You are unwell and perhaps tomorrow would be better."

"I want to know," she said, as they began to climb the stairs.

"Milady, truly, I would not wish to disturb you."

"Is it disturbing news then?" she asked, her eyes wide. "You have to tell me now. I insist. I could not sleep without knowing. I would stay awake all night and wonder."

They had reached the landing. "There has been another murder," Smythe said.

She stopped and gasped. "No! Who?"

Smythe moistened his lips. "Daniel Holland."

She almost fell. Smythe grabbed her around the waist, thinking she was really going to swoon this time. "Milady!"

She clutched at him. This time, not surprisingly, perhaps, her distress seemed quite genuine. She swallowed hard, then took a deep breath, which made her breasts swell very visibly in her low-cut bodice. Smythe caught himself and quickly looked away. He felt his face flushing.

"Daniel is dead? But . . ." she hesitated. "*When*? How did it happen?"

"Milady, perhaps we should not discuss this now—"

"I shall be all right. Now *tell* me!"

Smythe felt her closeness acutely and released her, but she retained a hold on his arm as they continued up the stairs. "He was murdered in the garden maze tonight. Run through with a rapier." He paused a moment, then added, " 'Tis not entirely clear what he was doing there, but it seems that someone must have followed him who meant to do him harm. I do not suppose you would have any idea who might have wished him ill?"

She shook her head. "No. No, not at all. Goodness, to think

that . . ." She caught herself. "To think that he is dead! First my sister, and now this! Poor Daniel!"

"It must have happened very quickly," Smythe said. "He could not have suffered."

"Well, that is some small consolation, perhaps. But just the same . . ." He felt her trembling. He could well understand why, though she, of course, had no idea that he knew. "How very frightening," she said. "To think that there is a vicious murderer amongst us . . . I feel so very vulnerable all of a sudden. This corridor is so empty . . . would you please escort me to my rooms?"

"Certainly, milady."

She put a finger to her lips. "We must be quiet, though," she said. "My sister's friend is in this room just ahead and to our right. I think that she is still awake and packing, preparing to depart first thing in the morning. I would not wish her to get the wrong idea, you understand."

"Of course, milady. Nor would I," Smythe said, with some alarm, wondering how Elizabeth would react if she came out and saw them together, walking arm-in-arm towards Blanche's bedroom. He was not sure she would believe his explanation. They walked past her door in silence.

"You are most understanding," Blanche said, after a moment, smiling at him. "You are a true gentleman."

"Alas, milady, I fear you have the wrong impression of me," he replied. "I am not a gentleman, merely a poor and lowly player."

"Oh, of course! Now I remember where I saw you! We met down by the river gate, when I arrived."

"Quite so, milady. I was among the Roman senators who were assigned to greet the guests."

"I remember. You looked much better in your toga than did any of the others."

"That is kind of you to say, milady."

Her face clouded over. " 'Twas when we all thought Catherine was dead," she said. "And then she turned out not to have been dead at all, only to be killed in her own tomb . . . how horrible! Oh, no, I must not think of it! I must think of something else, or I shall be quite undone. Tell me how it is to be a player."

"How it is to be a player?" Smythe repeated, not quite prepared for the question. "Ah. Well . . .'tis not that I possess a great deal of experience, milady. I am still quite new at it. But I am fortunate, indeed, to have found a position with the Queen's Men, who are the finest players in the land. 'Tis something I have dreamed of doing since I was but a boy."

"I thought that young boys were permitted to apprentice with the players," she said, "so that they might play the female roles before their voices change. Did you not do that?"

"Regretably, milady, my father did not approve of my becoming a player. He thought 'twas no fit occupation for a gentleman."

"Oh! So then you are a gentleman!"

"My father was a gentleman, milady. But he aspired to rise higher and become a knight, and in his efforts to pursue that lofty goal, he bankrupted himself and left me with nothing to inherit. Thus, I cannot claim to be a gentleman. I am but a simple farrier, a smith, an ostler, and now a player, though not, I fear, a very good one, though I do my humble best."

"Humility in any man is a most becoming trait," she said, with a smile. "And I can understand your story perhaps better than you know." They had reached her bedroom and she opened up the door as she spoke and went inside, but without releasing his arm, so that he was forced to enter with her. "Your father sounds very much like mine," she said, letting go his arm and closing the door behind them. "He is a most ambitious man. Appearances mean everything to him." She sounded bitter. "He gives more credence to what other people think than he does to the concerns of his own family. He drove my mother to an early grave with his obsessions. A proper lady does this, and a proper lady does that, and a proper lady would never do this, that, and the other. 'Tis enough to drive one mad."

As she spoke, as if without thinking, she slipped off her shoes and began unfastening her laces. For a moment, Smythe was too startled to speak, and then he could not quite find a way in which to get a word in edgewise.

"I can imagine how very frustrating it must have been for you, wanting so to be a player and never being allowed to pursue your heart's desire!" Blanche continued. "Always being told what a proper gentleman must or must not do! There are times, I am quite sure, when you thought that you might scream! Oh, how well I know that feeling. I understand, you see. I do. The two of us are very much alike."

She had now loosened her bodice and unlaced and removed the first of her petticoats, stepping out of it and letting it drop onto the floor. He was speechless, riveted to the spot. He could not believe that she was actually undressing in front of him. He looked around to see if there were any servants, but the two of them were quite alone. As she removed her second petticoat, Smythe saw that she was not wearing a farthingale, but a padded roll instead, which gave her skirts a softer drape and was probably more comfortable, especially when lying in a garden or upon a floor.

He swallowed hard. Blanche Middleton was a very beautiful young woman and she was exposing more of her beauty by the moment. It occurred to him that she fully intended to bed him, and it also occurred to him that he very much wanted to let her. But he could not go through with it.

"Milady, please, forgive me . . ." He said, interrupting her and holding out his hand in a staying motion. "This must stop now. Truly. I . . . I really must leave now. Please." He began to back away, toward the door.

She stopped and gazed at him, eyes wide. "Must you?" she said, softly.

His throat suddenly felt very dry. "In truth, I do not wish to," he replied, "but I must. Your beauty makes my heart race, but the truth is that I love another and could not bear to be unfaithful to her."

He reached the door and reached out behind him to open it.

"Tuck, wait," she said, coming toward him.

"Milady, please . . ." He opened the door and stepped back into the corridor.

She followed him, and came up close, and put her hands upon his chest. "You *are* a gentleman," she whispered. "The first true gentleman that I have met. And whoever she may be, I envy her." She rose up on her tiptoes and kissed him softly and lingeringly on the lips. "Good night, sweet Tuck." She smiled, stepped back inside, and shut the door.

For a moment, Tuck just stood there, his heart pounding, and then he heard the unmistakable sound of another door being shut behind him. He turned, quickly, but the corridor was empty now. He felt a knot form in his stomach as Blanche's words came back to him . . . *"My sister's friend is in this room just ahead and to our right. I think that she is still awake and packing, preparing to depart first thing in the morning. I would not wish her to get the wrong idea . . ."*

Elizabeth! Oh, God, he thought. What could she have seen? He had been coming out of Blanche's bedroom and she had followed him out into the corridor, barefoot and dressed in nothing but her undergarments, and she had kissed him on the lips and said good night . . .

He closed his eyes. She would never believe him if he told her what had truly happened. And for that matter, why should she? Guiltily, he realized that it had taken every ounce of willpower he had possessed to leave that room. He felt ashamed to admit it to himself, but he had wanted Blanche. And he could easily have had her. However, unlike every other male who came near her, he had managed to resist his baser urges. But would Elizabeth believe him?

He started to head down the corridor, toward her room, intent upon doing everything he could to convince her that he had not bedded Blanche, but suddenly he stopped.

What if it had *not* been Elizabeth, after all? What if the sound he had heard had merely been one of the other guests, going in to sleep after a late night? Whoever it was might not even have seen anything. It had only been an instant, after all. A mere moment. If he went to Elizabeth now, and protested his innocence, and it turned out that it had not been her, and she had not seen anything at all, then it would only make things worse.

Better to wait, he thought. After all, he had nothing to feel guilty for. He had not actually done anything wrong. He had merely escorted a lady back up to her room, and then had watched her strip down to her undergarments, said good night, and left. Well, she kissed him, but that was all, only a kiss, and a chaste one, at that. Hell, he thought, if she had seen only *that* much, Elizabeth would be furious. And he would know soon enough if she had seen him. It would be best to wait until he knew for certain. He took a deep breath, exhaled heavily, and headed for the stairs.

As Shakespeare followed Hughe Camden back downstairs, he had a feeling that he had left Smythe with his hands full. But then the lad was certainly old enough to be able to take care of himself. And if he couldn't, well, then Blanche Middleton was doubtless fully capable of taking care of him. What Shakespeare wanted to find out, if he could, was how long Camden had been in the library with Blanche. With any luck, Smythe would be asking Blanche exactly the same thing, so long as he was not distracted by her rather obvious attributes.

It would be nice to know if they both told the same story, and if the details coincided. But at the same time, Shakespeare thought, even if Smythe *was* distracted by the apparently perpetually randy Blanche Middleton, it might not necessarily prove to be a bad thing. It might get his mind off Elizabeth, if only for a little while. But even a little while could be enough, with any luck, to help effect a cure.

He did not really have anything against Elizabeth, personally. It was just that women were trouble. He knew that only too well. He thought of his Anne, back home in Stratford with the children, doubtless berating him soundly to anyone who would listen, and doubtless considering other likely prospects even as she did so. Not for the first time, he sighed with regret over his foolishness.

He would not forget his obligations. He would continue to send money, though at times, it placed a hardship on him he could ill endure. He did not really need fine clothes or lavish entertainments, and he could always eat a little less if it would allow him to drink a little more. And it was not as if things were not improving. He was certainly doing much better now than when he had first arrived in London. Having Smythe to help share the expenses eased some of the burden for them both, though at least Smythe did not have to support a family that he had never wanted. Although if Tuck did not watch out, he might easily get himself in trouble with young Blanche. But then, given Blanche's predilections and general lack of discretion, it would doubtless be impossible to fix the blame with any certainty. And from her father's point of view, any other candidate—except, perhaps, the neighbor's stableboy—would be a far more suitable scapegoat. No, Smythe was safe enough, thought Shakespeare.

Hughe Camden, on the other hand, would probably like nothing better than to place a bun inside that ready little oven. And even if a loaf was baked from someone else's dough, he might not object to claim it, for it would ensure a marriage, which in turn would ensure a fortune for him when Blanche's father died. There were no other heirs, and even if Godfrey Middleton decided to remarry in his dotage and sired a son with a new wife, Blanche's husband would still find himself in a very comfortable position. Aside from which, a man who had no compunction about killing would certainly not hesitate to dispose of any new young heirs. But what were the chances that Hughe Camden was that man?

They seemed rather remote, thought Shakespeare, as he followed Camden outside to the fairgrounds. Sir William seemed inclined to dismiss Camden as a suspect on the grounds of his pedigree, and on that basis alone, Camden could not be the man Smythe had overheard. That left Andrew Braithwaite and the Frenchman. One of them had to be the killer.

But which one?

12

SHAKESPEARE FOLLOWED HUGHE CAMDEN OUTSIDE and caught up to him as he was crossing the courtyard, heading towards the fairgrounds. By the time the poet fell in step beside him, the barrister had recovered much of his self-possession and gazed at Shakespeare with a look that conveyed both smug superiority and just the right amount of upper-class contempt.

Shakespeare did not find his snooty attitude even remotely unexpected. Camden was, after all, the son of a wealthy knight and he was given enough money that probably his greatest worry was how many times a month he could afford another suit of clothes or a fancy beaver hat, like those worn rakishly by all his colleagues at the Inns of Court. Then, too, as an inner barrister, he doubtless considered himself something of a connoisseur of theatrical productions, for the young gentlemen at the Inns of Court were well known for staging amateur theatricals in their halls for the better class of people, and the poets whose works they would perform were all university men such as Marlowe, Greene and Nashe. The Queen's Men and their ilk, who performed for the crass groundlings of the public theaters and often staged the very same plays, were looked upon by them as vulgar second-raters.

Camden raised a disdainful eyebrow at the poet, but did not deign to start a conversation. Presumably, thought Shakespeare, one did not speak first to one's inferiors. Fine, he thought, so be it. He simply smiled at Camden in a warm, comradely sort of way, and kept right on walking beside him, saying nothing. Camden cleared his throat after a moment, as if to prompt him, but Shakespeare merely smiled at him once more. This seemed to infuriate the barrister. His face flushed, the corners of his mouth turned down with scorn, and his aristocratic nostrils flared.

"If you suppose that there was any hint of impropriety in what you have just seen," said Camden, haughtily, "and that what you believe you may have witnessed has somehow placed you in some position of particular advantage over me, then I can assure you, sir, that you are very much mistaken on both counts."

"Oh, upon my word, that was well spoken!" Shakespeare said. "You flatter me, sir, to suppose such great complexity of thought to my most ordinary brain. Indeed, I can but scarcely apprehend your meaning. I can but hazard that your remarks just now were in some way concerned with your lying atop the lady in the library . . . or was it laying? S'trewth, lying, laying, I need my old schoolboy's hornbook, for I can never keep them straight."

"Now, see here . . ."

"Nay, milord, I was not seeking instruction, for doubtless you would know the difference, as you are a fine and educated gentleman of the Inns of Court. Eloquence, indeed, would be your proper province, whereas mine is but some foolish capering and posturing upon the stage. Odd's blood, what would I know, indeed?"

"Aye, well, not a very great deal, I should think," said Camden, stuffily.

"Not a great deal at all, I quite agree, I quite agree," said Shakespeare. "Which is why, of course, I make every effort to learn more and better myself at every opportunity, you see. And I could see, indeed, that back in yonder library, you were but doing what you could to comfort the young lady, who was doubtless overcome in her bereavement, what with the twin tragedies of the deaths of both her sister and her lover."

"Her *lover*, did you say?" Camden stopped abruptly, startled, but

Shakespeare purposely kept right on walking, as if he had not noticed, forcing the barrister to run several steps in order to catch up.

"Aye, her lover, too, slain so tragically on the very same day that her poor, dear sister was murdered, and not once, it seems, but twice! So in effect, I suppose one might say that there were three murders, save for the fact that there were but two victims."

"Wait a moment," Camden said, frowning, "what the devil are you talking about? What do you mean when you say her lover? That is to say, *whom* do you mean? And who is it that was slain and *how*? And, for that matter, *when*?"

"Oh, why, that would be Daniel Holland, I believe," said Shakespeare.

"*Holland!*"

"Aye, indeed, he is the very one."

"Good God! You mean to say that Holland was her lover?"

"Once again, sir, your education speaks, for indeed, 'twas *was*, not *is*, that is the proper form."

"*What?*"

"*Was*," said Shakespeare. "*Was* her lover, not *is* her lover, for as he is dead, he must perforce be was, not is."

"What in God's name are you babbling about?"

"Why, good grammar, I believe."

"God damn your grammar, sir!"

"I know, milord, 'tis atrocious, truly. I mangle each and every part and participle of speech. I am not fit to speak with educated gentlemen such as yourself. I am thoroughly ashamed. Forgive me, I shall be on my way and trouble you no longer."

"Stay, you impertinent rascal! Bestill yourself until I give you leave to go, you hear?"

"Why, certainly. Your servant, sir."

They had stopped just inside the fairgrounds, amidst the colorful pavilions and painted wood stalls decorated with particolored banners, painted cloths, and pennants showing the wares being displayed. The hour was late, but every single stall and tent was open and the grounds were crowded by the guests, none of whom, it seemed, had left for home or even gone to sleep for fear of missing any more excitement. The grounds were lit with flickering campfires and torches and the tents were lit with candles, giving the entire fair a festive glow. The cookfires were all burning brightly and the food vendors were all doing a brisk business. The air was full of tantalizing roasting and baking smells and Shakespeare suddenly realized that he was hungry. He could also do with a pint of ale or nice flagon of spiced wine. The trouble was, he had no money.

"Now, what is all this about Daniel Holland being Blanche's lover?" Camden demanded.

Shakespeare put a hand up to his brow, as if his head was paining him, and closed his eyes as he swayed slightly from side to side. "S'trewth, in all the excitement of the day, I fear I have not eaten anything. And here 'tis night and I am so famished that I nearly swoon with weakness. My stomach growls and I feel weak—"

"Very well then, come on and we shall get some food inside you," Camden said, leading him to the nearest stall that had a cookfire, "but you shall, by God, answer my questions afore I lose my patience!"

"God bless you, sir, you are a kind and noble soul," said Shakespeare, and within a moment he was munching contentedly upon a leg of mutton the vendor had been roasting.

"Now then," Camden said, "tell me what you know of this matter of Daniel Holland and Blanche Middleton."

"*Mmpf!*" said Shakespeare, clearing his throat several times, touching it as if something were caught there. "*Urggh . . . guggh . . .*"

"Oh, good God!" said Camden. "Here! You! Merchant! Some ale, and be quick about it!"

A moment later, the mutton was being washed down by a strong, dark ale and Shakespeare felt much better. "Ah! There, that seems to have dislodged it! I am much obliged to you, milord.

Doubtless, you have saved my life, else I would have choked to death right here upon the spot!"

"I shall bloody well choke you to death right here upon this spot unless you give me an answer to my question!" Camden nearly shouted. "Now what is all this about Holland?"

"Oh, well, he is dead," said Shakespeare, between bites of mutton leg. "He was killed, you see." He frowned, considering. "*Is* dead, *was* killed . . . aye, that seems to be correct, grammatically speaking."

"Speak whichever way you chose, you mountebank, but tell me how he was killed!"

"Run through, it seems," said Shakespeare, smacking his lips and taking a drink of ale. "Oh, this is most excellent. I truly thank you for your kindness, milord. I was so weak with hunger, I could scarcely stand."

"Stand and deliver me an answer, scoundrel! Run through by *whom?*" persisted Camden.

"Why, no one seems to know for certain," Shakespeare replied. He pointed to a stall a few yards off. "Why, look there! Would those be shepherds' pies?" He started walking towards a stall where an old man with an eye patch was laying out some freshly baked pies. "Ah, I can smell that tasty crust from here! My mouth waters with anticipation!"

Exasperated, Camden pursued him. "What do you mean, no one seems to know for certain? Do you mean that there is someone they suspect?"

"Oh, one of her suitors, I believe," said Shakespeare, coming up to the stall and looking over the pies the grizzled, one-eyed vendor had set out. "Blanche Middleton's suitors, that is. You know, the lady upon whom you were lying in the library. Or is that whom you were laying in the library? I am not quite certain. Both seem to me to be correct. Oh, my, these *do* look good . . ."

"Blast you! Here, you, vendor, let's have one of those pies."

"Certainly, milord," the old man said, bowing and wiping his hands on his leather apron. "Which one would you wish, yer worship?" He indicated a dozen steaming pies freshly set out on his display board.

"Any one, it does not matter," Camden said, impatiently.

"Oh, now, truly, sir, you do me honor . . ." Shakespeare said, as the old man selected one.

"Honor me with a reply and we shall both be satisfied." said Camden, tersely.

Shakespeare appraised the pie, which looked quite tempting, and then dubiously glanced at the old man, who seemed a bit bedraggled with his long, stringy, white hair and grimey, floppy hat, but whose hands, at least, looked reasonably clean. "Well, now, I shall need to set this ale down . . . or else, methinks, this mutton. . . ."

"Put it down upon the board," said Camden.

"But it does not look too clean, milord."

"Heaven help me!" Camden said, rolling his eyes. He threw some coins down for the pie. "Here, give me the mutton, and then you may take your blasted pie."

"But . . . I was not quite finished with the mutton, milord."

"Fine. Then I shall hold the ale, whilst you take the mutton and the pie."

"Ah . . . well, that may work, I suppose, but then I cannot drink, you see."

"Just *give* me the damned mutton leg!" said Camden through gritted teeth, snatching it away and brandishing it as if it were a club. "Now get *on* with it!"

"What was it I was saying, milord?"

"You were telling me who is suspected in the slaying of Daniel Holland!"

"Ah, well, one of the suitors, it seems, must have done it. Elimination of a rival, you see. They were seen together in the maze, it seems, that is to say, Holland and the lady . . . much as you and the lady were seen together in the library, and . . . oh, my goodness! I suppose that means that *you* could very well be next, milord!"

Camden paled. "What do you mean?"

"Well, if someone is killing off his rivals—"

"Then any one of us might well be next," said Braithwaite, from behind them. Camden turned so suddenly, he nearly struck Braithwaite with the leg of mutton. Braithwaite jerked back and Camden, alarmed by the sudden movement, instinctively raised the leg of mutton like a club.

"Have a care with that," said Braithwaite. " 'Twould be a waste to offer violence with a victual."

"You startled me, sir," said Camden, in an affronted tone.

" 'Twas never my intention, I assure you," Braithwaite said. "I could not help but overhear what you and Master Shakespeare were discussing. I had already heard the news, however. Everyone speaks of nothing else. 'Tis a shame about Dan Holland. He seemed a decent enough sort, I suppose, though if he did dishonor to the lady, then I cannot feel too sorry for him."

"Well, 'twould seem that I have been the very last to hear of his demise," said Camden, dryly.

"And yet I wonder if you were the very first to see it," Braithwaite replied, raising his eyebrow.

"What do you mean, sir?" Camden bridled at him. "Are you suggesting I had aught to do with it?"

"Well, one never knows, does one?" said Braithwaite. "As Master Shakespeare said, 'twould appear that one of us is anxious to eliminate his rivals and that one, for all we know, could very well be you."

"Or it could just as well be *you*," Camden retorted, angrily. "I deeply resent your implication, sir!"

"Well, a man who stands ready to club down a fellow with a leg of mutton could be capable of anything," said Braithwaite.

"You mock me, sir!"

"Tush, what use is there to mock a mockery?"

"*Will!*" Robert Speed came running up to them and, ignoring the two rivals, moved between them to tug at Shakespeare's sleeve. "Where the devil have you *been*? And where is Tuck, for Heaven's sake? Why, we have all been searching high and low for both of you!"

"Damn you!" said Camden, pale with fury. "I demand that you apologize at once!"

"Oh, forgive me, milord; I do humbly beg your pardon. I did not mean to interrupt," said Speed.

"Not *you*, you simpleton, I meant *this* gentleman!" said Camden, indicating Braithwaite. "I shall not stand here and suffer to be ridiculed!"

"And yet you do it so very well," said Braithwaite.

"Perhaps if we all took a moment—" Shakespeare began, but Speed began tugging on his sleeve again.

"We have set up the stage and have been trying to rehearse all day, but 'tis a near impossibility without our book holder and the author of our play!" said Speed. "Kemp has lost all patience and has refused to proceed without you, for he does not like his scenes and demands changes, and Burbage has ordered everyone to spread out through the estate and find you—"

"Will you *shut* up!" said Camden.

"—and now there is all this talk of murder once again and no one even knows if we are to perform tomorrow—"

"I said, *shut up*, you cursed fool!"

"Oh! Forgive me, milord," said Speed, "I do humbly beg your pardon, but I thought that you were speaking to the other gentleman again."

"*Idiot!*" said Camden, and lashed Speed viciously across the face with his leather glove.

"I say, that was uncalled for," Braithwaite said. "See how you like a taste of your own broth." He removed his glove and struck Camden in the face with it.

"Oh, God save us," said Shakespeare, backing away hurriedly and pulling Speed along with him.

Camden's rapier sang free of its scabbard. "You shall die for that, you villainous churl!"

"Lay on, barrister," said Braithwaite, drawing steel, "and damned be he that first cries, 'Hold, enough!' "

"A fight!" cried Speed.

"Gentlemen, please, put up your swords!" cried Shakespeare, but they were already engaged and a crowd quickly began to gather as the combatants dueled.

"Upon my word, what's this?" asked Burbage, joining the assemblage as Braithwaite and Camden exchanged thrusts and parries.

"More than I had bargained for, I fear," said Shakespeare.

"What had *you* to do with this?" asked Burbage.

"Everything and nothing," Shakespeare said. "I stirred up this brew, I fear, but now have naught to do with the result."

"I do believe they mean to kill each other," Burbage said.

"Aye, look at 'em go!" cried Speed, delighted with the spectacle, as indeed, were most of the observers, who cried out encouragement to one or the other of the combatants as they moved back and forth, their blades clanging against one another. The crowd surged back from them to give them room as they maneuvered. Camden lunged and Braithwaite parried, leaping backwards and knocking into the display board where the pies had been set out. Everything went crashing to the ground and the old man cried out and put his hands up to his head in consternation as his entire stall seemed in danger of collapsing, but Braithwaite recovered quickly and moved to the attack, and then Camden suddenly found himself on the defensive as he backed away, parrying furiously.

Shakespeare recalled that Smythe had said something about Camden wearing a duelist's rapier, and indeed, the barrister seemed skilled, but Braithwaite was no slouch with a blade, himself. The two seemed evenly matched. As they moved back and forth, the crowd moved with them, growing by the minute as everyone present on the fairgrounds responded to the noise and came to see what was occuring. Camden lunged again, but Braithwaite parried his thrust and riposted quickly, catching the barrister off balance. Camden staggered back awkwardly as Braithwaite lunged. Camden seemed to parry the stroke, but fell back into the crowd as he did so. There was a collective cry as they caught him and shoved him back up again, but then with a gasp, Camden fell to his knees.

"A touch! A touch!" several voices in the crowd cried out.

Braithwaite shook his head, perplexed. "Nay, I never pricked him!"

"But look, he bleeds!" cried Speed.

On his knees, Camden dropped his blade and brought a hand up to his side. It came away bloody. He gasped with pain, staring at Braithwaite with wide-eyed incomprehension.

"But . . .'twas not me!" Braithwaite said. He examined the tip of his sword, then held it out towards Shakespeare. "See for yourself! My blade is yet unblooded!"

"He speaks the truth," said Shakespeare.

Camden pitched forward onto his face and lay motionless.

"*Seize that man!*" The cry came from an anguished Sir Richard, who had arrived upon the scene just in time to see his son fall dead onto the ground. "*Seize him!* There is your murderer! And he has killed my son!"

"I have murdered no one! And he drew steel first!" protested Braithwaite, looking around with alarm at the throng surrounding him.

"You challenged him!" shouted someone in the crowd, and then a scuffle suddenly broke out. More people started shouting and in the next moment, a well-dressed, older man was shoved out of the crowd to fall sprawling next to the slain Hughe Camden, only he fell with a cry, followed by a grunt of pain on impact, demonstrating that he was still very much alive.

"*There* is your killer, Sir Richard!" a familiar voice called out, and Shakespeare stared in astonishment as the grizzled old pie vendor stepped out from the crowd, only now he was no longer stooped over, but stood straight and tall, and there was nothing even remotely subservient in his bearing. He reached up and removed his eyepatch and the wig he wore and stood revealed as none other than

Her Majesty's own councillor and confidante, Sir William Worley. "I saw the blackguard stab your son from behind with a dagger when he fell back into the crowd."

"Nay, 'tis not true!" the man cried out, as he got up to his knees. " 'Tis entirely innocent I am!"

"Why, 'tis the elder *Chevalier* Dubois!" Shakespeare exclaimed.

"Well, well," said Worley, standing over him. "And here we all thought you were deaf, *monsieur,* and did not speak because you could not hear. Yet you seem to have recovered miraculously. And 'tis even more miraculous that a nobleman from France should speak with a Cornish accent!"

From out of nowhere, it seemed, grim-faced men armed with swords and maces stepped out of the crowd and surrounded the faux Frenchman, and Shakespeare realized that Sir William had not returned alone, but had brought a squad of guardsmen with him. Dressed in ordinary clothing, they had blended with the crowd, standing by for Worley's signal. The man's face fell as he realized that his situation was completely hopeless.

"My apologies, sir," said Worley, turning to Braithwaite. "I had thought that the killer might be you, and in his haste to take advantage of your duel and make it seem as if *you* had killed a rival, this cowardly assassin very nearly made me sure of it. But although he tried to shelter himself within the crowd, I saw the fatal stroke when he stabbed Camden with this very bodkin." He displayed a bloody dagger that he had wrested from the killer. "Sir Richard . . ." He turned to the ashen-faced elder Camden. "I am most profoundly sorry for your loss, but in death, your son has helped us apprehend not only his own killer, but the murderer of both Catherine Middleton and Daniel Holland."

"*Nay!*" the killer shouted. "Nay, I tell you! S'trewth, I may be damned now, but I shall not bear the blame for what I have not done! God shall be my judge, for I did kill young Camden, but I swear I never killed the wench! And I never slew Holland, neither!

'Twas all *his* doing, I tell you! 'Twas all *his* plan from the start, and I'll not bear the blame for it alone!!"

"*Dubois!*" said Shakespeare.

The man spat upon the ground. "His name ain't no more Dubois than mine is. Why, he's no Frenchman. He—"

With a sharp, whizzing sound, a crossbow bolt penetrated his skull right between the eyes, causing his head to jerk back abruptly. He was dead before he hit the ground.

Pandemonium ensued as everyone started shouting at once and running in all directions. Most of the onlookers desperately fled the scene, fearful lest they should be the next targets of the unseen archer, but everyone ran in different directions, many of them colliding with one another, and the scene erupted into chaos in an instant.

Two of the guardsmen immediately threw themselves upon Sir William, bearing him down to the ground and covering him with their bodies, but he shoved them away, cursing furiously. "Never mind *me*, blast it! Search the fairgrounds! *Get me that archer!*"

So fascinated was he by everything that suddenly began happening around him that Shakespeare completely forgot to be frightened. He simply stood there watching as people ran shouting and screaming in different directions, tripping over one another and knocking each other down in their mad rush to get away.

The entire scene, somehow, took on the aspect of a dream to him. It was as if he were not a part of it, but stood on the outside somewhere, watching as if from a distance or from an audience. In his mind's eye, he replayed the scene of the assassin on his knees before them, at first protesting his innocence, then accepting his fate with resignation, then growing angry at the thought of being blamed for everything alone while his partner had planned it all . . . and then the slim, black bolt, flying straight and true, appearing to sprout all of a sudden from the killer's forehead. . . .

It had flown in at an angle.

For the archer to have made the shot, over the heads of the

crowd surrounding the assassin on his knees, he had to have been shooting from a height, an elevation. . . .

Shakespeare turned in the direction from which the arrow must have come, judging by the angle of the shot, and as he looked up the slope, back toward the house, he saw the stone wall that ran around the courtyard, and just beyond it, an open window.

It was an amazing shot to have come from atop that wall. Robin Hood himself could not have bettered it. And of course, it could only have been Phillipe Dubois . . . or whoever "Dubois" really was. He must have made the shot, then climbed in through that open window. It was astonishing marksmanship. But then, Tuck had said that whoever had shot that bolt at him had come within a hair's breadth of hitting his head from a good distance—

Good Lord, he thought, Tuck! The realization struck him suddenly that Tuck was still back at house. He turned, quickly. *"Sir William!"* he shouted. *"Sir William! This way! Hurry, for God's sake!"*

Smythe felt guilty, apprehensive and confused as he slowly descended the stairs to the first floor. What had happened, or nearly happened, with Blanche Middleton had quite unnerved him. Unlike Shakespeare, who already had a family of his own, he had no experience with women. When he was younger, there had been a few girls in his village who had cast coy glances in his direction a time or two, but he had always been too shy to do much else than avert his eyes and blush. Then he would hear their girlish laughter and that would only make it seem much worse the next time that it happened.

Since he came to London and started working at the theatre, there had been opportunities for him to gain a little more experience—and very likely more than a little, especially at The Toad and Badger, after their performances—but what had kept him from pursuing those opportunities were the feelings that he had for Elizabeth. On more than one occasion, Shakespeare had admonished him for his restraint, telling him that it was pointless and even ludicrous for him to remain faithful to a girl that he could never have, but that still had not changed his feelings or his constancy. He was in love with Elizabeth, and when one was in love, one remained true and faithful to that love. That was only as it should be.

What now should he make of his response to Blanche? Knowing full well that she was a wanton, he had nevertheless felt such a strong desire for her that it had made his head swim. What did that say about his character, and even more important, what did it say about his feelings towards Elizabeth?

If he had truly loved Elizabeth, he thought, then he should not have responded to Blanche the way he had. Certainly, there had been other times when he had not felt tempted by the saucy glances and the bawdy speech of the wenches at The Toad and Badger, but this had been completely different. It seemed to have taken every ounce of strength he had possessed to walk out of that room. And much to his chagrin, he realized that there was still a part of him—he knew only too well which part—that wanted very much to turn around and go back up the stairs, knock upon her door, and tell her that he had changed his mind. She had, quite simply, taken his breath away, and he had still not fully recovered.

What sort of man am I, he thought, who could profess love for one woman and yet be so basely tempted by another? Even now, after he had turned her down, having mustered all his strength of will to do so, he *still* wanted her, in spite of everything. If I am so weak, he thought, then truly, I must not be deserving of a good woman's love.

He stepped off the stairs into the deserted great hall of the manor. If Elizabeth had seen him leaving Blanche's room, then he was sure that nothing he could say would make the slightest bit of difference. For that matter, how could he protest his innocence when, in his heart, he knew that he was guilty, in thought if not in deed?

So preoccupied was he with his own thoughts that he almost

failed to respond to the sound he heard behind him, but in the silence of the empty hall, he could not fail to hear the footsteps coming down the stairs that he had just descended.

He froze, thinking that it could only be Elizabeth. Just as he had feared, it had, indeed, been she who had shut the door upstairs in the hall after seeing him coming out of Blanche's room, and now she had decided to come down and confront him. How would he ever convince her that he had not done anything? And then another possibility occurred to him. What if it were Blanche, coming after him to try to make him change his mind? Just the thought of it made his heart beat a little faster, and he felt ashamed for it. He took a deep breath and turned to face whoever it would be.

"So," said Godfrey Middleton, standing behind him at the foot of the stairs, "thought you could get away with it, did you?" He held a sword in his right hand. He raised it and held the blade pointed towards Smythe's chest as he advanced. "You saucy bastard. You thought you could dishonor my daughter and then boast about it to your friends, did you?"

Understanding dawned as Smythe realized that it had been Blanche's father who had seen him coming out of her room! Aghast, he hastened to explain himself.

"Sir, I assure you, there was nothing—" Smythe began, but Middleton would not let him finish.

"A pox on your assurances, you villain! Do you take me for a fool? I saw you coming out of my daughter's bedroom! How *dare* you! And in my own home! *Under my very nose!*"

"Sir, please," said Smythe, backing away as the blade came uncomfortably near his throat. The man was much too close. If he tried to draw steel to defend himself, Middleton would run him through on the instant. "Sir, please listen, you do not understand what truly—"

"I understand only too well!" Middleton said, his voice like a whipcrack. Smythe saw that he was breathing hard and his eyes were blazing with a fury akin to madness. And then Smythe suddenly noticed that the blade Middleton held was wet with blood. "I understand that I have taken serpents to my breast! *Serpents! Harlots! Sluts!* After all that I have done for them, after all those years of toil, *this* is how they have repayed me! By fornicating with common stable boys and players!"

Smythe was alarmed by the man's vehemence and filled with horror by the sight of the blood upon his blade, for he now realized what it had to mean. There was a hollow feeling in the pit of his stomach and his mouth suddenly felt dry. "Sir, I beg you to hear me out," he said. " 'Tis not at all what you think, I swear it in God's name!"

"You *dare* deny the truth to me when I have seen with mine own eyes, you scoundrel?" said Middleton, advancing on him. Smythe began to back away, still vainly trying to get a word in edgewise, but Middleton kept after him, the bloody blade hovering just inches from his throat. "Do you suppose that I shall suffer myself to be made a fool of in front of all these people? Do you think I shall allow myself to be dishonored and disgraced after all of the work that I have done? I shall see you in Hell first, along with both of those ungrateful bitches I have raised! Wanton sluts, just like their mother, may God curse her scarlet, strumpet soul! I sent that damned harlot to the Devil for her wickedness, hoping to spare my daughters from her evil influence, but I see now that they were poisoned within her very womb, for they both grew up just like her! *Sluts! Serpents!* And there is only one thing to be done with serpents!"

"My God," said Smythe, as the realization struck him like a thunderbolt. " 'Twas you! *You* killed Catherine!"

"The ungrateful little witch left me no choice! I *wept* for her, thinking she was dead! I had such high hopes for her! She could have been a real lady, the culmination of everything that I had striven for my whole life long! Do you have any idea what it took to find a suitable husband for her, a nobleman who would consent to marry a common woman with a reputation as a shrew? And yet, at long last, I found a nobleman who would have her and on her very wedding day, to my profound chagrin, she dies! I went back to the tomb to grieve for her and all that might have been, and I stood there, weeping, and asked her why she had to ruin everything and lo! She rose again before my very eyes! In fear, I fell onto my knees, thinking that she was a demon sent from Hell, or else a punishment from God, and I cowered before her and confessed her mother's murder and begged for her forgiveness! And then she screamed, and railed at me and struck me, and called me vile, unspeakable things, and told me how she had planned to fool me with the potion and run off with that stable boy! A *stable boy*! I realized then I had been made a fool of and so I struck the treacherous wench and said that I would kill her before I allowed her to disgrace me! 'Twas then that she produced the dagger, which that cursed stable boy had hidden by her mother's bier. . . . And so I had no choice, you see. No choice at all. She *made* me do it, just like her mother, and now her sinful sister. . . ."

"You shall hang for this, Middleton, even if you kill me," said Smythe, trying to avoid being backed against a wall. If he could only get a bit more room, a bit more space between them . . . "You have already locked up John Mason, so you cannot put the blame on him. And none of Blanche's suitors would ever seriously regard me as a rival, nor would they have any reason to kill Blanche. You shall never get away with this."

"Oh, I think I shall," Middleton replied, his eyes gleaming. "For 'twas *you* who had committed the foul deed! *You* followed Blanche up to her room and forced yourself upon her, and then you killed her so that she could not reveal what you had done, just like you killed her sister and the others, but I heard the noise, you see, and I pursued you down the stairs and . . ."

The bolt from the crossbow caught him in the hollow of his throat. He staggered back and dropped his blade, gurgling and gagging horribly and clutching at the wound, then he fell backward onto the floor, where he thrashed for a moment, then lay still.

"What the devil were you waiting for, you idiot?" said Dubois, lowering the crossbow. "He was about to kill you."

Smythe stared at him, speechless. It was Dubois, and yet . . . it was *not* Dubois. His posture and demeanor were completely different. Gone entirely was the French accent and the foppish manner. Even his voice sounded different. More resonant, more manly, more . . . *Irish*, of all things!

He expertly rewound the spring on the crossbow as he spoke and quickly fitted another bolt. "Strange how things turned out, eh? The bugger was quite mad, you know. And here I had gone to all that trouble to kill Holland and arrange for Camden's speedy dispatch, and now 'twas all for nothing. No doubt, I shall get the blame for Blanche's death, as well, unless you feel compelled to speak up on my behalf, seeing as how I saved your life just now. I do not kill women, you know. Not that it makes a great deal of difference, I suppose. They shall want me for murder just the same, seeing as how they saw me kill that fool I had for a partner. He would have spilled everything he knew about me. Couldn't have that. Anyway, do as you wish. Meanwhile, I would love to stay and chat, but there are a lot of people in pursuit of me right now and I really must run and steal a horse."

He raised the crossbow, aiming it at Smythe. "Now do stand still and allow me to go by, like a good fellow. And if you could find it in your heart to delay them just a bit, I truly would appreciate it. You might consider it evening the score, eh? *Au revoir.* Perhaps we shall meet again someday."

He grinned, gave Smythe a jaunty salute, then turned and ran towards the door. Smythe simply stood there, staring after him with disbelief, then he glanced down at Middleton's lifeless body. Another instant, and the man would have run him through. He felt a bit unsteady. He leaned back against the wall and took several deep breaths to steady his nerves.

A few moments later, he heard the sounds of running footsteps and men shouting. He stood and waited for them. They all came bursting into the great hall, led by Sir William, with Shakespeare right behind him.

"*Tuck!*" cried Shakespeare. "Thank Heaven! The Frenchman! Dubois! Have you seen him?"

"Aye, I have."

"Quickly, man, which way did he go?" asked Worley, and then his eyes widened as he saw Middleton's body lying on the floor. "Oh, good God! He has slain poor Godfrey!"

"Aye," said Smythe. "And in so doing, he has saved my life."

"*Dubois?*" said Shakespeare.

"Aye, for Godfrey Middleton was about to slay me," Smythe said. He pointed at Middleton's body as the hall became crowded with Dubois's pursuers. "He killed Catherine, for disgracing him with a stable boy, just as he had killed his wife for some like offense, whether real or imagined. He confessed it all to me. I fear that he has also murdered Blanche. That is doubtless her blood on his sword there. He was going to kill me, and then blame me for the deed."

"*What?*" said Worley, with astonishment.

"After we spoke in the library, and I told her about Daniel Holland's murder, Blanche was quite understandably distressed," Smythe explained. "I had escorted her back to her room, and when Middleton saw me leaving, he thought the worst of it. He followed me back downstairs and accused me of despoiling his daughter. He was enraged. He said . . . he said vile things that are best not repeated. There was a madness upon him. He told me how he had gone back to the tomb and saw Catherine awake as the effects of the potion wore off. He thought she was a demon or a spirit risen from the dead and so he fell upon his knees and confessed her mother's murder to her. She was horrified, and screamed at him, and in a rage told him how she had planned to stage her death and run off with young Mason. He struck her and then she produced the dagger Mason left there for her. He got it away from her and killed her with it. And he was about to kill me when Dubois came upon the scene and shot him down."

There was the sound of galloping hoofbeats outside on the cobbles and someone shouted out, *"Stop him! He is getting away!"*

"After him!" shouted someone else.

"Nay, let him go!" commanded Worley. "I'll not have men breaking their necks out there in the darkness, chasing after phantoms. 'Tis not worth the risk. I, for one, have seen quite enough corpses for one day. We shall deal with him another time . . . whoever he may be." He glanced at Smythe. "I do not suppose he told you that, did he?"

"No, Sir William, he did not," Smythe said, shaking his head. " 'Tis a mystery. But whoever he was, he was most certainly not French. He spoke to me with a most definite Irish accent."

"Irish!" Shakespeare said. "He was an *Irishman?*"

"Aye," said Smythe. "And he murdered Holland, I'm afraid."

"He arranged for Camden's murder, too," said Worley, "then shot down the man who did it, so that he could not reveal his name or bear witness against him. So while he may have saved your life, there are at least three murders for which we cannot forgive him."

"Indeed," said Smythe, dryly, "and there is one thing more which I cannot forgive him."

"But I thought you said the Irishman had saved your life?" said Shakespeare.

"Aye, he did at that," said Smythe, with a grimace. "But in the end, he turned out to be a much better actor than I could ever hope to be!"

EPILOGUE

T HE STAGE HAD BEEN TAKEN down and packed away, as had all of the tents and stalls that had stood upon the fairgrounds. Save for the players and a few merchants who were still putting away their wares, nearly everyone had left. The grounds were quite torn up, and it would apparently be some time before anyone thought about putting them right again. And given the way things had turned out, the festival at Middleton Manor would, indeed, be an event that people in London would talk about for a long, long time to come.

"Do you suppose that seeing his daughter apparently rising from the dead had unhinged his mind?" asked Shakespeare.

They stood together beneath some trees outside the house, not far from where the players' wagons waited. Worley sat in his light carriage, getting ready to drive back to Green Oaks, and from there, to rejoin the queen on her progress through the countryside.

"I suspect his madness came upon him long before." said Worley, "if, indeed, 'twas madness, for if it were, then he concealed it well. I think Tuck was closer to the truth when he said that it was rage. Godfrey Middleton was an ambitious, vain and selfish man. He wanted more than anything to be someone important, a gentleman, a courtier. Money alone was not enough. What he desired above all else was position. And it seemed that he would stop at nothing to achieve it. That was a sort of madness in itself, I suppose."

"And it seemed that all his daughters had desired was love," said Smythe. "Catherine had found it with a stable boy, and was willing to die for it. And poor Blanche kept looking for it everywhere, in vain."

"What will become of young Mason now?" asked Shakespeare.

"I shall take him back to work for me," said Worley. "Poor lad. He is quite undone with grief. I believe he shall get over it in time, but he is entirely blameless in the matter. I hold nothing against him. After all, all he did was fall in love above his station. He would not be the first to do that."

"Nor the last," said Smythe, softly, thinking of Elizabeth, who had left earlier with her father. She had never liked Blanche Middleton, but she had been deeply saddened by her death. For her, too, it would take time to recover from the tragic events that had occurred at Middleton Manor.

"Has there been any word about the Irishman?" asked Shakespeare.

Worley shook his head. " 'Twould appear that he has made good his escape. I have men out searching for him, but I suspect that coney will be quite difficult to catch. 'Tis quite a shame, really, such talent and resourcefulness, put to such base use. I could use a man like that in the queen's service."

"Perhaps Black Billy would have better luck in finding him than any of the queen's men," Smythe suggested.

Worley smiled. "Perhaps. We shall see."

"*Will! Tuck!*" called Burbage from the wagons. "Come on! We are ready to depart!"

"Well, your tour awaits," said Worley.

Shakespeare grimaced. " 'Twill seem quite tame after all this."

Smythe sighed. "I could do with something tame, methinks. I have had quite enough excitement for a while."

" 'Twas good of you to pay the players, Sir William," Shakespeare said.

Worley shrugged. " 'Twas not their fault they never had a chance to act their play. Besides, I shall make it back and then some from handling Her Majesty's disposal of the estate. There have already been several offers. Percival seems quite taken with the place. He said it has now attained a notorious reputation and no doubt the queen shall wish to come and see it."

"Well, the estate shall survive," said Shakespeare, dryly, "but I do not think I can say the same about my play. I do not regret not seeing it performed. 'Twas never any good, I fear."

"Oh, I would not say that, Will," Smythe replied. "Now, the beginning was quite promising, I thought. Perhaps you can keep that and use it somewhere else."

"Perhaps you can write a play about what happened here," said Worley, with a smile. " 'Twould be a tragedy, of course. Quite worthy of the Greeks, I should think. Murder, greed, imposture, lust and madness, dead bodies strewn everywhere about . . ."

"Been done," said Smythe.

"Still," said Shakespeare, scratching his chin thoughtfully, " 'tis an idea . . ."